Praise for Kimberley Troutte's
Catch Me in Castile

Gothic Journal Recommended Read

"...the mystery is intriguing, the characters are complicated and conflicted, and the action is intense. If you are looking for an eerie story to keep you up at night, this is it! I'm looking forward to more like this from this author!"
~ *Fallen Angels*

"...Catch Me in Castile will take you on a journey across the world and into the belly of an engrossing suspense. Kimberley Troutte also delivers on a heartfelt romance between a Spanish doctor and a woman who just needs something positive to happen in her life..."
~ *Night Owl Romance.*

"I thoroughly enjoyed this novel! Kimberley has a knack of entangling the reader into the storyline so it makes it impossible to put it down! Left me wanting more from this talented new author!"
~ *Reader Comment on Amazon*

"...Kimberly Troutte serves up romance with a heavy dose of danger in Catch Me in Castile. Santiago is the kind of hero that makes most women wish they could pay a visit to the doctor....Erin's an unusual heroine, in that for most of the book she isn't quite sure she has a full grip on her sanity (and with good reason). ...Ms. Troutte made me feel like I was being swept away to Spain, and I must admit, she also made me wish I had a Santiago waiting for me at journey's end."
~ *Joyfully Reviewed*

Look for these titles by
Kimberley Troutte

Now Available:

Soul Stealer

Catch Me in Castile

Kimberley Troutte

A SAṁHAIN PUḃLISHING, LṪD. publication.

Samhain Publishing, Ltd.
577 Mulberry Street, Suite 1520
Macon, GA 31201
www.samhainpublishing.com

Catch Me in Castile
Copyright © 2010 by Kimberley Troutte
Print ISBN: 978-1-60504-731-7
Digital ISBN: 978-1-60504-652-5

Cover by Angela Waters

First Samhain Publishing, Ltd. electronic publication: August 2009
First Samhain Publishing, Ltd. print publication: June 2010

Acknowledgements

Writing *Catch Me in Castile* was a twenty-year endurance race. I have lots of folks to thank for getting me to the finish line:

Deborah Nemeth, my coach, my editor, one in a million.

My beloved, Carlos. Love you, sweetheart. Thanks for the strong shoulders to lean on and for lifting me up when I ate dirt.

The greatest sons a mother could ask for gave sustenance-hugs to keep Mama going.

Mom and Dad paved the way, cheered from the sidelines and bought up tickets to every race. No daughter could be prouder of her parents.

Kori read this story more times than should have been humanly possible and became a great cyber-cheerleader.

My second parents set my feet in the starting blocks by taking me to Spain. They've also been an endless support of strength and pep-talks.

C.C. Wiley read all my stuff—the good, the bad and the ugly—and ran beside me.

Cynthia Appel, Leslie Dinaberg, Malena Lott, Leonard Tourney, Chicklit Writers of the World, Fiction that Sells, Romance Divas, and the Solvang Writers Group all kicked my butt down the track and offered water bottles when necessary.

My friends provided PowerBars, shoulder rubs and clean towels when the going got tough.

Thank you one and all.

Prologue

Alcázar, Segovia, Spain

Serena clapped her hand over her mouth to strangle the scream clawing up her throat. Someone was coming into the tower. Frantically, she searched for a way out, only to discover she was trapped. Voices boomed up the stairwell—her only means of escape.

¡Madre de Dios! Her mind flashed with terror and confusion. *They will kill me.*

She flew to the dark alcove behind the stairwell and pressed her back against the weathered stone wall. Holding her breath, she hoped against hope she had disappeared in the shadows.

"Careful, the steps are narrow," a Spaniard said.

"Is this the tower where the queen was beheaded?" a lady asked in a language both foreign and familiar to Serena.

"No, sugarplum. That was the castle in England," another man drawled.

"*Señores*, no queen lost her life in this tower."

Who are these people? Serena thought, and then a more important question exploded in her brain. *Dios mío... Who am I?*

"You say this tower is haunted?" The woman's voice echoed up the narrow, twisting flight of stairs.

Serena's eyes widened. *Haunted?*

"*Sí*, a ghost is here," was the answer.

What? Serena gulped. Itching to peek out from her hidey-hole, she forced herself to remain still. She did not have the luxury to fear spirits when her own life was at stake. She had been hiding in the tower for...days? Weeks? She frowned. Why couldn't she remember? Her mind was as heavy and slow as churned lard.

The clomping on the stairs produced a rather plump woman huffing from exertion. Her orange blouse was short in the sleeves and tight across her bosom. Serena wondered what sort of lady wore men's light blue hose.

After catching her breath, the woman exclaimed, "Holy Jiminy. The last time I was in a castle like this was at Disneyland. Ain't it pretty? Like steppin' into a fairy tale."

A man's pink face popped up the stairs behind her. He wore hose similar to the woman's and the largest hat Serena ever saw.

"It's somethin', ain't it?" The man—perhaps her husband, for he spoke like the woman—wiped his brow with a kerchief. "The brochure says Walt copied this castle, especially them blue spires."

"Lordy, look at all those red roofs down there. And there's the aqueduct thingy the Romans built. My oh my, we're on top of the world."

Serena's gaze followed the woman's pointing finger. An entire city had sprouted across the grassy fields. How was that possible?

Confused and scared, Serena wondered if she had awakened from a long slumber and found herself imprisoned in a foreign land. And yet...she squinted, slowly turning to take in her surroundings. No, not everything was different.

Her heart beat wildly. *Why am I still in the tower?*

She didn't dare question the strangers. She couldn't remember much but knew, deep down in her soul, that she was in terrible danger. Someone was trying to kill her.

If only I could remember who.

Making herself as small as possible, Serena peeked through a crack in the stone masonry and forced herself to be still. Perhaps these strangers could provide some answers.

"Built in the eleventh century by the Moors," the Spaniard recited, "the Alcázar was originally a fortress. Situated perfectly on the rocky banks of two rivers, the Eresma and Clamores—"

The husband waved a folder paper. "We can read, son. Tell

us somethin' that ain't in the brochure."

The guide paused. "Queen Isabel and King Fernando were married here in the fifteenth century. And Columbus came to this very castle to request permission from Queen Isabel to sail to—"

"Yep, here on page two." The husband tapped the paper. "Tell us somethin' different, like why on earth there are no bars coverin' this here winda? I'm an insurance man, son. Your winda is a liability. I could drive our Cadillac through that hole."

"*Señor*, please do not stand so close. It is dangerous."

The thick, gloved hand of terror grasped Serena's insides and squeezed. *Stay away from the window!*

"Not the Caddy, your Chevy maybe," his wife attested.

"Has anyone fallen out the winda?" the man asked the Spaniard.

"*Sí*. Five hundred years ago. A nursemaid in charge of Queen Isabel's heir was so overcome with grief when the young prince lost his life, she took her own."

Serena clutched her heart.

"You mean she jumped? Holy moly, that's one heck of a fall." The woman gripped her husband's arm and scooted toward the window. Slowly, carefully, she looked down.

Serena shut her eyes. She couldn't watch the woman lean over the ledge. A wave of horror rolled through her like a belly illness. Her head fell back against the cold wall with a jolt, ricocheting pain through her skull.

She saw stars for a moment and then...she began to remember. Rusty as an old blade, the memories slashed through her groggy brain—longing, lost love, betrayal. Each vision stabbed and stabbed until she was fully awake. And dying.

"Oh, Andrés," she wailed.

The woman, who was still bent at the waist over the window ledge, jerked up straight. "Did y'all hear that? I swear it sounded like a woman cryin'."

"Many have heard the nursemaid's cries, *señora*. A few have seen her."

The husband puffed up his barrel chest. "Ain't no such thing as ghosts."

"Don't be silly. Of course there are. We've got us one here, don't we?" Intensity burned in the woman's blue eyes.

"So says the legend."

The woman fisted her hands on her hips. "Why is the nursemaid still here? Ghosts don't stick around for five hundred years unless they've got some unfinished business. Hasn't anyone tried to help her move on?"

Serena fell silent.

"*Perdón*? I do not comprehend."

"My daughter, Erin could do it. We had us a ghost in the attic. A little séance and wham-bam-thank-ya-ma'am, no more moaning in the night."

Her husband slapped his forehead. "How many times do I have to say it? It was no ghost. The house was just settlin'."

"I'm sure Erin could help the cryin' spirit go on to the folks who love her. My Erin is smart as a whip. She's a stockbroker, you know."

The Spaniard shook his head, his face suddenly pale. "No, *señora*. Do not get too close to the ghost, or you will lose your mind."

"Whaaa—?" The woman's mouth fell open with such force the layer of fat under her jaw shook.

"Legend says one touch from the ghost will make you *loca*."

"*Loca*? You mean...oh no, crazy? Aaak!" The woman grabbed her husband's arm and yanked him toward the stairway. "Sorry, Mr. Tour Guide, we best be going now."

"Hey, slow up. We ain't finished the tour," the husband complained.

"I ain't stickin' around to end up like nutty Aunt Lulu, no sir."

Serena watched them leave with a sense of relief. She was alone. Now, where was she? The tower. Where it all happened. Her memories were fine goose down, floating on the wind. She had to do something before they blew away and she fell back into deep slumber. More than anything she longed to find Andrés. But how?

"Erin, Erin, Erin," she chanted softly. If fortune were with her, the next time she awoke she'd remember the name of her savior.

Chapter One

Dexter, Houghton, and Levine Brokerage, Los Angeles

I couldn't save myself. I was dying a gruesome, humiliating death that was far from over.

"There's no point in continuing the interview," the Big Guy said. "You're not handling this well, Erin."

Backed into the corner, my pride bleeding all over the place, I did what I had to do. "*I'm* not? Handle this: take your job and jam it straight up—"

He gripped my shoulder. "Be sensible."

"You want to keep that hand?" *Sensible?* Any sense had flown out the window fifteen minutes ago when the most important meeting of my life had turned into all-fiery hell. Never in my wildest dreams did I expect to pull out the "I Quit" card. This place, this job, was my life.

He tipped his palms up in his typical "let's negotiate" stance and turned on his plastic smile—the one he flashed before grinding opponents under his wingtips.

Had he forgotten I knew all his moves?

"Think about what you're doing. If you walk out of here, it's all over." His plastic smile slipped, just a hair.

I didn't want it to be over. Silently, I begged. *You want me to stay. You need me. Please, don't let me go.*

"It's your call. I won't stop you," he said.

"You think I should stick around to—what, rub my nose in your asinine decision?" I trembled with rage. He didn't want me...he never had.

His nostrils flared. "I was wrong. Obviously, you're not the best person for the job. I'm sorry."

He wasn't sorry. "The only thing obvious is I've been robbed." I narrowed my eyes at him. "No wait, screwed and then robbed. Sums it up, doesn't it?"

"You're acting like a crazy woman."

I leaned in close enough to kiss him. Or bite his nose off. "You haven't seen crazy yet." No one at the firm had, but I tilted dangerously in that direction.

Breathe, Erin, breathe. Don't lose control, my psychiatrist droned inside my head. I had never been so humiliated, or so viciously used by anyone before. This hurt.

YOU breathe, Dr. Stapleton. I want to pound something. Hard.

My gaze flicked down to the thick folder in my hand.

The Big Guy saw the look in my eye. "Erin, don't you dare. Those charts belong to DH&L."

Meaning that after eight years of devoting every waking hour to the brokerage, Erin Carter was no longer a part of the company. I'd become a non-entity.

My head threatened to explode.

I dumped the presentation I'd spent weeks preparing over his perfectly trimmed, meticulously styled salt-and-pepper hair. Life as I dreamed it rained down in glossy color and spanned out across the gray-flecked carpet. Trashed, all of it. Without looking back, I shoved the conference door open with a bang and hustled out of there before I strangled him with my bare hands.

Halfway down the corridor, reality set in. What had I done?

My stomach flopped. I was going to be sick. *Don't cry. Don't cry.*

I was numb and yet my legs were moving. Fast. The click of my heels on the faux-marble tiles sounded a lot like, "Screw up, screw up, screw up."

I grabbed my purse, fled through the lobby doors and ran like a demon chased me into the parking lot. Making it to my car, I shrank down in the front seat, covered my face with my hands and sobbed. The silk blouse I'd paid a kidney for was spotted with tears. How had things gotten so messed up? I felt...destroyed.

Rooting in the glove compartment for a package of Kleenex, my hand skimmed across the DH&L emblem blazoned on the Car's User Manual. That's when another important truth sank in—this wasn't my car. I drove the firm's navy blue Buick as a top commission producer. Some perk. I only drove it to and from work, even on weekends.

The windshield went fuzzy. Panic seized my brain and careened through my body like a high-speed police chase on the Hollywood Freeway. I wouldn't outrun the attack. This one was going to be colossal.

"Sweet God," I begged. "Not again."

Fingers of terror scraped down my spinal cord. A thirty-pound weight smashed the air out of my lungs. A strange sound filled the car's interior like air squeaking out of a busted balloon as I hyperventilated in the car that wasn't mine. The world spun madly. Gripping the steering wheel, I hung on, but nothing would stop the fall. No one would catch me.

My mind didn't snap. It exploded like an egg cooked on high in a microwave. Heartsick, panic-stricken and blinded with fury, I turned the key, stomped on the gas and floored the Buick.

Straight for the firm's lobby doors.

ℝ℞

I was lucky to be alive.

But with no love life, no career, and a jail cell in my near-future, luck was a relative term.

Truth be told, I was desperate, shattered, bone-achy and above all else, terrified. Craziness ran in my family, still no one on my family tree went nuts enough to become a suspect in an attempted vehicular manslaughter case. Before now.

Three days had passed in a blubbery haze involving sleep, food, wine, my pink-flowered pajamas and fuzzy socks. The delivery cartons and empty wine bottles grew and grew until the Hefty bag was too heavy to carry to the garbage bin. It sat there in the corner of my kitchen floor as bloated and worthless as I felt.

Standing in front of my open, empty refrigerator, I thought fleetingly about making an appointment with Dr. Stapleton. He'd have some ideas to drag me out of my depression, or at the very least stronger meds, but I didn't relish replaying the incident. There were no words to explain what happened.

Why did I do it? reverberated through my head like aftershocks. Panic bubbled up my throat like a soda can shaken to the point of exploding. I had to get my anxiety under control before I killed someone.

Dr. Stapleton's voice nagged inside my head. *You need to prioritize. Set some goals. Create a game plan.*

I ripped the drawers out of my desk and dumped them upside down in the middle of the den. All my client files would make a nice bonfire if I were crazy enough to set a match to them. I found the pale blue journal Mom had given me when I graduated from college. She'd always kept one to write her thoughts in. Mine was as empty as it was on graduation day.

I toddled off to the kitchen and dug into my purse for the purple pen with the gold letters saying *Stockbrokers do it with your share.* I cracked open the empty journal and wrote across the top of the first page, *Get a Life.*

Good. Exactly. Other people had normal lives, lovers and friends. Why couldn't I? I swung my legs under the barstool, tapped the back of the pen on the black-and-white speckled Corian countertop and concentrated really hard.

How does a woman who has completely crashed her life get a new one?

The phone rang by my elbow. I screeched in surprise and the pen took flight. My hands trembled as I checked the caller ID. *Maria.*

"I love talking to you, I do, but you don't have to call me every hour. Don't you have work to do? A life to live?"

"Hello to you too," Maria said. "I'm worried, *chica.* You keep saying you're fine but...that was some car crash."

"I know."

"Judy in Accounting called a zillion times. Why don't you pick up?"

My nerves had been too raw and jangled over the past three days to speak to anyone other than Maria. Checking emails was enough to douse me in cold sweat. Forget about going to the mailbox. Lord help me if I ended up a shut-in like my cousin Cate, who chopped down her mailbox and tossed out the garbage cans. She even boarded up the chimney to keep Santa out. One of my greatest fears was becoming cousin Cate, or any of my crazy relatives.

I wasn't there yet. Still, only Dr. Stapleton knew about my battle with anxiety disorder. How would it look? Erin Carter was supposed to be A-class partnership material, not a flipped-out basket case.

"I'll call her. Soon." *Maybe.*

"So? What are you doing with your spare time? Banging a cabana boy?"

I snorted. "Oh yeah, right after the gardener. I think you have me confused with a desperate housewife."

"You've got to get out of your condo before you become one of those old ladies who collects cats."

Great. I needed that image running through my head. "I'm fine."

"You're not. Get ready, I'm taking you to lunch."

I glanced at my watch. "Don't tell me Jerry lifted his hard-and-fast no-lunch-before-noon rule."

"About that, I dumped Jerry."

I jerked up straight. "No, you didn't."

"DH&L was boring as hell without Miss Stockbroker Supreme. Besides, the bullshit-flinging contests were getting tiresome."

"You heard something about the...accident?" A rock fell into my stomach.

She was silent for a moment. "There's an investigation, but it's only half-cheeked. Everyone knows what really happened."

"Investigation?" I squeaked.

"To find out why the accelerator stuck on you. Thank God those concrete posts were there, huh? A few feet to the left and you would have parked inside the lobby."

"What if they determine it wasn't an accelerator problem but..." I swallowed. "...a driver malfunction?" *Jail? The sanitarium for the insane and dangerous?*

"Come on, Erin, that's crazy. You were a little upset. We all heard you quit, or was it fired?" She waited, but I didn't volunteer an answer. "No one on this planet would buy that you crashed the car on purpose."

"I keep replaying the moment. It's all so messed up in my head. Oh Maria, what if someone had walked out of the lobby the moment when—?"

There was a sound on her end like a book slapping a table. "Stop it. No one got hurt, except an ugly American car and three concrete posts. It's over and done. I'll be there in twenty to take you to Chico's. Sounds like you could use lunch and a couple of margaritas." She hung up before I could protest.

I took a stuttering breath. Was it over?

ᎧᏆᏁᏆ

Maria and I sat on tall stools sipping our drinks and eating nachos while the Mexican music crescendoed into a bad polka nightmare. Getting out and doing normal things with a friend was what I needed. The thirty-pound weight on my chest had grown lighter. I could almost breathe.

Maria studied my beat-up face, concern telegraphing in her eyes. "That airbag really messed you up."

I shot her a dirty look. "You sure know how to make a girl feel pretty."

"Sorry. Look at those stitches in your lip. Didn't they have string that wasn't so blue?"

My heart performed a Riverdance beat. "Can we not talk about this?"

"Fine. Are you going to tell me what happened in that conference room, or do I have to sweat it out of the mail boy?"

I cocked an eyebrow at her. All the women at the firm lusted after the guy in the mailroom. "You'd like that, wouldn't you? Too bad you don't work there anymore."

"I've got his number." She smiled at my shock. "He's been over and has one of those tushes you just want to sink your teeth into, but that's beside the point. We're talking about you here."

"We are?" I fanned myself with the beer-and-wine menu. "I

lost my train of thought."

"You were just about to spill about the partner meeting."

It was no secret. Three months ago, one of our founding fathers had fallen prey to a sex kitten half his age. When he left the firm to sail around the world with his bouncing baby bride, a partner seat opened up. Every stockbroker within the fabric-covered cubicles of DH&L dreamed of adding their initial to the ten-foot sign out front. The battle to the top had been bloody. Coworkers lied, cheated and stabbed each other to be the last man standing. I would have killed for the promotion, and, Lord help me, almost did.

"You must have kicked some major male hiney during your presentation." Maria prodded for the blow-by-blow.

But I worried the truth would blow our friendship to kingdom come. I gulped a large sip of slushy margarita. "Oww. Ice cream headache."

"Who gulps margaritas?" She leaned in. "No one knew you left officially until yesterday. Of course the big boys did, but they are being suspiciously quiet."

Would Maria understand? I thought about my cousin, Betty. Did any of her friends understand when she drove her no-good, three-timing husband's pickup off the Santa Monica Pier? No, people usually don't get crazy.

"Okay, so you don't want to talk about it." She motioned to the empty seats around our table. "Don't cute guys eat lunch anymore?"

"Beats me. Purple-and-bloodshot eyes are all the rage." I did the game-show-model-finger-pointing to my shiners and split lip.

"Your eyes are golden-amber." She swirled melted cheese around on her chip. "When you haven't been intimately involved with an airbag."

"Ah well, but you have *the* exotic look with the black hair and blue eyes." The easy banter and normal conversation with Maria was good. Normal.

She spread her perfectly manicured hands wide. "We Spaniards all look like this. But you, Erin, are a sunny California sunset. Come to my country, you will be exotic."

"Me? Hmmm. I like the sound of that."

"So, it's settled. When do we leave?"

I stared at her a long moment. "Are you serious?"

"Serious as an IRS auditor with a hangover."

"Just pick up and go?"

"You've got some place to be? Face it, Erin. This is the best time to go."

I settled back in the stool. She was right. Spain sounded like the perfect place to get a life.

"You speak Spanish, don't you?" Maria asked.

"Three years of high school Spanish, plus two summers in Cuernavaca, Mexico. I get by."

"Castilian is a different dialect, but you'll pick it up. Oh, and you'll love Castile. Great museums, ancient castles, handsome Spaniards."

"Castles." I swallowed hard. "Nothing haunted, right?"

"Don't tell me you believe in ghosts."

"My mom scared the heebie-jeebies out of me. Can you imagine telling a ten-year-old kid a dead guy haunted the attic? Every night I went to bed expecting his cold dead hands around my neck." I shivered at the memory. "Mom decided we'd perform a séance to help the spirit move on. Séance." I snorted. "Like I knew what that was. Basically, I read out of this dusty leather-bound book while she did crazy mumbo-jumbo stuff with candles. Still freaks me out just thinking about it."

She rolled her eyes. "You can stay with me in Salamanca for the summer. You'll be perfectly safe. Unless..." She wagged her candy-apple-red-polished fingernail at me. "...your honey has other plans."

I half-choked on my margarita. "Excuse me?"

"Your main squeeze?" Her grin was downright devious. "I'm on to you, Erin. I know you have a boy toy of your own."

I died a thousand deaths. "You knew?"

"Suspected." She clicked her tongue. "Since you've worked so hard to cover your tracks, he's either horribly disfigured, or what? He's married?"

"Neither." I took a stuttering breath. "He's Jack."

"Do I know Jack?"

"You should. He signed your paycheck for five years."

"No!" She slammed her palms down on the table. "Our CFO?"

I scrubbed my face with my hands. "It started out simply. A glance. Easy flirtation. Nothing really, all in fun."

"You're dating the Big Cheese—"

"The Big Guy," I corrected.

She slit her eyes at me. "His anatomy aside, why didn't I know about this?" She plunked back in her barstool. "The partnership. That's it, isn't it?"

Shame warmed my cheeks. I played with the multicolored fringe on the placemat. "I didn't tell anyone. I was afraid it would look like I was messing with the Big Guy to obtain a leg up." I cleared my throat. "So to speak."

A chip loaded with melted cheese, beans and a sliding jalapeño remained frozen in air halfway to her mouth.

"I had to have the partner's seat. Don't you see, Maria? It was my one chance to prove..." *I wasn't losing my mind.* "...myself."

A strange look had replaced the shock on her face. It resembled admiration. "You've got *cajones*, woman." The chip finally made it to her mouth where it was crunched between her teeth. "What a story."

"It gets worse." I poked my umbrella into my glass, fracturing the stick. "I believed he was really into me. Insane, right?" I held up my hand. "Don't answer that."

"He's pretty darn cute. Who wouldn't want to believe it?"

"Because he's Jack. Hot sex for favors. We both knew the game going in." I made small circles on my forehead with my fingertips.

"Tell me."

"The meeting started out great. I proved I was the best candidate a hundred ways by multimedia presentation and glossy color handouts. When I was finished, he said, 'Let's go celebrate your victory, partner.' Maria, I did it. I'd won."

"Of course you did. You have the best client list and track record of anyone. Aw, *chica*, did you really think you had to sleep with the boss to prove yourself?"

"I didn't think it would hurt." I blew threw my lips. "Just

shows how wrong a girl can be. But at that moment, back in the conference room, I was euphoric. My letter *C* was going to be added to the ten-foot sign out front. I had it all, except...what I really need. What I've never had."

She leaned forward, all ears.

"A real life. This person I've become is messed up. I've lost myself. Do you understand?" I was looking at Maria when I said this, but remembering the look of horror on Jack's face.

"Sure, I get it. You've been killing yourself for the firm. You need to let up. Live a little."

I nodded. She did understand, part of it at least. "Making partner is important to me. Was. But I also want a semi-normal life with kids, family." *A whole night's sleep.* "I suggested we take things up a notch." I winced, reliving the daymare. "I might have used the L-word."

Her mouth hung open for a long minute. She knew Jack— the word *love* wasn't in his vocabulary. Finally, she snapped her mouth shut and managed, "What'd he say?"

"He laughed...hard." I covered my face with my hands. "When he realized I wasn't joking he said there wasn't much point in continuing the partnership interviews. Suddenly, I was far too emotional to be a company leader."

"Head of shit."

"Yeah, what you said." I didn't bother correcting her phrase, choosing instead to drain the final drip of slush from my bulbous, cactus-stemmed glass.

"Erin, what are you going to do?"

"It's already done." I threw up my hands. "I quit. Him and the company. Oh, and then I crashed their car into the building."

"*Madre de Dios!*" She lifted my empty glass. "Waiter, we need another over here."

Chapter Two

University Hospital of Salamanca, Spain

Hearing his name paged over the intercom system while making rounds, Santiago picked up the nearest wall phone. "*Bueno*, Doctor Botello."

"Do you live at that hospital?"

"Maria! Are you all right? Is everything—?"

"Fine. Everything's great. I'm coming home."

Santiago didn't say anything for a long moment. Shifting the receiver to his other hand, he leaned into the cold wall and lowered his voice. "No. Too dangerous."

"I'm tired of running from my own shadow."

"We all are. You know what's at stake."

"I want to come home. I miss life in Spain. I miss you."

Her voice sounded so thin and fragile that the childhood memories he was usually able to keep at bay came roaring back. Sorrow settled across the thousands of miles between them. "We've gone over this. I need you to stay in Los Angeles."

"I can't be afraid any longer, Santiago. I won't. I'm sorry you worry. You're my big brother, that's your job, but I'm a grown woman. Stronger than you think."

"Maria, this...thing...is bigger than you. Bigger than both of us. Stay in California where you will be protected. Please."

"Yeah, and what happens if the 'thing' gets me in California?"

His breath sucked in sharply. "Something happened. The darkness has come back?"

"No, God, relax. Just stating the obvious. California, Spain, what's the difference? It's over. Let it go, okay?"

"But—"

"Hey, I didn't tell you. I'm bringing a friend with me."

"To Spain? No, Maria. You can't."

"She's great. You're going to love her."

"Maria, listen to me. It's far too risky."

"I know the two of you will get along. She's very smart, funny. Well, usually. She's going through some emotional problems right now."

"Emotional problems." He ran his fingers through his hair. "So you met this friend at—"

"Work. She's a stockbroker at the firm. Was. Anyway, I like her, I want to help her get through this tough time, so I'm bringing her home with me for a few weeks."

"Not a good idea."

"It's a great idea. She needs help, I need to help someone. It's perfect. I'm tired of being the victim."

He pressed his palm to the headache burrowing deep behind his forehead. "What are you going to tell your friend?"

"Nothing."

"Maria."

"She's not strong right now. I don't want to scare her with horror stories."

"Tell her," he said firmly. "She might decide not to come if she knows the truth."

"I want her to come. It will be good for her. For us. Think of how much fun we can have, the places we'll show her."

He could only think about pending disaster. "At the very least, your friend should take precautions."

"She is *never* going to know! She's my best friend and I don't want to spook her needlessly."

"Holy Mother, I'm not saying scare the poor woman. Just...warn her."

"Let me handle this." Her voice screeched through the receiver. "Swear you won't tell her."

He closed his eyes. A clear memory of his little sister came to mind. She ran after him, desperately trying to keep in step. Wearing her favorite pink-flowered dress and matching ribbons tied around her bouncing pigtails, she was a tiny flash of color on a dark, dismal day. How innocent she was. They both were. The vision squeezed his heart. She was only nine when their lives exploded.

He hadn't wanted her running beside him then as he followed the coffin bearers into the cathedral. He'd been weak with grief and shame because he wasn't old enough to carry his father to rest. Too young to bear a man's body, but old enough to shoulder his responsibilities.

Though the bells had tolled so loudly that day he thought his broken heart might shatter in his chest, still he could hear his sister's voice.

"Swear everything's going to be all right." She had tugged on the sleeve of his only suit jacket.

It wasn't. Things would never be right for them again. But she was his little sister. His responsibility.

"Everything's going to be all right," he had promised. It was an oath he couldn't keep.

He blinked back the memories. "I swear I will not say anything to your friend unless something goes wrong."

"What could go wrong? Jeez, you worry like an old granny. I'm going to call you Old Lady Garcia. Remember how she used to glare at us through her window, her nasty wrinkled face spying on us every time we passed her ugly old house?" She laughed like a child.

He rarely laughed anymore and certainly not about this. "Maria, I wish you would reconsider. Stay in LA where I can keep you safe."

"Enough, Old Lady Garcia. A trip to Spain is what Erin needs right now. It's the best thing for her. And me. Love you."

He stood there a long moment with his forehead pressed to the cold wall, the receiver dead in his hand. Then he did something he hadn't done in a long time.

He made the sign of the cross over his chest and prayed.

ଔଞ

In my Get a Life Journal I had written: *1) I am not crazy. I will trust everything will work out for the best and go to Spain.*

Two weeks to the day of my meltdown, we were seated on the plane looking down on puffy clouds. I smiled at Maria. "It's not the corner office, but I finally have my window seat, don't I? At least for the duration of this flight."

"Coffee?" A flight attendant passed by with her little crash cart of caffeine.

"No," Maria said.

"She means yes." I smiled. "Preferably hot and dangerously, mind-melding strong."

"Since when do I drink coffee?" She frowned at me.

"You may be able to survive mornings without caffeine, but I can't."

"Aya, you remind me of my brother. He's a coffee fiend too."

"Sounds like my kind of guy."

"Not really. He's a nice guy."

"Ouch!" I pressed my hands to my heart. "I admit I don't have much experience with that sort of male, but I could learn to do nice."

"Excuse me?" She lifted her brow. "You're not *doing* this one. You haven't even met him yet."

"I didn't mean—"

She rolled her shoulder into mine. "Kidding. I hope you two do hit it off. You could both use a little...distraction."

"Uh-hmm," the flight attendant interrupted. "How about I get you your own cup?"

"Yes, do. And don't forget hers." I grinned.

The flight attendant poured both cups and handed them to me with a constipated smile. "You know I can refill these?"

"Good, maybe when you come back around. Thanks."

Maria shook her head at me. "She's going to spit in the next cup."

"Ewww." Silently, I sipped the hot elixir and slowly came alive, one nerve ending at a time. With closed eyes, I thought, *Saint Starbuck, you deserve a special seat in heaven.*

"You were too good for him, you know," Maria softly interrupted my near-orgasmic caffeine experience.

"Hmm?" Opening my eyes, I was surprised to see her leaning in, focusing intently on my face.

"Jack didn't deserve you. And you should do *nice* next time around."

Unwanted memories flooded my thoughts. The last image of Jack's handsome face swam into view. Slightly blurred by bitter, angry tears, it was lodged in my brain like a photo I had no business keeping.

The truth was, there was no *tomorrow* with Jack. Only now and maybe ten minutes from now. We'd been sinking in a kind of relationship quicksand where people don't move forward, or backward. They just sink. I crumpled the mental photo into a ball and tossed it back into the past.

"You know how they say hindsight is 20/20? Why does foresight have to be so darned blind?" I smiled weakly. "He offered to write a glowing letter of recommendation."

"Really? Which of your attributes was he going to recommend?"

I lifted my cup. "Head of shit."

"Forget him." She lifted "our" coffee cup and carefully clinked it with the one in my hand. "We'll have a blast in Salamanca. Focus on that."

Focus was one of Dr. Stapleton's buzzwords. The sound of it caught me off guard. "Should I find a hotel? I'd hate to impose on your family."

"Stop saying that. Are we, or are we not, friends?"

"The best." I smiled at the serious lines forming between her eyes.

"You'll be safe at my house. I promise."

Safe? "Is Salamanca crime-riddled?"

Her beautifully manicured fingers clutched the crucifix hanging around her neck. "I'm just saying sometimes people need a little looking after. I'm here for you. That's all."

My eyes watered. "You're wonderful."

"Yes, I am. Now, why don't you rest? You look dead tired."

I gave her a dirty look. "And you need to work on your flattery skills."

She shrugged. "It's the truth, Erin. You look like you haven't slept in weeks."

That was the truth, but I wasn't going to admit it. "Okay

Esteem-Builder. I'll rest." I kicked off my shoes, pulled my knees up and fluffed the little blue pillow as best as I could. Then I made the mistake of closing my eyes.

Dangling like a dried-up leaf, I hang onto the tower's window ledge by a single limb—my own bloody arm. None of my twenty-nine years flash before my eyes. What I see, hear and feel is spine-clawing fear. It tastes like acid on my tongue.

A gust of wind plasters me against the medieval tower. The rough sandstone scrapes my skin. My eyes begin to focus well enough to see the cream-colored castle with sharp spires and a blue-tiled roof. The window above me is big and as dark as a screaming mouth. The landscape is black beneath my bare feet. I can barely make out the rocks below the ledge I cling to for dear life. Jagged and sharp as a blade, those rocks can peel a person's skin like a grape. They are about to peel me.

I scream for help. Over and over. It will never come. No one will catch me.

Another gust shoves me against the tower, slashing fresh cuts. I cry out, but the scratches are the least of my injuries.

I'm dizzy and seeing flashes of lights. I shake my head, trying to clear my mind. Focus. Losing consciousness is not an option. What is that smell? The pungent odor filling my nostrils turns my stomach. I open my mouth, trying not to breathe through my nose.

Blood.

My blood is everywhere. It runs like a spilled bucket of water down the sandstone. I blink it out of my eyes. Warm and sticky, it drips through the cracks in my fingers, making them slicker by the second. I tighten my grip. It's no good. Nothing I do is ever any good.

I...am...slipping.

I scream, with every ounce of life left in me. And my fingers lose contact with the ledge.

"Hey." Maria nudged me. "You were crying out in your sleep."

The castle, the rocks, all gone. I was on the plane looking into Maria's horrified face. I wiped the drool off my cheek.

"Sorry."

"Damn that Jack! He's not worth losing sleep over. We need to find you a man who sees how special you really are, as a person, not just the best moneymaker in the place."

She sounded like a shrink. It warmed my heart. "You think I'm special?"

"You need a real man who worships you. Goddess status."

"What if—?" I blinked, swallowed hard. "What if I never find anyone like that?"

"You found a toad, why can't you find a prince?"

"Because the pond's crawling with toads?"

"Doesn't mean he's not out there." She wagged a finger at me.

Feeling better, I forced the dream down deep where I shoved all my horrors. The nightmares and the panic never stayed put in the recesses of my thoughts. They crouched, biding their time to strike when I was the most vulnerable. My worst nightmare was that one day they'd take over completely and I'd become as crazy as the rest of my relatives.

I shrugged off the heaviness settling between my shoulder blades. Terror wouldn't get me today. "I don't want to think about men. Tell me more about Spain. What happens after we land? Do we need to rent a car?"

"My brother's sending a car for us."

"The coffee fiend."

"Most respected doctor in the city. Too many awards to count."

"You must be very proud of him."

Her voice was soft. "After my father died, my brother took care of us. Mama was...distraught. There wasn't much money. A trust, yes, but we couldn't touch it until we became of age. My brother went to medical school and started his practice. Later, he sent me to school in the U.S. without touching my portion of the trust. Proud? There are no words."

"Sounds like an amazing guy."

"He is, but you'll probably find him a bit guarded."

No one did "guarded" better than I. "Does he need to be?" I asked.

"A handsome, big-hearted doctor? He's a magnet for every lowlife female crawling the earth."

"Ah. He's not married."

"Engaged once." She blew through her lips in disgust. "A train wreck. I warned him about her. But you know men, they all have a basic need to be taken care of, even if the woman, the situation, everything is all wrong."

I wondered about her theory. Did every man need a woman? Jack sure didn't need me. Much. He liked having me around for the fun times, but emotional need? No, Jack's need was not about me, or the organ he called his heart.

"That story doesn't have the happy-ever-after ring to it."

"She left him for another guy, maybe three whole days before the wedding. My brother was devastated."

"That's terrible."

"Past history. Good riddance." Her chin lifted. "Now it's little sister's chance to take care of him for a while. I'm dying to get home."

Butterflies of excitement tickled my insides, loosening the knot of dread lodged in my chest. I couldn't wait to get to Spain either. Forget about men, I thirsted for life. With any luck, I could outrun the misadventures of Erin Carter and start over fresh. I wouldn't screw it up this time.

I'm going to get a life, I promised myself. *Even if it kills me.*

CRESO

With twenty minutes to landing in Salamanca, I searched frantically for my hairbrush, which proved to do more harm than good.

"Ah jeez, look at my hair." My sandy-blond strands crackled and popped.

"Got a little electricity there?" Maria joked.

"Enough to power up a small city. Why does yours always look good?" I flipped my finger through her dark curls.

"Genes. You should have seen my mother's hair when she was young. Hey, speaking of jeans, you have a big stain on yours." She pointed to the burnished spot on the crotch of my pants.

"Coffee, courtesy of the Seat Bumper." I thumbed over my shoulder. "I swear if he kicks my chair one more time..."

She stole a peek at the guy behind me through the crack between our seats. "I don't know Erin, he's kind of burly, but if you think you can take him."

I grunted. "Thank God I don't know anyone in Salamanca."

Maria cleared her throat. "It's kind of a tradition..." She saw the murderous look I gave her. "Okay, a few people will be there to welcome me home. Friends, family, teachers, priest, neighbors. That sort of thing."

"What?"

"Relax. You look fine."

I opened my compact and was horrified at what peered back at me in the mirror. "You call this fine? No makeup. Hair gone badly wrong. Dark circles. Stained, wrinkled clothes—"

"The bruises are gone. And your lip looks better without the stitches, not so Bride of Frankenstein anymore. See? I'm working on that compliment thing."

"That's it. I'm not leaving this plane."

Maria turned a deaf ear to my protests. The instant we landed she jumped out of her seat. "Don't lag, Erin," she called, dragging me along with her carry-on luggage down the corridor toward the customs and baggage-claim areas.

I scrambled to keep up with her. A mass of humanity the size of Delaware was smashed in and around the gate outside the customs area, squealing her name. I had the odd sensation something bad was about to happen. Too late I reached for Maria's arm. I was unable to latch onto her before she was snatched away into a sea of cheek-kissers. Strange bodies pressed against me, sucking the oxygen out of the air with their foreign words. Ah, but then I saw *him*.

Whoa! My mind sighed. *Who is that?*

Easily the tallest in the crowd, a gorgeous hunk stood apart, as if the press of hot bodies pushing and shoving didn't concern him. His long fingers ran through neatly trimmed dark hair.

My breath caught when his stunning green eyes locked

onto mine. The expression in those eyes was intense—a broody mixture of regality or renegade. His jet-black eyebrows unfurrowed and a light flickered across his face.

Ooh-la-la.

I fluffed my hair and tucked the bit of T-shirt that had popped out back into my jeans. Nothing could be done about the coffee stains.

The moment was ruined when a security guard tapped the Spanish god on the shoulder and both turned to look at me.

Uh-oh. Was I in trouble? Could it be a crime in Spain to stare at an unbelievably handsome man?

Then it hit me like a car crash. I'd seen enough cop shows to know I was busted. The investigation of the accident was completed and an APB put out for my arrest. Spanish Security was coming to pick up the American wanted for attempted vehicular manslaughter. I'd be handcuffed and sent on the next flight home. They'd put me in the loony bin next to my nutty Aunt Lulu who ate her husband's socks. Oh dear Lord, my life was over.

I had to do something. Quickly. I didn't want life to be over, I had barely accomplished Step 1: Go to Spain. But what could I do? Both men were staring at me over the sea of people. The panic attack was a tornado building behind my eyeballs. I itched to shove my way through the crowd.

For the love of God, get me out of here.

A short exchange took place between the two men. It was my chance to escape.

Hunching down, I gathered my luggage and pushed toward the exit, keeping an eye out for Maria as I went. I had no plan other than to get away. I couldn't go back to the States and face the music. I'd almost made it to the door when—

"Oof! Excuse me. Oh."

I had smashed into the chest of the Spanish god. Startled as a possum on a highway, I gazed up at his green headlights. When he gave me the head-to-toe once-over I knew I was in big trouble. Yep, he was obviously an undercover cop. I was caught.

"Ms. Carter. Please come with me." He reached out and tried to take one of my suitcases out of my hand.

"Hey! Let go. I'm not going anywhere with you, buddy.

33

Show me the warrant." I sounded braver than I felt.

He released the suitcase. "Warrant?"

"Or whatever you call it here." I flipped the hair out of my eyes. "And identification. Pronto, mister."

"My apologies. I assumed you knew who I am." He took a step back and extended his hand. "I'm Santiago. Come with me to the car."

"I'm not going downtown in your paddy wagon, bud. Forget about it."

"Wagon?" His face registered confusion. "I believe it's a Buick."

"Oh sweet Lord." The blood in my face dropped to my feet.

"See?" He pointed out the glass window toward a beige car with an *Auto Servicio* sticker in the window. Car Service?

"You're not—?" The security guard had melted into the crowd. "I'm sorry, who are you?"

"Santiago. You need a car, right?"

Oh. The driver, I kicked myself for letting my imagination get the best of me. I took his hand in mine and shook. *Warm, firm grip. Nice. Very...* "Nice to meet you. I'm sorry, I thought... Um, yes, my friend and I need a car." I started to breathe again.

"Is this all?" He pointed at my luggage.

"It's more than enough. Don't you think?" Not sure what to bring, I had grossly over-packed. Ruffling through my Brighton wallet, I pulled out some bills to tip the poor guy.

"Erin, there you are—Santiago!" To my utter surprise, Maria flung her arms around the driver's neck. "This is my friend, Erin Carter."

"Yes. We've met," he said.

Another man walked up to us and Santiago handed him my bags. "The driver will take you home. I will see you later." With a curt nod, he strode back through the crowd.

How many drivers did we need? The tip money was still wadded up in my hand, but Santiago was gone.

"All of these." Maria showed driver number two our bags.

A weird foreboding washed over me. My skin prickled, tingling into my scalp like I was a B-actress in a horror flick waiting for evil to creep up behind her. It was ridiculous. My nervous system was still flooded with adrenaline after the security guard incident. I had to get a hold of myself.

A cry wailed in my ear and something poked my shoulder. I yelped and spun around. A tiny lady with vacant blue eyes lifted a covered object, ready to poke me with it again.

Evil? If so, I'd just been tagged.

Chapter Three

I let out the air I'd been holding and silently thanked God I hadn't used my self-defense moves on the poor old woman. *What was wrong with me?*

"No thanks, I'm not buying," I said in a trembling voice and turned away. My body still quaked.

She shoved the object under my nose.

"No thank you, really."

Her head shook fiercely. Silver strands of hair escaped from her tight bun, sticking out like electrified wires. There was something about her eyes—eerie, haunted, dead? She wasn't dirty, but had the shutdown look of someone in the shadows of an overpass curled up in a cardboard box. That look hit pretty close to home. I suddenly wanted to hug the poor thing and call her auntie.

"So, what is it you have there?" I asked. "A doll? *Muñeca?*" Her head bobbed up and down. "Sure, I'll take a peek at your, um, baby." I put my bag down, mesmerized by the great production she made of unfolding the dingy pink blanket. Slowly one side folded down, and then another, until the treasure was revealed. And what a sight it was.

Grisly is the best way to describe her doll. Both eyes had been poked out, the hair had been hacked off with some weapon, decidedly not scissors, the nose was missing and the tiny rosebud of a mouth had been opened to a forevermore gaping *O*. Even its cry sounded deranged, as if the voice box had been repeatedly run over by a baby's stroller.

Taken aback, I reacted. I'm not sure what my reaction was,

maybe my hand flew to my mouth, or I gasped, or both. Whatever I did, it was wrong.

Her eyes lit with fury. She raised the mutilated doll and whacked me over the head with it.

"Hey, stop that!" I rubbed my head.

She hugged the battered doll to her chest, glaring at me as if I had been the one to attack her. The doll's distorted cries sounded like hiccups when she rocked it back and forth.

"Okay. Moving on." I picked up my bags.

I didn't get far before she smashed her body against mine. It was like being belly-bumped in the back by a tiny Suma-wrestler. If there weren't so many people around us, I would surely have crashed to the floor alongside the bag that flew out of my hands.

"*Lo siento*, sorry," I said as total strangers helped right me again. I couldn't shake the grunting, belly-bumping woman with the hideous doll tucked under one arm. I was completely dumbstruck.

Maria rushed to my rescue. She clutched at the woman's bony shoulders. "Mama! Stop that."

Wait, what?

"It's Maria. I'm home. See? Stop bumping Erin."

Mrs. Botello rolled her thin shoulders to wriggle free from Maria's fingers and continued pestering me. It would have been comical if it were not so sad. I stopped trying to get away. Raising my eyebrows at Maria, I wondered what, if anything, I could do to help.

It was heartbreaking to see Maria's eyes misty with tears. "Please, Mama, look at my face."

"Mrs. Botello, I like your dolly, really—" I tried to reason with her, until she lifted the hapless thing to club me again.

Maria's face burned dark and angry. "That's it!" She yanked the doll out of her mother's hands. "Be nice."

Mrs. Botello turned her watery blue eyes on Maria. The wild fury immediately evaporated. She seemed to shrink, her tiny body collapsing.

"Oh, Mama." With a weak smile, Maria re-wrapped the doll in the grungy pink blanket and placed the whole lot in her mother's hands. "This is my friend, Erin. Remember, I told you she was coming to stay with us?"

Mrs. Botello scurried to her daughter's side. Using Maria as a body shield, she stole glances at me as if I were evil incarnate.

"Come on," Maria said to me. "She'll follow us." And she did, toddling along beside Maria like a two-year-old with the mangled *muñeca* in her left hand. "*Señora* Hernán!" Maria called to a woman in the crowd.

The woman hurried toward us looking panic-stricken. "*Lo siento,* she got away from me."

"It's all right. Nothing bad happened. This is my friend, Erin. Mrs. Hernán is the nurse who takes care of my mother."

When we got to the car, Maria buckled her mother in the backseat and kissed her forehead while I plopped my carry-on into the trunk. Maria met me at the back of the car. "Sorry. My mother is..." She searched for the right word and couldn't find it. "She does some funny things, but she's harmless. I think she liked you. Really."

It surprised me Maria had kept her mother's mental state a secret. We'd both hid our skeletons pretty well. "You think?"

"Definitely. You should see how she acts around people she doesn't like."

Maria had me sit up front with the driver. *Señora* Botello was still "getting to know me" which involved humming in a loud voice with her palms pressed to her ears. It was like being stuck in a car with the radio tuned full blast to the emergency broadcast signal.

"Sorry," Maria yelled over the monotone humming. "It's only a ten-minute ride to the house."

After the longest three-and-a-half minutes of my life, the humming ended abruptly. Mrs. Botello was asleep.

"Phew, the drugs finally kicked in. Why was she so agitated?" Maria asked.

Mrs. Hernán wouldn't meet her gaze. "She's been out of sorts since we received word you were coming home."

Maria fell silent.

"Nah, my hair probably freaked her out. Look at this disaster." I tugged at the mess sticking out from my head.

Maria smiled. "Oh yeah, you look hideous."

I shook my finger at her. "The compliment thing is not working out for you."

The driver took us through a giant roundabout. I gripped the dashboard. I'm used to the LA freeways, but this congested circle whipped cars out like a slingshot.

Maria was unfazed. "Oh, look, the *Parque de la Alamedilla.* My parents used to bring us to this park every summer. My brother and I tried catching pigeons for pets."

Buildings sprouted up at the edge of the park. Aged and majestic, many of the architectural structures were beautifully ornate with distinctive arches. The Spanish painters of old had been an agreeable bunch—the colors blurred together outside my window were varying shades of sand—from off-white to sunset pink. No shocking turquoise houses here. Red tiled roofs were the norm. Growing up in California I had been to many of the Spanish missions dotting the state, but none of them resembled this bustling city. It was all so *European.*

"Your city is beautiful," I said.

Maria smiled. "Salamanca has the oldest university in Spain. We'll take a tour one of these days. Here's my street."

I read the sign. *Calle de Gran Viva.* "Street of the Good Life."

The driver turned up a long cobblestone driveway overhung with ancient olive trees and parked in the circular driveway of a Mediterranean mansion. He got out and started removing our luggage from the trunk. Mrs. Hernán opened the door, speaking in soft, gentle words to the groggy Mrs. Botello. The two of them went inside the house.

Maria leaned against the car door. "Home. Finally."

"This is a palace. You never told me you were Spanish royalty."

Smiling, she hoisted a large bag over her shoulder. "You never asked."

We dragged our bags through the archway into an outside courtyard complete with a fountain and large fireplace. "You're a princess, right? Queen?"

She beamed from ear to ear. "My family had ties to the crown of Castile. Ask Santiago, he can give you all the gory details."

"Santiago?"

"My brother is a history buff."

"Oh dear." A sinking feeling rolled down my esophagus and landed in my stomach. "Santiago. The man I met at the airport. Is your brother?"

She rolled her eyes like a teenager. "Duh."

My face was hot with embarrassment. Good gosh, he must have thought I was a lunatic, demanding to see his warrant and then...had I pulled out tip money? No wonder he left in such a hurry.

"What's wrong? Did he say anything?" She studied my face.

"About...?"

She bit her lip. "Nothing."

"Yep, that pretty much covered our conversation. What was the deal with the security guard?"

She frowned.

A thought brought a low hum of panic up my spinal cord. *Was the guard really looking for me and Santiago somehow threw him off my trail?*

"You didn't see a guy in a uniform, about five foot eight, 160 pounds, stop to talk to him?"

"Nope. Santiago knows a ton of people in Salamanca. The guard was probably a patient."

Maria gave me the tour of her palace, pointing out various antiques and exquisite art pieces. There was a life-sized bronze woman holding a lily up to her nose in the living room. A golden head of an Arabian horse with flying mane, wild eyes and flared nostrils on a pedestal in the entry. Every wall was covered with paintings or tapestries.

"That painting there is a Borrassa, fourteenth century. Been in my family for generations."

"Impressive." We kept walking, me gaping, her beaming. "Your family has collected quite a few pieces."

"Yeah well, this is the Hall of Shame." She led me into a long hallway lined with photos.

"No way, I love family pictures."

"This is my favorite. It's the last one—" her voice caught,

"—of us all together."

"Awww, look how cute you were. Love those pigtails. A skiing vacation?"

"One of our trips to the Pyrenees." Maria peered closer at the picture. "I'm about nine there. See the look in Santiago's eye?"

I stared at the handsome young man. Yep, he was the guy from the airport, all right. Only now he was about a foot taller with impossibly wide shoulders, a sexy square jaw and to-die-for green eyes.

"He's about to smash a huge snowball on my head. He's hiding it behind his back, the rat. But I got my revenge." She laughed. "I always do."

"Is that your dad?"

"Yes," she said quietly. "Lord rest his soul."

"He was very handsome. Your mom sure seems happy." A much younger Mrs. Botello had wrapped her arms around her husband's waist. With her head tilted back, her dark hair cascaded over one shoulder. The photographer had captured the exact moment her laughter had erupted.

Maria turned her head away. "He was dead two months after this picture was taken."

"I'm sorry, Maria."

Her bottom lip quivered. "It's just hard, you know. The way things used to be, the way they are now. I barely recognize those people in the picture."

I hugged her.

She stiffened in my arms. "No. I promised myself I wouldn't do this." Pulling away, she angrily swiped at her eyes with the back of her hand. "Enough."

"It's okay, Maria, really."

With one quick shake of her head, she told me it wasn't okay.

"Listen, if you ever want to talk about it, or anything, I'm here, okay?"

"I know," she whispered. "As I am for you."

Sweet, but I wouldn't burden her with my problems. She had more than her share to deal with.

"Come on, let me show you your room. I can't wait to see what you think."

She made a big show of turning the doorknob. I had no idea what would be waiting for me behind the door.

CR&O

Serena pressed her cheek against the cold, stone masonry to fight off the lethargy. She was in the tower. Still. Locked in her eternal prison.

Yet the tower was preferable to the empty place, which resembled dreamless sleep, soundless, lonely. The emptiness pulled at her, stronger than any current, lulling her to slumber. But she could not afford to rest in a place which fed on her memories, sucking them dry. She needed her memories, no matter how terrifying and horrible they were. She had to find Andrés.

"No," she said and startled a little at the sound of her own voice echoing against the walls and bouncing off the sloped ceiling. "No," she repeated again, louder. "I will not close my eyes. Andrés! Where are you?"

There was no reply.

Taking the rosary out of her dress pocket she said her Hail Marys slowly by rote. When her fingers rolled across the last worn bead, she added a new prayer. "*Madre, ayúdame.*"

Shutting her eyes and concentrating with all her strength, Serena chanted, "Erin, Erin, Erin."

A swooping feeling hit her stomach like flying or, *Dios*, falling. She cried out, expecting the slashing pain, the breaking of her bones against the rocks, the agonizing last breaths. Nothing of the sort happened. A strange tearing sound, as if fabric had ripped in half, made her open her eyes again.

Wonder of wonders, she had escaped the tower. She was free!

But where was she? The room was empty save a few pieces of furniture. An armoire, large canopy-covered bed and a chair. Serena moved closer. The chair was familiar. It seemed like the one she used to sit upon when—

Her thoughts ended quickly. Someone was coming. Again.

CRISO

Maria let me go first. I walked into the light pink, paisley-wallpapered bedroom. It was a fairy princess room.

"This is it?" I faked disappointment. "I was planning to host a Lakers' Party in here."

Unsure, she peered at me closely. "You can have my room. It's a bit larger."

"I'm kidding. This room is much too good. Put me somewhere less elegant if you want and save this room for royalty."

"Nah, you're the most important guest here." She smiled brightly, all tears tamped down. "My room's next door. Why don't you rest a while before dinner?"

"Sounds lovely." I looked longingly at the queen-sized bed complete with four wooden posts and lacy canopy. The soft pink down comforter called my name.

"See you in a few hours." Maria closed the door behind her.

I yawned. I was ready for a nice long nap.

What the—?

Turning slowly, my gaze drifted across the bed, nightstand, wall mirror, antique velvet chair, cherry-wood armoire and back to the chair again. Flutters of familiarity tickled my brain and lifted the hairs on my scalp. I rubbed my arms. They were covered in goose bumps.

For no explainable reason, the antique chair continued to draw my attention.

The room tilted. I sat on the edge of the bed, balling the comforter up in my fists, hanging on as the room spun around me. *Damn, vertigo.* I'd had it once before when a cold virus infected my inner ear. Why now? What was happening to me?

Serena gasped. Before her a lady sat on the edge of the bed, holding on to blankets as if they were the sides of a boat being tossed on a merciless sea.

Virgin Mother, could this be her savior?

Serena forced herself to sit quietly on the chair waiting to see what her redeemer might do.

The lady was beautiful and strange in long hose similar to those of the other lady in the tower. And what of her hair? Unbound and chopped short, barely to her shoulders did it reach. The loose tendrils floated about her face like the soft feathers of a goose. Unheard of.

Does she not see me?

The lady's actions surprised her. Why did she press her fingertips into her temples as if her head pained her?

Serena began to fear the lady would never see her. Something had to be done.

Taking a deep breath, Serena steeled herself and whispered, "Erin?"

Hearing a noise, my head shot up faster than it should have. The room whirled like one of those teacup rides at Disneyland. It was all I could do not to be sick.

It was the craziest thing. The room wasn't really spinning, my inner ear had gone wonky on me. Keeping my head upright, I hoped the fluid in my ear would settle and behave. Needing to focus on something, my gaze drifted back to the antique chair. I had the sensation I wasn't alone.

"You're losing it, Erin."

No one was sitting on that stupid chair. To prove it, I carefully stood up, walked across the room and sat down.

The lady walked toward Serena.

Glory of glories, she sees me.

Happiness bloomed in her heart. Oh, to be free of the tower once and for all. She did not understand what a "say-on" was, but knew Erin could help her find her true love.

Andrés, we shall be together.

The lady said, "You're losing it, Erin."

Serena pressed her hands to her own heart. She did not know what was lost, but knew for certain her savior had been found. *Erin, you are my only hope. You must help me. You are...about to sit upon me? Stop.* "No!"

Serena's insides shook and she fell, landing hard. She

groaned and rubbed her sore backside.

I am back in the tower.

Staring up at the thick wood-beams, she panted to catch her breath. She was exhausted, but vowed to try it again once she had regained her strength. She would not remain in this place of death much longer.

Somehow, someway, she had to make Erin help her.

The spinning stopped and the déjà vu ended. I sat on the chair for a moment gathering my wits about me. It had to be exhaustion. I needed sleep. Desperately.

Kicking off my shoes, I dove under the thick down comforter. The satin sheets were cool and silky on my hot skin. Perfect. With thoughts of a handsome doctor dancing in my head, I closed my eyes. And dreamed.

I stand in a peaceful garden surrounded by blooming rose bushes. My heart thunders in my ears.

A breeze blows a warning across my skin. It whips my dark hair loose from the blue ribbon at the back of my neck and tugs on my long skirt. The rose bushes sway, revealing thorns beneath the satiny petals. Even here, in the gardens, evil exists.

Behind me is the castle. My refuge. I want to turn and flee back inside, but it is too late. I cannot move. Fear binds my legs and steals the air out of my chest.

If I can catch my breath, I will scream.

Death rides swiftly toward me like a man on a dark gray horse.

He is coming.

Chapter Four

What's the matter with me?

Why couldn't I stop thinking about those amazing green eyes, his jet-black hair, the way he moved in those charcoal colored pants... Oh Lordy.

Tossing clothes out of my suitcase, I searched for my nicest blouse while frantically, hand-pressing the wrinkles out of the black skirt.

It may have been a little soon after the Jack fiasco to fantasize about Santiago. But in a way, it felt healthy. Normal. Santiago came with no boost-me-up-the-ladder fringe benefits. It was simple girl-thinks-boy-is-yummy attraction.

This trip was about the normalization of Erin. If the healing process involved a hot studly Spaniard, all the better. I didn't need a man to clean up my life, or lack of life. No, I knew that responsibility rested solely on my shoulders. But Maria was right. Being a goddess, even for a few weeks, had a nice sound to it.

I rummaged through my carry-on and pulled out the blue notebook. Under *Get a Life* I wrote a second goal: *2) Relax. Flirt. Enjoy a man, just because. Become a goddess.*

"Goddess," I said to my reflection. The dark circles had faded to light smudges, but my eyes were still tired, my complexion too pale. "Yeah, right."

Straightening my back, lifting my shoulders, I swiped a little pink lip gloss on my lips. Fingers of excitement tingled down my back and twisted my stomach in knots.

Get a hold of yourself, Erin, I chided myself. *It's just dinner.*

I took a big breath and turned out the light.

CR£O

When she walked into the room, Santiago's heart did a painful miss-beat against his breastplate, as if it stopped dead in his chest only to start again with her smile.

He'd been sitting on the edge of the sofa impatiently waiting for Maria's friend to show herself. He wanted to speak with her alone, while Maria showered, to determine the woman's mental state. She had acted so oddly at the airport. His sister had hinted at some sort of breakdown and he could not, in good conscience, leave a fragile female in this house. It was far too dangerous.

He had enough trouble taking care of his mother and shielding his sister from the darkness. How in the hell could he protect another woman? He couldn't. He'd insist she move out.

But when he saw her...

Sweet Mother, when he saw her all rational thought ended.

"Hello again." Her voice was as smooth and promising as satin sheets.

His gaze traveled across her curves. She didn't look fragile. No, she looked good enough to eat. She lifted an eyebrow, shooting him a look loaded with hunger. Need coursed through his own veins. Her smile produced a punch of heat to his groin.

Mierda, he was in trouble.

"*Buenos tardes.* Did you have a nice rest?" He asked.

"Yes, and, I um—" she moved closer, her cheeks flushed, "—need to apologize for earlier at the airport. I made a perfect ass of myself."

She came around the couch to sit and he noted how perfect her ass was. His gut twisted. "No apologies necessary." He forced himself to study her clinically, searching for grounds to throw her out of the mansion. It didn't take a Chief of Medicine to notice her pale skin and dark-rimmed eyes. "Are you feeling all right?"

Her crooked smile told him she knew she was being examined. "Well, doctor, I've had better years." Her laughter was husky and rich. "But I'm determined to get a life. No time like the present, right?"

He was mesmerized by what sparked from her tired eyes. She was determined and more—she was courageous. Something horrible had happened to her. He could see she hadn't slept well in days, maybe weeks, and yet she smiled. How had she accomplished that? He longed to dig deeper, to know her secrets. The muscles and nerves in his cheeks rarely turned upwards anymore. Laughter was a thing of the past.

"Hey guys. Glad you two are getting to know each other," Maria called from the hallway.

He jumped to his feet and met his sister halfway across the room. "Wonderful to have you home, sis."

Maria hugged him. "I can't tell you how it feels to be here. Staying for dinner?"

He cast a look over his shoulder towards Erin, feeling the hunger rumble in his bones. He had to get away from her, fast. "No, I'm meeting Helena tonight."

"Helena?" Maria asked.

He couldn't take his eyes off Erin when he said, "She's a volunteer at the hospital. A friend. We're discussing an intern program over dinner."

"I see," Maria said.

"Nice to speak with you, Ms. Carter." He willed his legs to walk him right out the door. Instead, he found himself standing before her, his hand outstretched. She rose and placed her hand in his. They didn't shake. Instead, their eyes locked and he bent and placed a kiss on her cheek.

"You too." Her eyes were on his lips. "See you soon?"

He was still holding her hand. No woman had captivated him so quickly, so completely. She was trouble. Big trouble. He had to get out of there. "Soon."

Finally, somehow, he made it to the front door.

Maria's voice carried all the way from the living room and bounced off the entry walls. "Surprise of surprises. My brother has a girlfriend. Hospital Helena. Great, huh?"

"Um, yeah, great." Erin's voice floated to him like a breeze.

Frowning, he turned the knob and left.

"Um, yeah, great." I didn't add, *For Helena.*

My heart was still beating too fast. I sat down before I fell down. *My gosh, he kissed me.* On the cheek, sure, but it was a kiss.

"Maybe the planets have aligned or something." Maria plopped on the couch next to me. "Hey, will my luck change too? Kind of a familial lucky streak?"

"Looking for love, are we?"

"Love? I'm talking about getting lucky. A hot Spanish hunk rolling around under my goose-down comforter? Yum, that's what I'd call dessert."

"You go, girl." I laughed. "What about commitment? Do you ever think about the long-term stuff?"

"During sex?"

"Ever?"

"I did once..." She let the sentiment hang there a moment.

"And?"

"And hot sex is more fun to think about."

"Maria, *está lista?*" A voice called from the kitchen.

"Come on, dinner's ready. I'm starved."

I tagged along behind Maria, my hand to my cheek.

We gorged on spicy vegetable soup, an almond-crusted calamari steak, and chicken breast swimming in a dark mole sauce. All of it to die for.

After dinner we brought our dishes into the kitchen. Maria threw her arms around a short dark seventy-ish woman. "Thank you, Rosa. Everything was delicious. *Dios mío*, how I've missed your meals."

"*De nada, mi amor.*"

"Erin, this is Rosa, the true woman of the house."

"*Sí, Señorita* Ereen, I is dat," she said in her broken English. "I is de cooker, cleaner and peacekeeper. Lord knows what dey do widout ol' Rosa." She took our dishes and began hand washing them.

"And you speak English. Here, let me help with those," I offered.

"She's taking an online course," Maria said.

Rosa shook her head firmly. "No *Señorita* Ereen. I don' need no help."

"Good try," Maria said to me. "Rosa is queen of the kitchen. We just stay out of her way." Maria scooted her rear up onto the kitchen counter and motioned for me to join her.

"If I is de queen, dan why you no listen to me?" She pointed at Maria. "You knows, I no like when you sit up there."

"I knows it," Maria teased.

"So why you want my heart to a-stop wid worry?"

"I always sit up here to listen to your stories." Maria winked at me.

Rosa muttered under her breath, but I could tell it was only a halfhearted protest. I had a sneaky suspicion she'd missed the bantering ritual with Maria.

"Do yous want to hear about de time Santiago and Maria put de snake in me bed?"

"Fun times, fun times," Maria joked and a bemused smile softened Rosa's wrinkled face.

I laughed. "I want to hear it all."

Rosa recalled many funny stories in the Botello household, while careful not to reveal anything too personal about the people she worked for some thirty-odd years. The time flew by.

"Okay, *chicas*," Maria slid down off the counter. "Beddy-bye time."

"What's dis? I's jus about to tell de first time Maria gets kissed by a boy."

"Have a heart," Maria whined, raising her hand. "How many times should I be forced to relive the moment Jorge Lupes's nose nearly poked out my eye?"

I covered my mouth with my hand.

"Laugh all you want. I had a black eye for a week and still have nightmares." She shuddered. "Damn, if Jorge Lupes is on the menu, think I'll skip the dessert." Kissing Rosa's cheek, she waved to me. "See you *mañana*."

I couldn't drag myself away. Rosa reminded me of an older version of my favorite aunt, a beautiful woman who died much too young of breast cancer. "I've been thinking about Mr. Botello...Santiago. He's a man of few words, isn't he?" I was still worried I'd offended him at the airport.

Rosa's face fell. She wrung the towel in her hands. "He is dat way now wid everybody. He holds hisself back from de people."

"You'll probably find him a bit guarded," Maria had said.

"I would be too after what happened to him."

Color drained from Rosa's face as if a ghost had leaped out from behind the counter. "You...know?"

"About the disappearing fiancée? Yes, Maria told me. Pretty heartless to dump Santiago three days before the wedding."

"I should not talk about dis," she whispered.

"It's none of my business. But I do like him, I mean, he seemed..." *hot,* "...like a nice man. That woman must have really hurt him."

Rosa's eyes flew open in surprise. "Cristina? Dat girl, aye, was *una bella*—oh how you say?—a beauty. She and Santiago, *fantástico!*" She clapped her hands together before her heart. "A couple made by de Lord hisself."

"She left him."

"No, *Señorita* Ereen, do not believe all dis you hear." She looked cautiously around the empty kitchen. "Please, do not speak of this anymore."

"Now I'm worried about him. Please tell me what happened."

Rosa's brows relaxed and her lips turned up slightly at the corners. "I should not say anything, but I tell you more because of *tus ojos.*"

"My eyes?"

"Glory be to God." She folded her hands together and lifted her face toward the ceiling. "He has answered old Rosa's prayers. And sent an angel."

"I'm not following you."

She cupped her leathery hands around my cheeks, studying my face. "Ereen, don' tell nobody dis." She leaned her tiny frame against the counter next to me. Mixed emotions flooded her dark face—propriety, desire to unburden her secret, and fear—the strongest of these being fear. "Peoples saying she ran away, but is impossible, Cristina loves Santiago."

"Okay..."

"Someting bery bad happened to Cristina. I knows it. Santiago knows too. It changes him. His papa dies, his mama is sick, den dis. My heart breaks inside my body for him."

I blinked, trying to figure out what she was not telling me. "Surely there was a police investigation. Didn't someone try to find her?"

"Oh, *Dios mío, sí.* Santiago searched everywhere. He hired men to look. Offered rewards. Many months. *Nada.* When de police give up, Santiago keeps looking. Knocking on doors, searching de hospitals."

"What about her family?"

"No one heard from her again."

"Wow." I exhaled, leaning back against the cabinet. "What does Santiago think happened to her?"

"He no talk about dat. Peoples saying she finds a new man. I don' believe it."

I lifted myself off the counter and landed lightly on the floor before her. "What do you believe?"

Her voice was low. "Der's only one reason why Cristina no marry Santiago." She crooked her finger. When I bent down to her level, she whispered in my ear, "All dey going to find is her bones. Evil done steal her away."

I backed up in astonishment. "You suspect someone—?"

"Someting," she corrected. Her lips trembled. "We call it de darkness. It can take any of us. Quickly and without mercy."

"Darkness?"

"Now go," she said. "I have much work to do."

"But—"

Forcibly she turned me by my shoulders and headed me toward the door. Goodness, she was strong for a woman her age. "Go!" She shooed me with the kitchen towel, her soft warning behind me. "Ereen, *cuidado.*"

Be careful? A new man making my pulse race, strange déjà vu, and a spooked housekeeper talking of a missing woman's bones. What was there to be careful about?

೧೭৪୭

Serena opened her eyes. She found herself curled up against a rock wall in a dark alcove, somewhere faintly familiar. Her mind scrambled to recall where she was. Who she was. Fear, dark and deadly as a blade pressed to her throat, made it difficult to breathe.

Why was she afraid?

Her gaze traveled up the dark wall searching for answers. She narrowed her eyes and peered deeper into the corner of the alcove.

"What is this?" Her voice echoed off the stone walls.

There, written in the dust on the floor, was one word.

She stared at it a moment, puzzled. Lifting her hand, she was surprised to find her finger coated in dust. If she had written the word before she fell asleep, then it must have been important. Hope flooded her senses.

She yelled the word as loudly as she could. And suddenly the tower was gone.

Where am I?

Darkness blinded her eyes. She was sitting on a chair. Something rustled nearby, breathing deeply. Serena sat still, waiting for her eyes to adjust. When they did, she recognized the bedchamber, the chair, and the bed with the large lump in the middle of it.

Espera, the lump in the bed is...moving.

Serena tiptoed to the bed. "*Perdón,* can you help me?"

The woman in the bed stirred. "Whaa—?"

"*Por favor,* do the say-on." Serena poked the lump in what she hoped was a shoulder.

The woman opened one eye. "Go away."

"I shall, if you do your duty."

"Damn dreams." Erin's eyes were glassy, unfocused. "Let me sleep for once."

"I am no dream. At least, I do not believe so. Truth be told, I do not know who I am." She sighed. "What I am."

"I'm dead tired," Erin mumbled. "Self-discover elsewhere."

Serena's mouth fell open. "Are you dead? You see, I've been wondering if perhaps I am as well. It is all so unclear.

Sometimes, I remember—" she swallowed hard, "—horrible things. Other times, I can remember not a thing. Except Andrés. I must find him."

Erin didn't say a word. Her breathing had deepened.

"Awaken! You must do your say-on."

The woman who was supposed to reunite her with her everlasting love was snoring loudly.

As Serena sat back down on the chair to ponder what to do next, the room started to spin around her. The next thing she knew, she was back in the tower. Crying. Again.

CȜƧꙨ

"Rise and shine!" Maria called out much too cheerfully. Startled, I sat up in bed clutching the blankets around my chest. My pulse raced. I wasn't quite sure where I was.

"Jeez, you look like you've seen a ghost. Do you always wake up like that?"

I plopped back down, yanking the pillow over my head. "Please go away."

"Snooze later, Erin." The sound of the shades being lifted grated in my ears. "Time to shop for man-killer gowns."

"Gowns?" I sat back up. "Are you serious?"

"Serious as a—"

"Hung-over IRS Auditor?"

"No. My brother when he wants to get his groove on."

I was awake now. "Huh?"

"He's throwing a welcome home party. For me." She made a circular movement with her finger. "For both of us. "It's going to be huge. Everyone's coming. Come on, get up already." I groaned into my pillow. "Here." She pulled the covers back and produced a tray. "Coffee and hot rolls. Now hurry."

An hour later we were walking into town. "See that place? The one with the shells?" Maria pointed to an unusual-looking house with something odd stuck all over the front of it.

"Those are shells?"

"Carved from stone." We crossed the street and went for a

closer look. "This was originally a palace built in the fifteen hundreds for a knight. My brother loves this place. He used to call it his because the shells were the emblems for the Santiago Order the knight belonged to. Cool, huh? It's a library now. Maybe one day when we have more time we'll go in. Today we're on a mission."

A few blocks later we came to a large plaza containing a giant four-story, rectangular conglomeration of shops and romantic cafes. It looked hundreds of years old, and the open area in the middle went on forever.

"Holy cow! Would you look at this place?"

"I knew you'd like it. This is the Plaza Mayor, basically the heart of the city."

"It's gorgeous." I tipped my head to see as high up as I could. "The architecture is unbelievable. I feel like I'm in a palace courtyard. I could spend all day here."

"Another day. We're late." She took my arm and we walked through the Plaza Mayor and out the other side.

"Whoa, wait. What is the delicious smell?"

"Mmm, *jamón serrano*. Only the best ham in the world." We followed our noses to a butcher store with all sorts of amazing animal parts swinging in the window. "That's *jamón serrano*."

"A big chunk of pig leg?"

"This ham has been curing for about eighteen months. Just wait until you try it. My gosh, of all the things I have missed, this ranks in the top ten."

"Eighteen-month-old pig? I'll take your word for it."

"No way *chica*, you've got to try this for yourself. We're already late, I guess a few more minutes won't hurt."

The butcher scraped off thin strips of ham, somewhat like prosciutto, but a thousand times better. It was sweet, dry and earthy all at once.

"I'm in love," I sighed.

"Told ya so." She licked her fingers. "Heavenly. Okay, let's roll."

As we passed an ancient sandstone cathedral, I saw a man watching us from across the street. He seemed familiar.

"Do you see that guy?" I whispered to Maria. "Across the

street, pretending to look in the shoe store?"

"Yeah, so?"

"I think he's following us. See? He's looking again."

"Oh come on," she laughed. "Of course he's looking. We're h-o-t."

I didn't laugh. "Does he look like a cop to you?"

"No. Why would a cop follow us?"

I couldn't meet her eyes. "Stupid, huh?"

"A little paranoid, maybe. Hello!" She waved at the man. He waved back and went inside the shoe store. "See? Nothing to worry about," she said.

"I guess so." Still, he was familiar and he was following us. I was sure.

The bells from the cathedral began ringing loudly, methodically calling worshippers to noontime mass. I loved the way the ancient and the modern intertwined.

"We're here. Lucas Felatilla's. My favorite dressmaker in Spain," Maria said. We ducked under a rock arch covered by a heavy vine and stepped into a quaint shop smelling faintly of old building and strongly of rich fabrics.

"Is it really you, Maria?" A sixty-ish gentleman stretched out his arms.

Maria hugged him. "In the flesh. How are you, Lucas?"

"Wonderful, *bella,* since you have returned." Lucas was an aging Ichabod Crane, thin and lanky. His hair was parted near his left ear and dragged across his balding scalp. While his hair was silly, his gray pinstriped pleated pants and dark shirt suited him to a tee. "And who is this lovely creature?"

"Erin, my friend from California. Do you have any gowns already made in our sizes? What? Stop looking at me that way. I would have given you more time if I had it."

"Only once did you allow me the luxury to be creative for you." He pouted. "Ah, but the gown for your brother's wedding was one of the most exquisite designs I ever created—" He stopped abruptly. A heavy stillness settled on the room. "A thousand pardons. I should not have mentioned that sorrowful time."

"No worries. My brother is fine, really." She patted his arm.

His silver eyebrows hiked up for just a moment before he forced indifference across his face. "She was found, then?"

"She's somewhere, sinking her claws into a richer man. My brother gives most of his money away to charity."

"Ah," he said noncommittally.

"Now, what about it?" Maria asked. "Do you have anything my friend and I can try on?"

"We shall see. Come this way." Lucas eyeballed me. "You're a size, what, eight in the United States?" he said in perfect English.

"Why, yes." I was stunned.

"I have something for you to try." He ushered me into a dressing room and asked me to wait. I could hear the two of them chatting. Gowns rustled as I imagined his long fingers filtering through them. "Maria, why have you stayed away so long? I missed you."

"It couldn't be helped, but now I'm back. To stay."

"Fabulous. Here you go, I think you will like this one best, but knowing you, you'll try them all. I'll bring this gown to your friend."

"Only one for her?" Maria asked.

"Ah *bella*, wait until you see it." Gently, as if it were a baby made of lace, he handed the gown to me. He tugged the curtain closed with a loud scraping of hooks on a metal rod. "Call if you need any help fastening the back."

After putting it on, I stood for a long moment staring at the mirror. I'd never seen anything so beautiful in all my life.

The pearl-colored chiffon flowed to the floor. The scooped neck bared the upper part of my shoulders. The dress plummeted lower than I really dared to go in the back, ending a few scant centimeters above the tip of my tailbone. It was fitted, but not grossly snug, across my hips. A slit traveled decadently up the right side to my thigh. The whole thing fastened together delicately by a single gold chain dangling down the length of my back. A handful of pearls elegantly finished off the chain, which dipped and swayed against me as I moved.

"Erin, what's taking so long?" Maria poked her head into my dressing room. "Oh my God. Buy it. Buy it now."

The closest I'd come recently to a night on the town was pizza delivery in Jack's office. Not the sort of place where ball gowns were mandatory attire. I mentally wiped the slate clean.

Jack is the past. The new Erin, goddess in training, simply had to have the gown.

"So?" Maria asked impatiently.

"One question—does Lucas sell matching shoes?"

Maria clapped her hands together gleefully, "Of course." Her chin tipped up proudly. "You have not lived until you've worn Spanish stilettos."

"That's what I want. To live in Spanish stilettos."

Chapter Five

After making our purchases, we sat in an outdoor café in the Plaza Mayor and watched hundreds of people pass by. The Spanish people were attractive and well-groomed even when shopping in the heat of the summer. I smiled at a little boy who could not have been more than five skipping along at his mother's side. His socks were color coordinated to his shorts and hat.

"Maria, how in the world could you trade this paradise for the fabric-walled cubicles at DH&L?"

She shrugged. "What can I say? Karma catches up with you sometimes and boots your fat ass to California."

I snorted. "Fat? Ple-ease."

"All right. Cute, perky, near-perfect ass."

"Near-perfect?"

"I've got a mole."

"Of course. So? Tell me about the karma part."

Her hand swished through the air like she was batting a fly. "Long story."

"I've got time." I took a sip of my *agua con gas*.

"You forget, we've got a huge party tonight."

"That's hours away. You're subject changing. What's the story?"

"It's not just long, it's nasty. Who wants to put a damper on such a beautiful day?"

"Come on, you can't mess up this day. Did you see the shoes I bought?" I lifted the tote bag. "I've died and gone to heaven. So spit it out, why did you spend five years in what I now see was the pit of hell?"

She frowned. "It's not important. I'm here now, back where I belong. And I'm lucky to have such a great friend."

My, my how she could redirect the conversation. "Yes, you are, however I am luckier. You rescued me from likely death by takeout and brought me to this romantic café." I waved my hand at the view. "Our friendship would be perfect if you were a little fatter and uglier."

"Perfect for you." She playfully slapped my hand.

"Seriously Maria, you don't have to be so strong, you know. You can talk to me about anything, remember?"

She stared at me a long moment, debating, chewing on her pink lip. "Five years ago I had this...it was...kind of like a..." her laughter was raspy, "...great big disastrous meltdown."

I scooted closer to her. "What happened?"

She fell silent, unwilling, or unable, to go on.

"Why don't you try me?" I gave her my best, encouraging smile. "I know my way around a meltdown or two."

"I...I can't," she whispered. "It hurts."

"It was a guy, wasn't it?"

Her face fell, distorting before my eyes like a melting candle. She started fiddling with her things.

"Oh Maria, don't go—"

"I can't talk about this." She snatched up all her bags and stood. "Bad memories are like rotting trash. Best to throw them out."

CR&SO

"Santiago used to laugh when I played 'makeup'." Maria applied the finishing touches of rouge on my cheeks. "This is fun. Kind of like having a sister."

I smiled. "Better. All the fun, no one stealing my clothes."

"Oh, I don't know. I might rip that dress right off your body when you're not looking. I like this thing—" she ran her hands down the slinky black satin clinging to her hips, "—but yours is the second-best dress Lucas ever made."

"The first being the one he made for Santiago's wedding?"

She nodded, a strange look rippling across her face.

"Well, sorry, sis. This one won't fit you. If I could squeeze into your size two, and we took this one in a bit, I might want to trade next time."

"If there is a next time. Santiago is a lot of things, but party animal he is not." She nodded. "Okay Cinderella, stand up. Let's have a look at you." When I rose, she clapped her hand to her heart. "Simply gorgeous."

"You too, my friend. You too." After our conversation in the Plaza Mayor, I'd vowed to help Maria find a great guy. She deserved someone who could make her smile and had nice wide shoulders to lean on. Lord willing, Mr. Great would show up at the party tonight.

"Boy, if Jack could see you now," she said.

"Shit, do I know a Jack?" I mimicked her, batting my mascara-thick eyelashes.

"Good attitude."

"No, really, hardly thought of him at all."

"No?" She cocked her head trying to read me, "Good. He doesn't deserve a single thought. Sorry I brought him up."

I took some deep breaths. No matter how brave I sounded, the nerves were voracious mice gnawing at my stomach. It had been a decade since I'd been to a non-working party.

I grabbed my Get a Life Journal and wrote: *3) Be the goddess. Be the goddess. Be the goddess.* Then I added. *And don't go crazy.*

"Hey, what's that?" Maria tried to peek over my shoulder.

"Nothing." I quickly shoved the journal in my drawer. "Ready to go?"

We glided down the winding stairwell. I have to admit, several heads did turn when we made our entrance. To my delight, the one head I wanted to spin looked straight at us.

"You both look gorgeous. Quiet everybody, please." Santiago's eloquent Spanish filled the air. "A toast to my sister, who has come home at last, and to her American friend, Erin Carter. Rumor has it, gentlemen, these two beauties are unattached. If I were you, I would acquaint myself with them *pronto.*"

Laughter filled the hall, especially after Maria elbowed her brother in the ribs.

"Okay, okay." Santiago laughed. "Now, we celebrate!"

The crowd cheered and the music began again. While we were getting ready, a crew had come in and moved all the sofas and chairs from the living room. The rugs had been rolled up and a square wooden dance floor brought in. The large formal table had been replaced by half a dozen round ones, each covered with light pink tablecloths, Maria's favorite color. Several bouquets of pink roses and lilies mixed with white gardenias had been scattered around the house. Candles and luminaries lit up the inside while strands of twinkling lights were draped across the balcony. Tuxedoed bartenders manned two long rectangular bars. Another table was covered with a divine spread including jumbo shrimps, dips and cheeses.

When it came to a party, Santiago didn't mess around.

Maria was quickly whisked away to dance. I wasn't alone for long. Like bashful barracudas the gentlemen encircled me, slowly coming in for the kill. When I proved able to converse in their native tongue, the dance proposals flooded in one after the other. The Spanish gentlemen eyed me eagerly, curious about the new *chica* who knew her moves.

I was thrilled. Dancing has always been one of my passions. While the other girls in my college dormitory spent their free time at the gym, I learned ballroom, swing, jazz and salsa.

I enjoyed the attention, was flattered by their smiles and wolfish grins, but my thoughts kept drifting toward the dark-haired man with dreamy emerald eyes. Every now and then, I would sneak glances his way. He was spending most of his time with a redheaded beauty.

Helena.

I scrutinized the way they conversed with the eye of a jealous lover. Helena was a chatterbox. Even on the dance floor, she wouldn't shut up. Man, with a chance to wrap her arms around that hunky guy, she chose to yap instead? What was she thinking?

More than once Santiago's gaze swung my way. And when he smiled at me? Oh Lordy, how that man could make my legs weak.

"I beg your pardon?" I asked, realizing I was not paying attention to the four men talking to me. "No, thank you, I have some champagne right here." I reached behind me and retrieved my glass from the table and took a sip.

Mmm, champagne, my favorite, and not some cheap brand either. The lord of the manor sure knows how to throw a swanky party.

I took another sip. While pretending to be immersed in the group conversation, my eyes wandered again.

Uh-oh. Santiago and Helena were no longer on the dance floor.

Maria was, though, right in the in the middle, gyrating like crazy. The band was playing an old B-52 favorite, "Rock Lobster", and Maria was dancing with two—no, make it three handsome men. The bun I had so fastidiously worked into place had come loose. Her black hair was swinging wildly about her head as her feet pranced to the fast beat. I smiled. *Good for her.* With any luck, Mr. Great was one of the three. Oh heck, make it all three.

Helena wandered off to speak with an acquaintance. Santiago moved off the dance floor.

"Hey, bro," Maria called to him. "Great party."

He smiled at her. "Looks like you're having fun."

"These three hunks?" She winked at the men she was dancing with. "Nobody moves a girl like a Spanish man."

He grimaced. "Never say stuff like that to your brother."

She turned to the men. "Can you get me something to drink?"

Santiago shook his head as all three men fast-walked to be the first to the bar. "Disgusting. I used to like those guys."

"Ah, don't fault them. They missed me. So? What do you think of my friend?"

"Erin? Uh, Carter?"

He didn't like her knowing smile. "Yep. The one you've been making goo-goo eyes at all evening. Why don't you ask her to dance?"

His face warmed. "She's a little out of my league. Have you seen her out there?"

Maria snorted. "Oh, please. Who watched *Dirty Dancing* seven times?"

"It was six. And stop smiling at me."

Her smile got bigger. "I knew you would like her. So what's the problem? Go for it, Swayze."

He narrowed his eyes at her. "Didn't you say she has issues?"

"Don't we all?"

He crossed his arms and gave her a look.

She patted his shoulder. "Relax, she has teensy-weensy run-of-the-mill problems. And she's only staying for a short time, why don't you have some fun for a change?"

His mind couldn't stop replaying past history. Whenever he let his guard down, the worst always happened. No matter how hard he tried, he couldn't save any of the women he loved. He wasn't strong enough. "Fun?"

"Yeah, you know what that is, don't you?"

He ran his fingers through his hair. "It's certainly not dating a woman with—" He stopped short of saying, *emotional problems.*

"What?" Maria asked.

"With all the women here. Why limit myself? You haven't." He nodded at the three men pushing through the crowds toward them, bumping into each other to be first to Maria's side. Each was carrying two glasses of champagne.

"True. As long as you're happy." Her wink was wicked. "Oh, good. Erin's having fun too. And so is Raúl."

Erin was dancing with Santiago's childhood friend. Raúl had a stupid grin on his face and his hands were heading too far south down Erin's back. Santiago had the sudden desire to punch the daylights out of Raúl.

"Sorry, sis. I've got to—"

Raúl's damn hands slipped further. Against his better judgment, Santiago raced across the dance floor to rescue another woman he had no business saving.

"May I cut in?" Santiago's voice came up behind me, sending electric fingers up my spine.

Thank God. I had just moved my dance partner's hands off my ass for the fifth time. "Absolutely. *Gracias,* um, Raúl?" The man gave me a lecherous smile and moved off the dance floor.

I put my hands on Santiago's shoulders. A shiver of delight sparked through me when his hands rested on my waist.

"I've been watching you," he said.

"You have?" I squeaked.

"You're a great dancer."

"Oh. That. Well, you're no slouch yourself," I teased, forcing my voice back to normal. "I've been watching you too."

He grinned. "Shall we show the others how it's done?"

He took my hand, twirling me under his arm. We danced one song, and then another, moving effortlessly from swing to salsa. His hips were poetry in motion, his long fingers hooking mine like a dream. He was good, really good, and together we sizzled. He was so smooth, so elegant, so...sexy.

I let go of my inhibitions and our movements went from innocent to the R-rated version, dipping closer and closer to X. It was exhilarating and, as Maria would say, *h-o-t.* When the rumba started, his hands slid further down until his thumbs rested on my hipbones. My pelvis swiveled under his fingers. I had the crazy desire to slide his hands lower, lower, until he caressed my...

When a few onlookers clapped, Santiago's cheeks colored. "Would you like to rest?"

Um, not exactly what I wanted to do at the moment. "Sure."

We sat at a small table a few feet off the floor and watched the others dance. I gloated. None of them could cut the rug nearly as well as we did.

A large open-mouthed vase filled with floating pink candles sat in the middle of the table between us. Candlelight glowed in his eyes. I toyed with the base of my champagne flute, trying to control myself. Somehow simple things, like breathing, were more difficult when he looked at me like that.

Serena was shocked and thrilled to find herself at some

sort of a ball. Wandering through the crowd, she searched for familiar faces. She did not recognize a soul. The music was so loud it hurt her ears and reverberated through her entire body. When she put up her hands to block the sound, she bumped a man carrying a silver tray loaded with food morsels.

"*Perdón*," she said.

The man did not answer and the tray did not waver. Strange, he acted as if he hadn't seen her at all.

Erin sat at a round table gazing lovingly into the face of a handsome nobleman.

Ah, he is her love. Serena made her way to Erin's side.

"You worked with Maria?" Santiago asked.

"I am...was...am a stockbroker." I laughed. "It's a little confusing right now. I'm taking a break from it all." I sat back. "Call it a vacation."

"Ah," was his polite answer. He probably suspected I'd been canned. I let him think whatever he wanted. Somehow being fired from my job would have been better than losing my mind, heart, and soul to it.

"It's a difficult business, especially for a woman."

My hackles rose. "For a *woman*?"

His eyebrows rose to match my tone. "It's not?"

"It's a hard business for many. A woman dedicated to succeeding in her career can handle it just fine."

"You're a career woman."

"I most certainly am—hey, watch out!" A fist to my shoulder blade rudely cut off my thoughts. Spinning around in my chair, I was ready to scream at the brute who had the audacity to sock a woman in the back. Oddly, no one was there.

Dear God, I'm imagining things?

"Are you all right?" he asked.

Facing him again, my hackles had gone down, replaced by goose bumps all over my skin. "Did you see who hit me in the—?" I closed my mouth.

His dark eyebrows hitched up in confusion.

No, I scolded myself, *Stick to Plan 3 in my Get a Life Journal—don't go crazy.*

"Nothing." The old fight to stand up for myself and my gender was gone. I sighed. "To answer your question, I'm trying to be all right. Sometimes...it's hard."

Emotion I couldn't decipher passed over his face. "I know."

He had his own hardships to bear. I wasn't about to drop mine in his lap. "Santiago, all I want to be right now is on vacation. I need a break from my life. When I get home, I'll try to sort out what I want to be when I grow up."

"Fair enough." He still eyed me suspiciously. "How long will you be staying?"

"Trying to get rid of me already?" I teased, but thought it might be true.

"No. How long will we be fortunate to have your company?"

"Ah, a charmer you are. My condo is rented out for the summer, so I have three months to play around. I'll probably travel Spain a bit. See the sights."

"Why don't you stay here the whole time?" His mouth opened in surprise as if he hadn't meant to say that at all.

"Here? In your home?"

His lips parted, but no sounds came out.

I kept my answer light. "That would be imposing. Something my mother tells me not to do."

He pinched the bridge of his nose, thinking. What in the world was he debating in that glorious head of his? Finally he said, "The house is big. I'd appreciate it if you keep Maria company while she settles back in. It will be good for her to look after you. I'm not here often. I have a flat downtown, closer to the hospital."

"Oh."

"Please consider staying. Here."

"You and Maria are very kind. I'll think about it."

Oh man, that devastating grin.

We switched gears and I asked him about his career, while the candlelight shimmered in his eyes. He had a general practice, was trained in internal medicine and elected to the position of Chief Medical Doctor at the Salamanca hospital.

I smelled modesty. "Impressive. Where'd you go to school?"

"I graduated from UCLA. Pre-Med. My graduate work was

here, in Salamanca."

"You must know Dr. John Stapleton at UCLA," flew out of my mouth before I had a chance to rein it in.

He thought a moment. "Doesn't ring a bell. Which medical department is he in?"

Holy crap, please tell me I did not drop my psychiatrist's name into casual conversation with the sexiest man on the planet.

I ran my hand up the back of my neck. "Um, not sure." *Think, Erin, think.* "Hey, I almost went to UCLA too. USC has a better Economics department." I drew lazy eights on the glass table with my fingers, trying to calm myself. "Too bad I can't speak to you ever again."

"What?"

"We're rivals."

"I hope not. You make me look good on the dance floor."

Nope, did that all by himself. I wondered for a millisecond about Helena. Had she gone home? Could I be so lucky? "I, uh, noticed you dancing with a lovely lady over there."

"With beautiful red hair?"

"That would be the one." I resisted touching my own sandy locks. "Is she, are you two, you know?"

"Helena is a friend of mine who volunteers at the hospital."

"Say no more." I held up my hand. "Been there myself."

He frowned, studying my face. "Been where? The hospital?"

I blushed. "No, I meant you don't need to tell me about your relationship. I understand the need for—" I searched for the appropriate word, "—discretion at work."

He smiled and leaned a little closer. "Helena and I are friends. You had male friends at your last job, right?"

Dry gulp. "Not friends, exactly. More like spiteful, vicious— Ow!"

"What's wrong?"

I rubbed my shoulder. "Something pinched me. Do you have mosquitoes here?"

His face was serious "What happened in your job? Did someone hurt you?"

He seemed determined to make me tell him the gory

details. I wasn't going there. Not anymore. I looked into his sensitive eyes. "My life is..." I thought about Maria, "...littered. I'm trying to clean it up. And I will. For now, I'm seizing the day one moment at a time. Starting with this one."

I flattened my palms on the round table and leaned closer. He watched curiously as I moved toward him until we were face to face. Softly, I kissed his lips. Calculating career woman would never dare do such a thing. The newly developing goddess in me was feeling reckless. Alive.

I meant for it to be a soft peck, a gentle caress. I had absolutely no intensions of flicking the tip of my tongue across his bottom lip, deepening the kiss, sucking his delicious bottom lip into my mouth, and running my fingers through his glorious black hair. None at all. But the best laid plans...

Chapter Six

The attraction raged like a storm out of control, snapping and crackling under Santiago's skin. He couldn't help it. The dancing had warmed his blood and the fire roaring inside the woman threatened to consume him.

Erin was beautiful beyond words. She was also smart, sensitive, and courageous. But he saw something else behind those deep honey eyes that scared him. Every now and then he caught a flash of anguish, a twist of her pain, buried deep in her psyche.

It ate at him. He wasn't good at sitting idly by while a beautiful woman was tortured before his eyes. And why she kept looking over her shoulder was beyond him. Hallucinations? Post-traumatic disorder?

Damn it! What happened to her?

Don't get involved, he warned himself. *I can't fix her.*

Besides, he had more than enough problems to worry about. No, he had to squelch the firestorm spreading through his veins. For both their sakes.

But when her lips met his...

Dear God, when she kissed him electricity sparked through his nervous system and lightning struck his heart. It was as if he'd been zapped by the hospital's defibrillator. His mind was five seconds behind, trying to comprehend the situation. And when her tongue ran across his bottom lip, slowly, sensually...*mierda*, he had to learn how to breathe all over again.

Erin Carter was a force of nature, unlike anything he'd ever seen. Lord help him, he wanted to seize the lightning in his fists and dive headlong into the storm.

Pulling back slowly, still inches from his lips, I asked, "Any more questions?"

I was thrilled to see the dangerous sparkle in his eyes. "What questions?" He rose quickly and offered his hand. "Dance with me."

Happy all the way down to my little dancing toes, I took his hand. As if on cue, the band played a slow song and someone dimmed the lights. We rocked slowly to the music. Delicious heat spread through me when he turned his head toward mine and gazed deeply into my eyes.

I thought we were floating on a cloud until the corner of my eye caught a glimpse of "beautiful red hair".

Great, here comes hospital gal-pal, Helena.

I ground my back molars together and warned myself not to get suckered. If he had something even remotely serious going on with Helena, I should walk away...right...now. I stopped dancing.

"You okay?"

"I really shouldn't get in the middle of..." I looked around and Helena was gone. Funny, Santiago hadn't paid any attention to her at all. *Walk away now,* I warned myself. *N-o-w.* "...the dance floor, it's pretty crowded." My legs simply refused to listen to logic.

"Need fresh air?" he asked.

"Absolutely." Funny, how easy it was to walk away from the dance floor *with* him. Traitorous legs.

He grabbed two flute glasses and led me toward the French doors.

"On the balcony?" I croaked.

He stretched his hand toward me. "The view of Salamanca is amazing. Especially when it's this clear." His gaze raked over me. "And beautiful."

I took his hand in mine and stepped haltingly over the threshold. He was right. It was beautiful, in a gut-wrenching sort of way.

Fear slid into my chest and gripped my heart. I fought back against the panic attack. I was suddenly afraid of heights? How had *that* happened? I'd scaled Half Dome in college, for heaven's sake.

Don't go crazy, don't go crazy...

I flattened myself against the wall, miles from the edge of the balcony. He leaned against the wall too. Turned on his side, his shoulder rested against the smooth stucco. His lips were tantalizingly close.

Tipping his glass toward mine, he toasted, "*Amigos nuevos.*"

"New friends." Our glasses clinked together. A slight breeze cooled the heat on my face. Tiny white lights twinkled all around us. I started to feel calmer with my back to the wall. "Thank you so much for throwing this party."

"My pleasure. I enjoy being with you."

"Really?"

"Fun, smart, beautiful." He tapped the tip of my nose lightly with his index finger. "What's not to like?"

From inside the house the first few notes played of "Hero" by Enrique Iglesias.

I pressed my palms against Santiago's chest and feigned melting. "I love this song."

He took the glass from my other hand and placed it with his on the balcony ledge. Turning around, he smiled, wrapped one arm around my waist and held the other out for me to take. "We have to dance to your favorite song."

"Here?" I squeaked.

"Why not?" He cocked his head at me.

"No reason." Except maybe for an overwhelming, irrational fear of plunging to my death. What in the world was the matter with me?

He pulled me closer and sang the words softly in my ear. Santiago's voice was deep and sensual. Suddenly, it wasn't fear taking my breath away.

A slow burn spread inside me. His warm hand pressed the small of my back, drawing me even closer. Our hips moved against each other, smooth as warm caramel. Resting my head on his shoulder, our bodies molded together, moving in perfect rhythm. My heart thumped wildly against him and my chest rose and fell with his.

When the song ended we held each other for a long delicious moment, the air pure electricity between us. Santiago dipped me. My lips were a breath away from his. His intense gaze lingered there before wandering back to my eyes.

He wanted to kiss me. Badly. He brought me back up. "We'd better go inside."

"Um, sure, okay." My cheeks were, without a doubt, flushed scarlet. Heat surged through my body with no place to go. I dropped my gaze to the tiles to hide the pure desire in my eyes and collided into him.

"Oh, sorry, I didn't see you'd stopped—" I was bewildered by the expression on his face. "What's up?"

"Erin, I'm stuck on you."

Did he mean he was attracted to me? When he moved his hand, my whole gown moved too. *Darn, he was being literal.*

"Hey, hold on there, cowboy." I clutched the front of the dress.

"My cufflink is entangled."

Nice twist of fate. I wondered if I could keep him forever. "Careful. That strand of pearls you've hooked is keeping my dress on. If you pull too hard, this American might really embarrass herself in your country."

"Come inside." His arm remaining where it was, he gently guided me inside though the crowded hall and into a guest lounge. "Sorry. I don't think it wise to go much further." He had trouble meeting my gaze.

"Good thinking. I'll turn around and you try to free yourself."

I rotated slowly to face the mirror. His knees pressed against the back of my legs. In the mirror, I could see his fingers working with a surgeon's skill on the pearls.

Oh. My. God. Strong, capable and gentle all at once, a girl could fantasize all day long about those hands.

Down, girl. A whole party was waiting outside the door.

"Don't worry, the chances of the dress falling apart are

slim," I joked.

There was a significant pause before he spoke. The smile he gave me was loaded with heat. "How slim?"

In the mirror, my eyes locked onto his. "One could hope?"

He bent and placed his lips on the back of my neck for a long, luscious moment.

"What if I can't free myself from you?" he whispered. His free hand wrapped around my midsection and hugged me to him. "What then?"

I let my head fall back against his chest, savoring the feel of him. The rise and fall of his breath blowing gently on the back of my neck made loose tendrils of my hair dance.

"Then the dress will have to come off. And your tux."

His free hand was making slow circles on my abdomen. Looking into the mirror, his gaze fixated on my parted lips. "The tux has to go?"

"It's only fair," I teased, my voice huskier than normal. "Every last stitch."

He spun me around and kissed me. Hard.

I'd waited my entire life for that kiss. My arms curled around his neck, pulling him closer. His cologne, musky and manly, wafted up to my nose. His champagne lips were more potent than anything I'd ever tasted. I was swamped with passion. His. Mine. Ours. The world fell away. I soared, hanging onto him as my only connection to this earth.

One of his hands pressed into the small of my back, skin on skin, as if we were still dancing. The other cupped my cheek, gently, lovingly. It blew my mind he could be gentle even as his lips seared mine. Is this how it felt when someone actually cared?

Dear God, what I've been missing.

Our tongues met and a whole new dance began—faster, hotter, a salsa too sexy to be rated. Gentleness was consumed by need, want trumped all. His emerald eyes were dark, almost black as they bored into mine.

He kissed my lower lip, sucking gently and then releasing. My heart broke when he pulled those lips away and soared again when they moved to the sweet spot beneath my jaw. He kissed, sucked, and nibbled my earlobe.

My breath caught. I threw my head back, waves of excitement making my head spin. I wanted those magical lips everywhere, all at once. Desperate to feel his skin, I snaked my hands underneath his tuxedo jacket. Far too much material came between us. I wanted it gone. All of it. *Now.*

His breath was warm and heavy in my ear. "Erin."

"Hmmm?" *Damn it! How do these buttons work?*

"Erin, we can't." He pressed his hands to mine, just as one of the buttons gave way.

"Can't?" I breathed in his manly cologne. My heart threatened to arrest.

Gently, ever so gently, he lifted a loose strand of hair off my cheek and tucked it behind my ear. He groaned. "We better go back."

Did he mean back to the party or back to where we were before we kissed? I forced myself to play it lightly, "At least you're free."

He frowned, not understanding.

"Your cufflink?" I lifted his arm and flicked the gold link.

"How did that happen?"

"I have no idea."

Behind them, Serena smiled.

CR80

Many hours later the band went home and I hauled my tired body off to bed. I was exhausted and fell asleep almost as soon as my head hit the pillow. As I slipped into REM, a barb of fear jabbed through my subconscious. Something was waiting for me. Something scary.

With a throbbing urgency, I was dragged to a place I didn't want to go. My sleepy brain dug in its heels, fighting as best as it could, but was no match for whatever was sucking me in. In the deepest part of sleep, my muscles were paralyzed when I saw her.

Sitting on a high-backed velvet chair, a young woman runs a brush through her black hair with long, deliberate strokes. Her gown is centuries old and the color of the sky. The eyes gazing into the silver-framed mirror flash gray in the candlelight. Her features are delicate, beautiful, haunting.

Who is she? She doesn't see me at all. I am a spirit floating on a dream. I move closer.

The chair, the mirror, the gown are all very old. She can't be more than seventeen or eighteen, but hardship has etched her face and aged her eyes. Standing behind her, I am close enough to smell a hint of violets drifting up from her hair. I want her to see me and tell me why she's so sad. I reach out to tap her shoulder. A lock of jet-black hair twists around my finger. It's like touching fog. I can only feel the essence of the curl, mostly the damp and cold. I let it go.

Who are you?

"Serena," she answers my thoughts. "I will help you win your love, if you help me find mine. Please say-on."

"I don't understand."

In the mirror her face twists with pain. Sorrow, deep and raw, consumes her and I know instantly she will not survive it. No one could bear such agony.

"You will not say-on?"

"I have no idea what you mean."

Sadness rises up from her like a frigid mist, lifting from her hair and circling all around me. It pulls me closer. I feel lost, disoriented. I can't see through the cold, cold haze. My world falls away. I am lost.

When the mist clears, I gasp. I am the one sitting on the velvet high-backed chair gazing into the silver-framed mirror with eyes the color of fog. My blood runs cold.

I'm dead.

CR80

"Evil done steal her away," Rosa had said. "We call it de darkness. And it can take any one of us."

My eyes popped open.

"Holy crap." I rolled over to see the clock. "Five thirty?"

I'd only been asleep for three hours. Who could go back to sleep after that dream?

I wrapped myself in a midnight-blue silk robe showered with delicate pink-and-white flowers. Maria had generously loaned it to me the day she came to my house to help me pack. Yanking the red-hot silk number Jack had given me out of the go-to-Spain pile, she had said, "No unnecessary reminders, Erin. I'll loan you one."

Quietly, I barefooted down to the kitchen. A box of chamomile tea sat on the counter proclaiming to be calming, so I made a cup and carried it out onto the dew-drenched balcony. Flattening my back against the wall, I morning-dreamed about one enchanting evening.

I replayed it all in my head—the smile on his face when he first saw me, his laughter, the smell of him, his hand pressing the small of my back, the intensity in his eyes, those magical lips... What a night.

Santiago's deep, urgent voice interrupted my thoughts. "We need to talk."

When I turned around, I was shocked to see the dangerous look on his face—deadly if you factor in how fast my pulse was racing. A person could expire from so much brooding gorgeousness.

"Erin! In this light you looked like— Never mind, sorry I startled you."

"Not at all." I tried on a smile, but my lips would not cooperate. I was a little hurt that he'd planned to meet someone else on *our* balcony. *Had Helena stayed the night?*

I kept the question to myself and drank up the glorious sight before me. Even at six o'clock in the morning, barefoot, with hair sticking up on the right side of his head, he was beautiful. The man who had been weak-in-my-knees delectable in a tuxedo was now singe-the-hairs-off-my-skin delicious in gray sweatpants and a half-zipped sweat-jacket.

His hands were in his pockets and he rocked slightly on his heels. "Trouble sleeping?"

The scary dream replayed itself in my head. "A little. How about you? Do you usually get up this early after hosting a late-night party?"

"I don't sleep much. An old habit from medical school." He shrugged. "And I don't host many parties."

"You should, you're good at it. I had a wonderful time."

He grinned. "Me too."

"Maybe if you make parties a regular sort of thing you can kick that no-sleeping habit of yours. A person can only take so much champagne and dancing before a few late-rising mornings begin to creep in."

"Possibly." He chuckled. "I'd miss seeing the start of the day." He turned toward the waking city lit by soft orange light. The stillness of it all was lovely and calming. "Each sunrise reminds me I am alive."

He wasn't the only one feeling alive at the moment, and I wasn't looking at the sunrise. Oh, that strong jaw, straight nose, long dark lashes. And the serious eyes filled with—*oh, jeez*—amusement?

Was I projecting my raw desire too clearly? I hugged my arms.

"Cold?" He began unzipping his sweat-jacket.

Even though I would have paid every last penny in my savings account to see him bare-chested, I held up my hand, "No, I couldn't take your jacket."

He raised one finger and went back inside, returning quickly. "Try this." Coming up behind me, he wrapped a soft dark green fleece blanket around my shoulders.

"Did you just pull that off your bed?"

I wanted to cheer. His personal blanket was cozy and smelled faintly of his musky cologne, but those weren't the best things about it. Even though several dozen women were at the party last night, Santiago had gone to bed alone. No man would ever yank a blanket off Helena or any other woman sleeping in his bed.

He moved around to face me while tugging the warm fleece over my shoulders and smoothing it against me. "Better?" His forgotten hands remained where they were, locking the blanket against my breasts.

Holy moly, yes. "Much."

He adjusted his stance, moving closer. "Last night you were gorgeous in your cufflink-catching gown."

"I swear I don't know how that happened."

"I don't either, but that's not my point. What I'm trying to say is—" he moved even closer, "—I've never seen anything more beautiful than you are. Right now. In my blanket."

His lips were so close. His gaze traveled from my mouth to my eyes and back to my mouth. I parted my lips and angled my head, giving him the perfect opportunity. He moved in for the kiss.

Something rustled inside the house. His head snapped toward the noise and his hands flew off me.

"Someone's up," I said.

He stepped back, listening a moment. Neither one of us heard anything more.

"The wind?" I offered.

His hands found their way back to his pockets and he was rocking on his heels again. "I'll go see. My mother has been known to wander the house at night."

I sighed. "Yeah, I'll go in too. Might as well get dressed. I can't go back to sleep now."

He put his hand on the door handle and turned to face me. "Would you like some breakfast?"

I smiled. "You can cook?"

He lifted his chin, pretending to be insulted. "You doubt it?"

"Hmm. I'm willing to see for myself."

CX80

"Almost ready." He seemed perfectly domestic in front of the stove.

Man, a gorgeous hottie fixing me breakfast? A girl could get used to that.

"What can I do?"

"You can tell me how you like your *huevos*."

I coughed. "Isn't that part of the male anatomy?"

He laughed out loud. "You've heard that expression? I meant your eggs. Scrambled okay?"

"Oh. Sure, however you're making them is fine."

I took our plates with the eggs and potatoes into the dining room. He followed behind with the rest. We sat at the table across from each other.

"It's the first time I've beaten Maria out of bed," I said.

"I doubt she'll be up any time soon. She celebrated pretty hard last night."

Laughing and cuddling up next to a handsome man at the end of the party, she had waved at me over his shoulder as I headed up the stairs to stumble into bed. Then to my surprise, she pointed at him and mouthed, "Jorge Lupes."

Well, well, well, he was dessert after all. I couldn't wait to get the story from her later.

"What's that you're drinking?"

He pronounced it chok-o-la-tay. "Try this." He dipped a long pastry into the thick-as-pudding drink.

"Mmm, chocolate. Breakfast of champions."

He licked the thick brown goodness from his lips like a kid. "Rosa always makes this for me. It reminds me of good times we had when I was a boy." His face was wistful.

"For me, it's hot Cinnamon Spiced Tea. My mom made it for special times. Holidays, sick days, when Grandma came. Gosh, I miss Cinnamon Spiced Tea."

"Maybe one day we can share recipes. My chocolate for your tea."

"Throw in one of these pastry thingies and you've got a deal." I tasted the *huevos* and *papas*. "Hey, you really can cook."

"I can't believe you doubted my skills."

"You're a man of many talents, Santiago." I dipped my pastry into the chocolate.

"Maria will sleep the day away. Would you care to join me? I have this thing I do every Saturday morning."

"Thing?" The pastry slipped from my fingers and stuck in the drink. "Care to elaborate?" I asked while I fished it out.

"Just a little something I do." He crossed his arms and grinned at me.

"Ah. Tells me pretty much nothing. Intriguing. Yes, I would

love to do the Saturday morning thing with you."

"Great." His eyes twinkled.

"Am I dressed properly for this top-secret adventure?" I had on my favorite butt-hugging Lucky jeans, a pink T-shirt with *Bebe* written across the chest and short black boots. It was my best attempt at casual-slash-smokin'.

From the look in his eye, I was successful.

"You look great."

I took a choppy breath. "Thanks."

He forced his gaze from mine by checking his watch. "Just about time to go. Are you ready?"

"Give me a couple minutes."

I ran back upstairs, brushed my teeth and hair, dabbed on a little perfume, swiped on pink lipstick and raced outside.

"Oh no." I stopped in my tracks. "We're not going on *that*."

"What? You're afraid of motorcycles? It is the best way to get where we are going."

"Where? Hell?"

"Ah, come on. Are you really afraid?"

I opened my thumb and pointer finger a pinch and peeked through the space. "An itsy-bitsy bit."

He rubbed my shoulder and gazed sincerely into my eyes. "I'll take care of you, Erin. I promise."

And I thought, if you've got to go, it might as well be clinging to the broad back of a dreamy tall dark Spaniard with sparkling green eyes, surgeon hands and to-die-for lips.

I put my hand out, motioning toward the extra helmet. "All right. Let's go do the thing."

Chapter Seven

He slowed down and parked in front of a field. "We're here." He put his foot down to steady the bike, took his helmet off and combed his fingers through his hair. Then he helped me with my helmet.

I shook my hair. "We're going to watch a soccer game?"

"Watch? No." He grinned. "Look, here comes the team now."

A horde of young teenage boys filtered in through a narrow gate and stomped onto the field. A quiet moment turned loud with laughter, shouts and kid noises.

I smiled. "What's this all about?"

"Those are my boys." His smile was endearing. "I coach the Salamanca Devils, the local *fútbol* team. They're good, really good. Haven't lost a game this season. This year we're going to the Junior Cup, I just know it."

"That's wonderful."

His face was soft, caring. "Most of these kids come from tough backgrounds. No dads, poor grades, alcohol, abuses, low end of the economic scale. Bad stuff. But they all live and breathe *fútbol*. To play they must keep good grades, I won't let them on the field unless they do."

"Hi, men," he called, turning his attention toward the approaching gaggle of twelve boys. "Ready to play?"

"Who's the lady?" asked a light-haired boy who was kicking a ball up in the air and bouncing it on his head.

"Let me introduce my assistant coach for the day, Miss Carter."

I shot a glance at him. Assistant coach? More like mascot.

"Nice to meet you all." The curious faces seared me up and down.

"All right, men, pick your teams and let's get started."

"We're short, Coach," a little guy with long dark hair complained. "Hector and Ramón are sick."

A skinny redheaded boy coated with freckles piped up, "Yeah, their mom made them eat poison." He grabbed his stomach and bent over in mock abdominal distress.

"Twin brothers with *food* poisoning," Santiago explained. "I checked on them yesterday. They'll be fine by tomorrow."

Pretty soon all the boys were grabbing their stomachs. The morning air was pierced with a chorus of the crudest retching sounds ever made.

"Looks like an epidemic," I said.

"Enough! We have a lady here today. Pretend like we know how to behave, okay?" The boys straightened up immediately.

"So what are we going to do, Coach?" The redhead asked. "We can't play a full team without Hector and Ramon."

"Well, I've got an idea if Miss Carter is willing." Santiago's smile was beyond mischievous.

"Oh, no you don't." I shook my head. "What do I know about soccer?"

"*Fútbol*," he corrected. "We will teach you. Right men?"

"Sure, Coach Botello." Their smiles were innocent, but those eyes sparked evilly. "We'll show the lady."

"Why do I feel like this is going to end badly?" I grumbled.

"Come on, Erin," he said to me in English. "It will be fun. So what do you want to be skins or shirts?"

"What?"

"My team are skins. Miss Carter's group is keeping their shirts on." Santiago ripped his off. "Pick sides already and let's play."

With one glance at his glorious chest, ripped abs and perfectly defined pecs, I thought, *fútbol? Yeah, I can do that.*

I had no idea what I was doing, but if playing this game would keep Santiago running half-naked across the field then I'd do my best.

Five minutes into the game, a holy terror with short

cropped black hair came straight for me. He dribbled the ball with his feet down the field while gunning for me. I stood my ground, ready to block him and make an attempt at the ball.

He was nearly on top of me when the kid passed the ball to his teammate. Strangely, though, he kept coming at me. Fast. He didn't slow until he knocked me to the ground. Air huffed out of my chest as my butt made contact with the grass.

"Hey!" I yelled.

The boy shrugged at his teammates and walked a little taller when they all cheered. Apparently, flattening Assistant Coach Carter was the goal all along.

The blast from Santiago's whistle made us all jump. "Foul! José Luis, what do you think you are doing?"

"Nothing, Coach." The boy became smaller and more like his twelve years than the devil's spawn who ran me down. "Just playing *fútbol.*"

Santiago gave me his hand and helped me up. "Are you all right?"

I was suddenly inches away from his muscular shirtless body. "Yeah, just a little—" my eyes lifted slowly from his glorious rippling abs, up that delicious chest to his concerned face, "—winded."

He put a warm hand on my shoulder. "Do you want to quit?"

"What? Carters don't use the Q-word." *We prefer to crash and burn.*

"Penalty kick, Miss Carter. Take your shot." Santiago glared at the boys to behave themselves.

I squinted my eyes at the goal, took a running start and kicked that sucker as hard as I could. Unbelievably, the ball shot past the goalie and straight into the net.

Santiago clapped. "All right, Miss Carter."

The boys all sang in unison, "Goalllllll!"

The game continued and one of my teammates actually passed the ball to me. It was my chance. I ran down the field trying my best to dribble the ball as the boys had done. José Luis moved forward to block me.

"Perfect," I said under my breath. "Bring it on." I raced

forward and bumped into his shoulder, leaving the ball behind me on the grass.

José Luis didn't fall over because I purposefully didn't hit him as hard as he walloped me. He stood there stunned, his mouth hanging open in astonishment.

Santiago's whistle pierced the air again. "Miss Carter!" His face was full of shock mixed with admiration. "What are you doing?"

"Nothing, Coach." I cut my eyes toward the group of boys gathering around. "Just playing *fútbol*."

Laughter erupted like a rash of explosions. I offered my hand to José Luis.

He faltered for a moment and then shook it. "I like this lady, Coach. She can be on my team next time."

I smiled. "It's a deal. Go on, take your free shot."

Santiago shook his head. "You are one tough lady, Miss Carter." The look on his face made my insides turn to mush.

"Yeah? You should have seen me about a month ago."

When the match was over, we made our way toward the drinking fountains, the skins team tugging shirts over their heads as they walked.

The redheaded boy ran up next to us, matching our stride. "Where are you taking Miss Carter after this?"

Santiago gave me the head-to-toe once-over. "I don't know, Javy, she looks a little tired."

I checked out the damage. I had grass stains on the butt of my Lucky jeans, dirt embedded in my nails, and my hair was probably doing its own wild thing, but tired? "No. I feel great. Seriously. I can't remember when I've had so much fun."

"I'm glad. Not many women would want to come out here and go toe-to-toe with a bunch of twelve and thirteen-year-old boys."

"I'm not just any woman."

He took a moment and studied my face, his eyes boring into mine. "I know," he said softly. "That much, I know."

"So?" asked Javy, the boy I'd forgotten was walking next to me. "Where are you taking her? She's probably hungry—"

"Yeah, and thirsty too," a skinny boy chimed in behind us.

"Someplace nice," José Luis offered from the other side of Santiago and then blushed when I smiled at him.

"Hey, what's this all about?" Santiago asked.

"Come on, Coach. You bring a nice lady to the field who can actually *play fútbol*? Don't you want to marry her or something?" a chubby kid said.

Santiago laughed. "Miss Carter does deserve a special lunch after all the hard effort she put in with you monkeys. How about it, Erin? Can I treat you?"

"Sounds wonderful. I am pretty hungry. And thirsty. Thanks boys, for a fun morning."

"*Adiós*, Miss Carter. See you next time," they called out as they filtered back out through the narrow gate. It was sad to see them go.

"Shall we be on our way?" He tucked his shirt back into his pants.

"Where?"

"The best place I can think of."

"Pretty much tells me nothing. Is surprise the theme of the day?"

His eyes twinkled. "It might take a couple hours to get there."

Hmm, clinging to that hunk of a man for two hours on his bike? "Works for me."

We were going sound-barrier-breaking fast. Any sane woman would be terrified out of her wits. Even if she was wrapped around a Spanish god who rode like he was one with the motorcycle. Santiago weaved us around cars on the congested two-lane highway. He'd confessed to being a national motorcycle champion in his younger days and hardly ever crashed. *Hardly ever.* Was that supposed to make me feel better?

It took a little while, but soon I began to enjoy the speed and the rush.

He pulled over to the side of the road, letting the cars whiz passed us. "We're almost there," he said loudly over his shoulder to me. "Keep your eyes open for an amazing sight."

"Where are we going?"

"Segovia. I'll give you the tour once we get off this highway."

As we entered the city, he pulled onto a quieter street and parked the bike.

"Holy smokes! What's that?" I pointed toward an intricate structure several stories high, arches upon arches as far as my eyes could see.

He grinned. "Amazing, right? It's the largest and best-preserved Roman aqueduct of its kind in the world. And it still works. The coolest thing? None of those stone blocks are held together by mortar or concrete."

Cool, yes, but it didn't compare with his eyes glowing with excitement. A girl could be bowled over by so much boyish exuberance. Those dimples brought a punch of heat to my belly.

"Wow," I said, and meant it.

He got off the bike and took my hand. "There's so much I want to show you."

We walked hand in hand down the cobblestone streets through romantic coves and hideaways.

"Hear that?" he asked. "The bells from the sixteenth century cathedral still call worshippers to mass. No matter what direction you come into Segovia, you can see it. I think the bishops wanted to make sure God was the first and last thing on your mind when you arrived here."

"Has anyone ever told you what a wonderful tour guide you are?"

"You're the first person I've taken on this tour."

"Really? I love this city." Happiness threatened to burst out of my chest. "It's so old, modern, romantic."

"I've been here many times." He put his arm around my shoulders. "But this is my favorite."

Mercy! My heart pounded.

"Hungry? The restaurant I'm taking you to is world-famous for paella."

"Starved."

When we got there, the restaurant was packed and my stomach was already eating itself. I didn't know how much longer I could wait before I passed out.

He held up a finger, motioning for me to wait outside. Through the windows I saw him lean over the podium and whisper into the hostess's ear. The hostess was far too pretty, with her gazelle legs and short skirt. Jealousy punched me in the gut when the pretty young thing threw her arms around Santiago's broad shoulders and hugged him.

"What the—?" I snapped my mouth shut and moved away from the window as he made his way back through the crowd to little old normal-legged me.

"It's our lucky day." Santiago pointed to a table being cleared next to the window.

"What did you have to do, give up a kidney?" I whispered as we walked passed the line.

"Nothing so dramatic," was all he'd say.

The hostess stood by the table beaming at him.

My word, she is young. And gorgeous. And curvy.

"Thank you, Daniela, this is great," he said.

She handed us the menus as we sat. "If there is anything more you need..." She gave Santiago's shoulder a little rub. "Anything..." The word hung in the air.

Heat rose in my cheeks. My fists balled under the table. *Hello? I'm sitting right here.*

She turned her dark eyes toward me for the first time. "Doctor Botello saved my brother's life. My family will always be in his debt. Enjoy your meal."

He watched her walk away. "Nice girl."

"Indeed." I smiled at him. "And quite pretty."

"Yes, she'll be a beauty when she grows up."

When she grows up. Man, I liked this guy.

"Hey, your back is to the window. You can't see the great view from there." I pointed to the segment of the Roman aqueduct arches framed by the window.

"Not true. I have the best view in the place." He was looking at me.

I blushed and opened the menu. "Uh-oh."

His black eyebrows notched up.

"Having a little trouble understanding some of these

Spanish dishes." I lifted the menu. "For example, what is *morcilla*?"

He grimaced. "Not sure you want to know, unless you like sausage balls filled with blood."

"Eeww." I shuddered. "Passing on *morcilla*. What about this, *'calamares en su tinta'*?"

"Squid in its ink."

"Double eeww."

He laughed. "Shall I order for us?"

"Thank you." I breathed a sigh of relief.

"Have you decided?" the waiter asked. I glanced up from my menu to see a short man, on the downhill side of fifty, with slender shoulders and a voluptuous belly flopping over his belt. He was the first overweight person I had seen in Spain.

Straight-faced, Santiago said that we wanted the blood sausage and squid loaded with ink.

"What?" I gasped.

"*Mentiras*. Just joking. Salad, American style. Oysters. And, oh yes, paella."

"American?" The waiter asked me.

"Guilty as charged."

"You have come for the Tour?" he asked.

I frowned.

"The Tour de France," Santiago explained.

"Isn't that a bike race?" I asked.

The men exchanged glances. Santiago rolled his eyes. The waiter crossed his arms. "Not just any bike race, *señorita*. The best, most important race in the world."

"Americans are more occupied with that game they call football and that other one where they hit a ball with a stick to follow a real sport. Ignorance." Santiago's lips curled above the glass when he took a sip of wine.

"Hey! You're getting entirely too much enjoyment out of this," I grumbled at him.

He winked.

"*Señorita*, your American, Lance Armstrong, won the Tour seven times. An impossible feat never accomplished before. He is a world champion! An American hero. All that after conquering cancer. How can you not be a fan?"

"Well, sure, I know who Lance Armstrong is—"

Santiago leaned toward the waiter conspiratorially. "When I lived in America, the Tour de France was hardly televised."

Shaking his head, the waiter huffed all the way back to the kitchen.

"Jeez, you would think I made a derogatory remark about his restaurant. Or his mother. Why is he upset about a bike ride in France?"

"Race," he corrected. "We take our European sports very seriously. I am happy we were not asked to leave."

"You're kidding."

"Yes, I am." He laughed. "Still, he's the owner, try to stay on his good side. He might spit in your paella."

"Maria says that too. I can't believe that you Spanish people go around spitting in each other's food."

"What? I was kidding."

"Gotcha." I laughed. "All right. I promise to be on my best behavior."

When he took a long drink, a wave of insanity washed over me. I forced myself to peel my eyes off the Adam's apple moving with each swallow and vanquish all thoughts of nibbling kisses along his smooth neck.

"Why haven't you brought more women here, to this beautiful spot?"

Those green eyes bored into mine. "Segovia is a special place for me. My parents used to bring us here for the day before going up the mountains to ski. After the accident, I didn't want to share Segovia with anyone else. Before today."

"Oh, Santiago, that means a lot to me. Thank you."

After a long moment he said, "I was engaged to be married. Once."

Cristina. "I know."

His eyes widened. "You do?"

"I'm sorry. I can't imagine what you went through. You never heard from her again?"

He shook his head, staring at the fork he twirled with his fingers.

"What do you think happened?"

"I wish I knew, Erin. I hope she's happy. Wherever she is." Pain was etched in his eyes.

Lightly, I put my hand on his. "You deserve happiness too."

A shadow passed over his face. He turned his hand over so our fingers were linked. "What about you? A beautiful woman such as yourself must have many *novios*."

"Not when she's married to her career." Sadness crept in and settled heavily in my chest. "There's not much time for a social life."

"Sounds lonely."

"I have a fish named Hairy."

He grinned. "Never known a woman to be in love with a fish."

I snorted and the wine I had just sipped went up my nose. "You've never met Hairy. The world's most handsome Beta."

"Hmm. Is it strange to be jealous of a Beta?" The darned twinkle in his eyes was getting my hopes up.

"What about Helena? Nothing romantic between you two?" I stared long and hard at him, searching every pore for the truth.

He didn't flinch under the scrutiny. "We dated a while. She's a wonderful lady, just not what I'm looking for."

"Ah." I swallowed. "Looking for someone in particular, are you?"

"Yes." His gaze was intense, his answer saying it all. "I'm tired of being alone."

Me too. The thought popped up so fast in my brain I almost shouted it. Was the loneliness driving me insane?

He studied my face as if something remarkable and/or scary had just flashed across it.

Good grief, had I said any of that out loud?

I groped for humor to diffuse the situation. "So who is she? Describe this woman you seek. Or better yet, let me do it."

He sat back in his chair, the grin slowly spreading. "All right."

"Okay." I pretended to push up my short sleeves and rubbed my palms together. "She's got to be perfect, right? Size four everywhere, but the top."

91

"Not necessarily. Someone your size would certainly do."

That nearly knocked me off my chair. "Okay, so body perfection is not the issue. Let's see. How about intelligence?"

"Smart, yes. For thought-provoking conversations, such as this one we are having right now. Who says your body isn't perfect?"

I cleared my throat. "All right then. How about a woman who is devoted to her career and better at business than most men?"

He shook his head. "I'd love a woman who is good at whatever she does, even staying home and being a mother—"

"Oh no." I groaned loudly. "You want a stay-at-home mother, preferably pregnant and barefoot, right?"

He raised his hand. "She can wear shoes."

"Just what I thought." I shook my head. "Most men either want a vixen, or a mother. You're looking for—"

"A beautiful woman, inside and out, to help me provide a loving, stable, safe home for our family." His gaze dropped with his voice. "All the things I never had."

That got me. "Oh."

"I don't mind if she has a career, only our life together comes first. That's all. She could be a stockbroker."

"A stockbroker?" The bravado in my voice was gone.

"As long as she comes home at a decent hour each night. To me."

I took a deep breath, willing my heart to beat slower before it arrested.

To him?

Thoughts of meeting him at the front door with nothing on but a hot pink negligee danced in my head. But then, that meant I would be the one at home waiting. Career-woman waited for no man.

Still, the goddess in me liked the pretty dream.

The waiter placed the basket of piping hot bread on the table.

"Good gravy! Did he just glare at me?" I whispered.

"Think so. You'd better try some of the fancy sweet talk you Americans are famous for." Santiago grinned in earnest.

When he tore off a piece of bread I had another lovely opportunity to watch him. God, what a gorgeous man. That square jaw, those perfect lips... *Jeez, it's hot in here.*

"Tell me about your family." He offered me the chunk of bread.

I took a few sips of ice water before answering. "My parents are both retired. They love to travel and even came to Spain a few years back. Now they're off in some remote area of Africa. Peace Corps."

"Very honorable. And you resemble, your father, or mother?" He studied my face, which was becoming warmer by the minute.

"Mom and I are like sisters. Except for the Southern drawl thing. We moved to California when I was two, but Mom still has the Texas-belle goin' on."

"You miss them."

"Terribly. Mom and I talked every day until they ventured off to places where the land lines are few and cell phones rarely get signals."

"No brothers or sisters?"

"Maria's the closest I have to a sister."

A flood of emotion washed over his face. "I can't tell you how happy I am to hear that. She's had some difficult times."

"I know," I said softly.

"You do? All of it?"

"She told me how you took care of things after your father passed away."

His jaw tightened.

"What is your mother's...condition?"

He took a deep breath. "A long story."

I covered my mouth with my hand. "I didn't mean to pry. Forget I asked."

He held up his hand. "It's okay. Mama can be frightening at times."

"I am not afraid of her—well, not really anyway, a little, maybe. Is there anything that can be done?"

"The medicines for schizophrenia help with the symptoms but are no cure."

I rubbed his knuckles with my thumb. *Poor guy, he's got a lot to deal with.*

"The cold gray months of winter are the hardest on her. My father was the only one who could draw my mother out of the darkness. When he passed away..." He swallowed hard. "Papa was the love of her life. He died in a head-on car crash."

"I am so sorry."

"It was too much. Papa kept all the strings together in her head." He laced his fingers together. "With his passing, her mind..." He opened his fingers and let his hands fall to the table.

"A great loss like that can ruin the best of us." My Uncle Charlie stopped wearing clothes after Aunt Nancy passed.

"When the person is already fragile, like Mama was, it can break them."

I thought about Maria and her rotting memories. "Can a person have a breakdown much later after a tragic loss?"

"Post-traumatic stress can show up years afterwards. This sort of thing happens to war veterans or survivors of a natural disaster."

Hmm. Was Maria's breakdown a result of her father's death after all?

"Mama just slipped away from us. At seventeen I was suddenly responsible for Mama, Maria, me, everything. Then the doctors took over." He turned his head from me.

I wanted to curl up in his lap, tell him everything was going to be fine and kiss away his pain.

When he turned his face to me again, I was shocked to the core. There was murderous fury in his eyes when he said, "Have you ever wanted to kill someone?"

Chapter Eight

"What do you mean?" Did he know about my recent desire to drive a car through a building?

"The doctors made me commit my mother to a mental hospital. Not a nice one, Erin. A place of torture, neglect, putrid death. That's where they put my broken mother." He choked up.

My hand flew to my mouth in shock.

After swiping at his eyes, he focused on his glass. He swirled his wine. I didn't say a word. I knew he would talk through the pain on his own terms. People ate and laughed around the crowded room. At our table the silence grew thick between us. Dishes clanking all the way in the kitchen sounded loud.

His voice was low and hoarse when he continued, "My mother stayed three months before Maria and I were allowed to visit. They told us she was a danger to herself and to us." He blew threw his lips in disgust. "We trusted the doctors. Doctors who didn't care if she lived or died."

He gulped his wine like it was water. I reached out and touched his hand.

His eyes didn't meet mine as he relived the memory. "Clothes hung off her body, her hair was matted. Bedsores oozed across her back and legs. She stank like something unimaginable. Her eyes—"

I stopped him. I couldn't bear for him to say more. "Horrible. What did you do?"

When his eyes rose from his glass to finally meet mine they

were narrowed slits full of dark rage. "I carried her out of there. The doctors and nurses ran after me. I was young and scared, but I would not let them have her. I threatened to bring the police. Or a gun."

"Did you have a gun?"

"There was one in Papa's cabinet," he said quietly. "I wasn't sure how to use it, but I would have done anything to protect Mama."

"Even if it meant going to jail?"

Fury washed across his face, coloring his cheeks, tightening his jaw. He slammed his fist down on the table, rattling the plates and glasses. "I wanted to kill them for what they did to her."

I took his fist and opened it, my fingers lacing into his. Time passed slowly as I waited for him to recover himself. Eyes closed, he pressed his other hand to his forehead for a long moment. When he opened them, they were bloodshot and weary.

"Sorry," he said quietly, the rage seeping away.

"Please, don't apologize. You were very brave."

"I swore to her she would never see inside one of those places again. That's why I keep her at home, with a nurse. I became a doctor because no one deserves to be treated like old garbage. No one."

"You're a good man." I blinked back the wetness filling my eyes.

Taking my hand, he brought it up to his cheek and rested his head on it. "I try to be, but some things are out of my control." He turned my hand over and gently pressed his lips against my palm. "Thank you for your kindness."

"I promise not to bring up any more difficult topics."

"No problem, *querida*. I'll answer any question you have." He squeezed my hand gently.

The warmth from his touch rushed through my core. My whole body hummed. It didn't make much sense to be falling so hard for a guy I had only known for a few days.

Not just any guy, I told myself. *Look at that gorgeous, sweet, courageous, complex man. Who wouldn't fall for him?*

The waiter slopped my oysters down before me. Something had to be done. "*Señor*, listen." I tugged on his shirtsleeve. "What if I promise to watch the, um...Tour...on television?"

"You can do better," he said.

"What?"

"You two must come to my family's lodge in the Sierra de Guadarrama foothills. In the morning my family and friends come to the lodge and we watch the race on a big-screen TV."

"What?" It was Santiago's turn to be surprised.

"Tomorrow is an important day," he said. "One of the hardest stages, up the Pyrenees. The racers cross the border from France to Spain. You come and watch the greatest bike race in the world. With us."

We both stared at him.

"Daniela tells me you saved her brother's life," he continued. "Diego is a national hero. He was chosen for the national *fútbol* team and will assuredly go to the Cup next year. We all owe you a debt, Doctor. Let us repay you a tiny portion."

Santiago actually blushed. "Your offer is generous. Unfortunately, we came up from Salamanca for the day only."

The man pressed on. "How do you expect your *novia* to learn? She needs to watch the Tour with Europeans to learn the nuances. The intrigue. Besides, we will have *tostón*—roasted suckling pig and *judiones*—huge white beans. You'll never taste anything better."

"Oh, the last time I had *tostón*—" Santiago's eyes glazed over.

"It sounds like fun," I said.

"You want to go?"

"Sure. I mean, if you do." My ears were still echoing the "novia" part. "I'm on vacation, remember? You're the one with responsibilities." I folded my hands in my lap and waited for a sign. If he had feelings for me, he wouldn't turn this opportunity down. I waited, biting on my lip.

He swirled the wine in his glass, his face unreadable. Debating. Weighing something in his mind, but what?

"*Señor*, do you have rooms to spare?" Santiago asked.

"Call me Rodrigo. My brother and I close the lodge in July

for vacation, so friends and family can come and stay to watch the Tour together. You will enjoy it."

"Very generous. Thank you." Santiago's smile was crooked. It was obvious this new predicament had caught him completely off guard.

"We love company. Although, beware my wife. She's liable to talk your ear right off. I'll go now and bring the salad—American style."

I was afraid to ask how "American salad" differed from what the Spaniards ate.

Santiago shook his head in disbelief. "This is the first weekend I've had off in a month."

I raised my glass. "To fate then."

His smile remained crooked. What was going on up there in that beautiful head of his?

When Rodrigo brought the salad he smiled generously at me and I found a little rosebud alongside my plate.

"You've done it. He's in love," Santiago whispered.

"Don't know, but maybe he won't spit in my paella."

"Unless he already did." His dimples deepened.

"Santiago! You're incorrigible."

He leaned forward. "And you have amazing eyes. Sometimes brown, green, the color of honey. I've never seen eyes like yours."

Maria had said something about my eyes too. Her comment had not made me giddy nor dried my throat so I could barely swallow my delicious food.

Along with the bill, Rodrigo shoved a makeshift map into Santiago's palm. "Here are the directions. No one will be there until tomorrow, so—"

"No one?" Santiago repeated.

"You two enjoy. Please feel at home," Rodrigo said.

"I can't believe this. Thank you so much," I said.

"It is nothing, *bella*. Until tomorrow." He kissed my cheek.

We walked out into the bright sunlight. I waved to Rodrigo who was still watching as we crossed the street.

"Come on, there's more to see before we head up to the lodge."

"Another surprise?" Swinging my leg over his bike, I wrapped my arms around him. *This day gets better and better.*

"I have to admit, I'm enjoying this bike of yours," I whispered in his ear.

He parked the bike. "Gets under your skin doesn't it?"

"It plays havoc with my hair, that's for sure." I unstrapped my helmet and ran my fingers up my scalp to fluff the flattened strands.

"I'll let you drive next time." He waved the keys before my nose.

"Ah, no. Thank you. No."

"It's easy. I'll teach you."

"Nope. I'll only ride this thing with an expert on the front. And you, Mr. National Champion—" I tossed the helmet to him, "—are the only expert I know."

He grinned like a schoolboy. "Good."

"I still can't believe you raced, though. Motorcycle racing looks suicidal. What made you want to do that?"

The dimples disappeared, making me sorry I'd asked.

"When you feel out of control, when life turns on you..." He cupped my cheek with his hand. "You fight back. It seems reckless, but I didn't want to die. Riding, fast and furious, was my way of punching death in the face." He smiled, just a little. "I stole back the control he stole from me. And lived."

I pressed my hands to my chest to still the tremor of panic.

He frowned. "Doesn't make much sense, does it?"

I nodded like a bobble-headed doll. "I've been out of control." And strangely enough, my response was to drive fast and furious too. "Before."

His thumb caressed my cheekbone. "Want to talk about it?"

I blew out the breath I didn't know I was holding. "Not in this lifetime."

He took a moment longer to read my face. "All right. I want to take you somewhere special."

We walked several blocks. Every now and again I'd steal glances at him and he'd smile at me. It felt so...right. Like we'd always walked this way, my fingers curled around his. I couldn't stop smiling.

"That's it up there, the Alcázar," he said.

The cream-colored palace with its sharply sloping blue-tiled roof was out of a dream, or off a Hollywood set. A wave of something not so fairytale-ish passed over me. "I've seen this palace before."

"Disneyland? Walt Disney used this castle for his inspiration."

"That's probably it," I lied.

"Come, let us go inside." Santiago took my hand.

I hesitated on the stone bridge draping across a deep ravine. Dear God, a moat. A dry, unbelievably deep moat. I swallowed hard as a wave of phobia rolled over me again, just as it had on the balcony.

Stop this, I screamed at myself. Just because Grandma Grace suddenly developed a fear of elevators while on one—requiring three men to carry her off by her elbows—did not mean I was catching a fear-of-heights. *I won't allow it.*

With half-closed eyes I took halting baby steps, concentrating on Santiago's broad back until I'd made it across.

Santiago paid for a guide to take us on a private tour. He and I walked hand-in-hand behind the man, who rattled off historical events and the names of kings and queens who'd ruled Spain.

I murmured to Santiago, "The only Spanish monarchs I've heard about are Queen Isabel and King Ferdinand. Because of Columbus, of course."

"Please to follow me," the guide said. "Careful inside. The steps are narrow."

"Steps?" I squeaked. "We're going inside the tower?"

Santiago lightly touched my shoulder. "Do you want me to go first?"

"Can I wait down here?"

"And miss the amazing view?"

I gritted my teeth, focused on my feet climbing the stairs and wondered how in the world I was going to live through this one. It wasn't just the heights. Something worse was triggering my panic button.

tailbone and fingered its way up to my scalp. An orange-sized lump of hot panic burned my throat. I couldn't breathe. I held the scream inside my chest where it scraped to get out. Terror bucked through me like a wild thing out of control. Something horrible clung to the edge of my consciousness, just out of my reach.

"Stay away from the window," a voice screeched on the wind.

Everything rolled all around me. My stomach lurched.

Oh God.

"Erin, are you all right? You're pale." Santiago tried to move me away from the window. I was frozen in place, gripping his arm as if my life depended on it.

"Step back, before it is too late!" The voice was screaming at me.

"I can't." My knees wobbled.

"That's right. Lean on me. I've got you," Santiago was saying in a soothing voice.

"Erin, Erin, run!" The ghost's scream was a nail scraping my brain.

"Stop it, please," I begged.

"Stop what?" Santiago asked.

"Oh God!" I cried. "I'm dying."

I turned my face toward him, but the spinning in my head was so strong I couldn't focus. Shooting yellow and red lights whizzed past my eyes. I sailed into a black, whirling hole full of muffled voices and shrill ringing sounds. Feeling myself go limp, I fleetingly thought about how much it would hurt when my body hit the ground.

From a tunnel far, far away, someone yelled. "I remember this. Look!"

Chapter Nine

Spring of 1494, Alcázar, Segovia

Serena strolls with Clara through the palace rose gardens, enjoying the warmth of the sun after an unseasonably cold winter.

"Aunt Beatriz is determined to make a fine lady-in-waiting of me," Clara says. "Even if the waiting part bores me to tears. I had to feign belly illness to sneak away."

"The marquesa is bound to find you out. Perhaps we should go back so you may continue your lessons."

"And miss this lovely celebration? Never." Clara pulls a hard roll out of the folds of her satin gown. "Cook said it is your birthday."

"Aya, Clara. You've got honey on your gown." Serena uses the apron of her own plain dress to swipe at the stain.

"Why fuss? It is just a gown."

Serena's gaze drops to the dirt beneath her worn shoes. Clara has many gowns. All beautiful.

Taking Serena's elbow, Clara pulls her toward the shade of a lacy oak. "This looks like a fine spot to begin the festivities."

"Hmmm. Why do I think you are using me as an excuse to forego your training?" Serena shakes a finger at her.

Clara pouts. "That is not fair."

"What was it this time? Letter penning?"

"Far worse. Embroidery." Clara grimaces. "Aunt Beatriz says it teaches poise, patience and beauty. Holy Madre, I'd rather poke out my eye with a needle than have to add another stitch to her pillow."

Serena cannot help herself. She laughs aloud.

"What handsome gentleman cares if I make a pretty stitch? It is my pretty figure that will catch his eye. Is it not?" Clara says as she sashays around the tree.

"You ask me? I know little about being a lady."

"This is the truth. Your manners are greatly lacking. Will you eat your gift, or not?"

Serena spreads her dress out behind her and motions for Clara to sit beside her in the soft, cool grass. Breaking the sweet roll in half, they eat it, licking the honey from their fingers.

"Aya, Serena, Cook must really care for you. She never remembers my birthday."

Serena's voice is soft when she says, "This is the first time I can remember anyone marking the day." In her memory she sees parties with presents, laughter, and song. And feels the sorrow. When the other girls at the Convent of Santa Ana celebrated with each other, she was never included.

Clara wipes her hands on the grass and twists her long cream-colored braid around her finger. "So, fourteen years ago today Serena Muñoz was born in a smelly fishing village." She points the end of her braid at Serena. "You are a long way from home, *amiga.*"

Serena shakes her head so hard her raven curls fall forward to partially cover her gray eyes. "I do not have a home." She sighs. "I wish I had a mother to kiss my cheek on this day."

"Why do you pine for a mother who gave you that scar? You are better off here."

Serena palms the ugly mark cutting a jagged course down her cheek. "Not true, at least not the way you mean. Mother Catarina told me the story, do you wish to hear it?"

"Tell me, it will keep me all the longer from needlepoint."

"A neighbor lady gathering berries heard a baby's cries coming from my family's underground cellar. She was terrified to go into the yard. Black death had killed half the residents in my fishing village. The lady thought no one had survived in the Muñoz house. Was it truly a baby, or a spirit's cries? Being a woman of good heart, she could not bear to leave. With trembling hands, she lifted the cellar door and found me screaming with hunger and fright. The woman almost fled when she saw the gash on my cheek and my hair matted with dried blood, but she had no daughters of her own and longed to keep me.

"Her husband would not allow me to stay in their home. Everyone wondered how I had escaped from a house where the bodies of my family were still strewn across the mattresses and floors. The plague had attacked like a wolf in the night. How had I survived?"

Clara leans forward in awe. "You never told me this story."

"The villagers thought I was cursed and sought to be rid of me. Death had left its claw mark upon my countenance, had it not? Would it return to collect me and all those nearby? As it so happened, a nun from the Convent of Santa Ana came to see the miracle with her own two eyes."

Serena stops to take a breath. The memory is hard to relive, even when it is only the stories the sisters told she recalls.

"So?" Clara nudges Serena's shoulder. "What miracle?"

"Sister Agnes arrived moments before the villagers set my house aflame. She saw my mother's swollen arm draped over the window ledge. When the sister's gaze traveled from the window and across the yard to the underground cellar, she knew at once what had occurred.

"My mother knew the villagers would never rescue a baby from a death house. The villagers would set fire to the house with me still inside. In her final moments of agony, my mother threw me out the window. She used her last drop of life to save mine."

Clara dabs at the corners of her eyes with her kerchief. "That is perhaps the sweetest story I have ever heard. But then, how did you come to live here, at the palace?"

"My guardian, Lord rest her soul, arranged it with your aunt. The Marquesa de Moya was kind enough to take me in."

"To my good fortune. Without you I would never taste a pastry like the one we just shared." Clara licks the sweetness still clinging to her lips.

Serena smiles. "It was good. I shall have to thank Cook for her thoughtfulness."

"Mmm, do. Perhaps she'll give you another." Clara stands up quickly. "*Mira*, do you see what I see?"

Serena pushes her hair back and follows her friend's pointing finger. A young man is riding his charcoal horse across the bridge toward the Alcázar with the confidence and speed of a warrior.

"Who is he?" Serena squints as hard as she can.

"Over here!" Clara dances on her tippy-toes. "Aya, he saw me."

Serena's heart pounds when the young man slows his horse. She has the urge to run back inside the castle, but her feet root themselves into the grass and her eyes refuse to look anywhere other than at the young man.

He wears a dark blue tunic with matching hose and felt hat. Sitting tall upon his gray horse, he resembles a statue of a soldier in the plaza. He is perhaps the most beautiful creature she has ever seen.

"Good day, ladies," he says.

He has a deep, rich voice that sings sweeter to her heart than any melody she has ever heard, including those Father Simón sings during Mass. The thought brings terror to her chest and she half-expects to be struck down where she stands for blasphemy.

"Why, is that really you, Andrés?" Clara runs to him. The tight bodice of her gown strains with every breath she takes. "I thought you were off fighting great battles for our king."

"Surely a swordsman, even the greatest of them all—" he winks, "—cannot always be fighting." His gaze fixes upon Serena, traveling from the tip of her head down to her tiny feet. No part of her has moved since his arrival.

"Tell me all the news." Clara twists her long blond braid around her finger. "I want to hear everything."

"But, cousin, where are your manners?" When he removes his hat, dark hair falls across his brow. He swings his leg off the horse, landing lightly in front of the silent Serena. "Are you not going to introduce me to this beautiful *señorita*?"

Serena's face burns. Her gaze quickly pulls away from the warm brown eyes boring into her soul.

"Apologies," Clara says. "Serena Muñoz de Avila, this

handsome brute is my cousin, Andrés, the Marques de Moya."

He bows deeply. "Pleased to make your acquaintance."

Serena makes a small curtsy in response, but cannot manage a word. In her fourteen years, she has never conversed with a young man, let alone a handsome nobleman. Until this moment, she has not stared one directly in the eye either. Her hot cheeks grow hotter. She is aghast to feel tears threatening to flow.

Andrés seems not to notice her discomfort. "Serena from Avila, is it? My mother did not send word that a lovely lady was staying in the Alcázar. I might have taken my two-week leave from the king's army earlier."

Serena's eyes widen. It is as if a dozen tiny birds have suddenly taken flight inside her chest. She looks up from the ground and is instantly captivated by his handsome face.

"Will you be staying in Segovia long?" He leans toward her.

It is difficult to swallow. The young man's face becomes distorted through tears of embarrassment welling in her eyes. After an unbearable moment of silence, she opens her mouth and garbles, "I...uh...um..."

Clara rushes to her rescue. "Do not tease her so. She is from the convent and not accustomed to your charm."

His mouth opens in surprise. "This beautiful young lady is from the convent?"

Serena's hand flies to her hot cheek. The nobleman must not have seen the scar, or he would not use the words "beautiful" and "lovely".

"Remember when your mother's friend adopted a girl? Serena is that girl. She's living at the palace until she is of age and finds a suitable husband," Clara said.

"A suitable husband?" He grins.

"Certainly, perhaps a smithy, or we could hope for a merchant of wares." Even though Clara leans close to Andrés's ear, Serena hears her friend whisper, "The poor girl has no dowry, no family."

Andrés is taken aback. "I see."

Serena feels herself melting into the dirt.

"She is fortunate to be under your mother's care." Clara

pats Serena's shoulder. "Even if a nobleman is out of her reach."

Serena blinks hard, but the tears fall anyway. She has heard stories of lightning striking people. Why cannot a bolt hit her now and put an end to this misery?

"*Dios mío*, are you ill?" Clara asks.

Still Serena cannot find her tongue to speak.

Andrés shifts uncomfortably from boot to boot. "I should, that is to say, I must..." He clears his throat. Turning toward his horse, he finds the excuse to take his leave. "...be off to the stables. *Buenos tardes.*" In a flurry of motion, he swings up onto the saddle and is gone.

"Holy Mother, Serena! Did a spirit brush against your soul?" Clara chides.

"Sorry," she sniffles. "No man has spoken directly to me. Save the priest during confession. And he is behind the curtain."

"Sweet Mother!" Clara laughs. "Not to worry. Andrés did not mean you any harm. He compliments all the *señoritas*. It is part of his nature. Noblemen are like that." She chuckles again. "Only the priest, *rico*. You have lived a sheltered life. But let me tell you mine has not been too different.

"When I was a girl, my mother sent me here to learn how to be a real lady. And—as you have seen with your own eyes— Aunt Beatriz is a harsh woman. Not so loving as my own mother. I tell you true, Andrés was my saving grace. He invited me to play the games of hide and chase with himself, Prince Juan and the royal princesses. He made me feel at home. So you see, he is no monster to fear. And I shall teach you how to speak to the next nobleman who passes by."

Serena doubts she will ever be able to speak to a nobleman. Pressing her hand to her breast, she wonders at how fast her heart is beating. It has never raced so.

CR&D

He was checking my pulse. My blood raced under those gentle fingertips.

"Open your eyes, *querida*. That's better." Santiago's

109

handsome face was taut with concern.

"What happened?" Disoriented, and embarrassed, I tried to sit up.

"Slowly," he warned.

Resting my head back on his lap, I blinked my eyes, trying to clear my blurry vision. My chest was tight with an unnamed panic. I had the strangest desire to get up and run like mad.

With him peering into my eyes with such feeling, what sane woman would flee?

"Do you know who I am?" he asked softly.

"The man of my dreams?"

Santiago smiled. "Good, you're feeling better?"

My thoughts were fuzzy. A heavy sense of dread pounded through my veins. Fear had left a foreboding aftertaste. "We have to get out of here," I mumbled.

"Do you know where you are?" He looked closely at my pupils.

I was stretched out on a very hard floor staring up at an old, sloping, wood-beamed ceiling. I'd been here hundreds of times before. Well, not exactly in his lap, but in this tower. Place of death. "Yes," I said weakly. "Disneyland."

"Close enough." His face was gentle. I imagined he used this soothing tone on scared children in the hospital. "I should've listened. You really are afraid of heights."

"Just today." And the other day on the balcony. Oh...no, I was developing a phobia.

"You fainted." The tour guide's head popped up over Santiago's shoulder.

"That's impossible. I don't faint." My indignant words sounded like they came from inside a tunnel.

"Did she touch you?" the guide asked me. His face was screwed up in fear.

Santiago glanced over his shoulder. "Who?"

"The Tower Ghost. They say one touch and the victim goes insane."

"No. Still sane," I replied. At least I hoped I was.

"Shew," the guide mumbled. "I'd hate to lose another one."

"Do you mind?" Santiago asked. "She needs air."

"Of course. Sorry." The guide stepped back.

Santiago gently moved the hair out of my eyes. "Racing pulse, hyperventilation, temporary loss of consciousness? All classic signs of extreme phobia. You were very brave. I shouldn't have pressed you to look out the window. Forgive me."

"I feel like a total idiot."

He helped me up and held me in his arms for a moment. He was waiting until I was stable on my feet, but being held like that could wobble any girl's legs.

"Do you want to see the rest of the castle?" The guide asked.

"No," we replied in unison.

Santiago wrapped his arm around my shoulders. "I think the princess has had enough of the tower."

"More than enough, Knight of the Santiago Order."

His mouth fell open. "How did you... Oh, Maria took you to the House of Shells." He grinned. "All right then, I'm rescuing you, fair princess. Let's go."

Outside the castle, I peeked back up at the dark window. A cold chill prickled my skin.

"Ghosts." I shivered. "The screaming got to me."

He touched my shoulder lightly. "It was only the wind."

Um, no, the wind didn't usually yell at me to get away in a woman's voice.

"You're feeling normal now?" He gently rubbed my arm as if he were calming a frightened wild pony. We walked back to the parking lot.

Normal? I almost snorted. Extreme phobias coming and going, hearing screaming ghosts, being inside the death castle of my nightmares? Being insane was the only sane answer. Sweet God, the craziness that ran in my family was catching me.

"Better."

"Climb on, princess." He handed me a helmet and motioned for me to sit behind him on the motorcycle.

I hopped on, feeling very much like a princess hugging her handsome prince. Only the strong steed we rode was a hog, of the motorcycle breed.

The scenery flew by, changing from tall buildings to long stretches of green countryside to small mountain villages dotting the foothills at the base of sharply angled mountains.

Santiago stopped once to call Maria and check Rodrigo's crude map and then we were off again. It was early evening by the time we reached the lodge. Nestled against the foothills with pines all around was a stunning A-frame with high ceilings, large windows and the biggest log beams I'd ever seen.

"This is it?" I read the sign. "La Querida de las Montañas."

"Sweetheart of the Mountains." He patted the helmet on my head. "Like you." After unlocking the ornate wood door, he stepped back so I could go first and flipped the lights on behind me.

The entrance was lovely. Overhead a large crystal chandelier hung from the high-beamed ceiling. Oil paintings of the Spanish countryside decorated the walls. A red carpet lay across the tiled floor. To our right was the dark cherry-wood check-in-counter. Scattered throughout the lobby were several intimate spots where couples could cuddle up on leather couches, drink hot toddies and warm their bodies by the huge rock fireplace.

"Santiago, look at this view."

He followed me to a gigantic window. We stood shoulder to shoulder in awed reverence. The last of the afternoon sunshine slanting through the window warmed our bodies and painted the snow-capped mountains with its soft yellow glow.

"Are those the Pyrenees? They don't look real," I marveled.

"They're full of magic," he said softly.

I raised my eyebrows.

"We have a saying: once brushed by the magic of the Pyrenees, good fortune will follow."

"Have you been brushed by their magic?"

A secret smile played on those full lips. "I've been at the feet of the sleeping giants and felt their magic."

"And the fortune?"

Slowly he turned to face me. "We're here together."

It was suddenly hard to swallow. I edged closer. "Thank you for bringing me."

"Why thank me? We wouldn't have come if you weren't so ignorant about sports," he teased.

I socked his shoulder. "I'm not ignorant about all sports. Just silly European ones."

"Hey!" He rubbed his arm. "You'd better take that back. We Spaniards don't do anything silly."

"No? What's up with that?" With my fingers drumming my hips, I shook my head sadly. "Lame sports and no sense of fun? That's messed up."

He squinted at me. "Are you insulting my countrymen?"

"Stating facts. I do have an idea how we can bring a little silly into your life."

He crossed his arms over that glorious chest. "Plop down in front of—forgive my language—the boob-tube? Catch one of those highly intelligent American reality shows?"

"Not a show. Just catch—" I shoved him and took off running, "—me."

Being alone in the lobby gave my feet wings. My shoes made slapping sounds, echoing off the high ceilings as the carpet changed to hardwood and then tile and back to carpet again beneath my feet. I didn't look back.

Startled at first, he quickly jumped into the game and was in hot pursuit. I squealed. Career woman was long gone. I was deliriously free. Breathing heavily, I rounded a red leather couch. We circled the couch a few times, warily eyeing each other.

"There's no way you're going to catch me," I taunted. "Might as well give it up."

"Think so?"

To my amazement he leapt over the back of the couch, landing square in front of me, graceful as a cat. "Track team." He smiled triumphantly. "Hurdles."

"Hey, no fair!" I protested when he repeated my move by pushing me backwards onto the couch. I stopped protesting the moment he landed lightly on top of me.

"Wrestling team too." He pinned my arms and legs beneath

his hot body. "Any other macho sports you wish me to demonstrate?"

I was laughing so hard I could barely breathe. His deep laughter joined mine and resonated throughout the lobby. I hadn't heard him laugh like that before. It was music to my ears.

"Say it."

"What?" My chest heaved up and down against his.

"'Spaniards are the best.'"

"At?"

"This..." His lips met mine.

Chapter Ten

Lord Almighty. It was like being dragged under water, without the kicking and screaming part. Everything spun out of control. I couldn't breathe, didn't know which way was up, didn't care. I hung on, letting the hot current take me with him.

He kissed like a man in need. Desperate, burning need. His lips laid claim to me like he owned me. I kissed him back, giving in to all the want flooding through my body. Desire, hunger, joy I've never known, all swirled together in a heady mix making my head spin.

I wanted more, much, much more. Melting into the couch, I was a puddle of boneless, burning electricity. I opened my eyes halfway to gaze at him. Oh man, the way this man kissed. Glorious. Beauty. Haaawwt. I closed my eyes again and let him take me away.

Then tragedy struck.

He ripped his lips from mine and bolted upright. "Why'd you do that?" He rubbed his cheek as if he'd been stung.

"Um, you kissed me. Not that I mind."

His face was a mixture of surprise and alarm. "Your hands. I pinned them."

I wiggled my arms out from under him. "You did, but I doubt you'd be able to do it again," I taunted playfully. "Here they are. Free. Try to get them."

"But how did you...?"

"Are you okay? You've gone all pale on me. Except for...hey, what's that mark on your cheek?"

He had on his serious doctor eyes. "Maria told me what

happened in Los Angeles."

"Maria told you?" *That little skunk.* "Everything?"

"You've been through an emotional trauma."

"That's true..." I had no idea where he was going with this.

"If you're confused about being here with me. I understand."

"Wait. What?"

He rubbed his cheek. "It's not your fault. You're vulnerable. I shouldn't have pinned your arms."

I sat up. "I'm not as vulnerable as you'd think. Come here, let me prove it to you." I started to wrap my arms around his neck, but he ducked under them and flew off the couch.

"I'll see if there's any food in the kitchen. You rest." He pointed to the couch. "After the fainting spell in the tower, you shouldn't have been running."

In shock, I watched him go. "Oh, wow," I sighed, sinking back into the couch. How in the world was I ever going to get through to such a man? His barriers were so darn thick.

My body was still sizzling. I ran a finger across my lips, praying he would come back and kiss me again.

He searched the refrigerator. Bare. The pantry. Not much. Cabinets. A box of crackers. Standing in the middle of the kitchen, hands on his hips, he caught sight of his reflection in the chrome oven handle. He moved closer and peered at his distorted face. The outline of a handprint was clearly visible.

Why'd she do it? And the fainting episode—clearly she was more unstable than he'd originally thought. What in the hell was her mental state? Phobia, for sure, a hint of bipolar disorder as well? Maria said Erin was depressed after losing her job, was she now swinging toward manic? And what about the voice she'd heard in the tower? Dear God, was she schizophrenic too?

He blew out a heavy breath. He liked her. Too damn much. But he couldn't get involved. No matter what Maria said, it would be cruel to date a woman in emotional distress knowing full well he'd never commit to her. Better to end things now, before they got out of hand.

He would be a friend to her—obviously she needed one. But a *novio*? No, that honor he would leave to a better man. He just couldn't do it.

CRSO

Serena squinted at the man before her. Santiago, was it? Dangerous, is what he was.

Her senses were growing stronger and more acute the longer she stayed awake. And what she sensed now made her blood boil.

Serena smelled death on the man. He stank of murder and deceit.

Why does Erin care for him?

It did not matter. Serena knew Erin was her only pathway to Andrés. In the short time she had been near Erin, Serena recalled bits and pieces of her life. Her memories were weaving together like a tapestry. How wonderful to remember her childhood and the fateful day she met her beloved.

Serena sighed. *I cannot forget again.*

She knew what she must do. She would cling to Erin until all the memories came back—the good ones and those which terrified her. Once she remembered everything, she would know how to find Andrés.

There was only one problem—Santiago, the man of death.

She studied him as he slammed cabinet doors. He was a danger to her plans and to Erin's life. She had to stop him.

Glaring at Santiago, she whispered, "I shall strike you again if I have to. Leave my savior alone."

CRSO

The banging in the kitchen proved he was trying to put some distance between us. Oh, I knew why he was slamming cabinet doors, or at least I thought I did.

The women he loved had hurt him, badly. His mother, his fiancée, possibly even Helena had all inflicted damage in their own way. His defense mechanisms had flown up like the Great Wall of China around his heart.

I've got to get through to him.

I don't know how it happened so fast, but I was in love. Head-over-heels, ready-to-fall-on-my-butt sort of love. Now all I had to do was convince Santiago to take the fall with me.

If I had my Get a Life Journal, I would write:

4) Get through to Santiago, if it kills me. And stop flipping out.

"Not much here to eat," he called, as he walked down the hall.

I rose to meet him. "You're hungry? I'm still full from lunch."

"What about dinner and breakfast? There's no food. I'll ride to one of the mountain villages for supplies."

"Now? It'll be dark soon."

"That's why I'm leaving now."

Is it? "Do you want me to go with you?"

"It's been a long day. Why don't you take a bath, get some rest. I'll be back soon."

Cleaning up had a nice ring to it, plus I didn't relish getting back on that bike so soon. "If you're sure."

"Lock the front door. I have the key."

Moments later the whine of his motorcycle echoed down the canyon. I had never heard such a lonely sound.

⊂అ⊋

Santiago stopped his bike in a turnout. He wasn't interested in the amazing view. He had a long-distance call to make.

"Martin, it's me," he said.

"Santiago? What's wrong?"

"I'm not sure yet. Do you know Erin Carter?"

"No. Should I?"

Santiago exhaled his relief. "How about a Dr. Stapleton at UCLA?"

"John? Sure, he's one of the best psychiatrists in the area. Why? What's this all about?"

His heart sank. His suspicions about Erin's mental state

were true.

"What's his specialty? Bipolar disorder? Schizophrenia?" He steeled himself for the worst.

"Insomnia, actually," Martin said. "He's been doing some radical experiments for sleep disorders."

Santiago smiled. Insomnia he could deal with.

"Are you going to tell me why you called to talk about John after midnight your time? Santiago, what's going on?"

"Sorry, Martin. Forget I called."

"Right. Like I can. You're worried, aren't you?"

Santiago sat back hard against the motorcycle seat. The darkness. That was it. He was worried the thing cursing his family had gotten its bloody tentacles around Erin too. It was crazy. Wasn't it?

"I told you," Martin was saying. "We got it this time. I promise."

Santiago winced. In his experience promises were broken. And people died. "You're sure?"

"I performed all the tests five times each. We're clear. So, relax, will ya? My advice to you is to get on with your life. Live a little."

A vision of Erin's beautiful, warm body came to mind. And a kiss, so delicious...

"Santiago? Are you there?"

"Thanks, Martin. I'm going to take your advice."

C380

Taking the universal room key from the hook behind the check-in counter, I cruised from room to room to find the best. All the suites were beautiful, each offered differing views of the mountains and the valleys below.

Then I found the one. It was a cozy suite with a king-sized bed situated perfectly beneath glass ceilings. Stargazing took on a whole new meaning in a room like this. There was an adjoining suite for Santiago. I was not going to assume anything, especially after his mad flight down the mountain.

I ran the water and poured a packet of pear bubble bath

into the tub. Sinking into the steamy water I let my thoughts drift. What a day. Beautiful, exhilarating, romantic. The bubbles rose, tickling and popping under my chin. The sweet smell of pear was divine. I closed my eyes and soaked in the hot water, reliving Santiago's lips on mine.

Then I remembered the tower. Had I really heard a ghost?

I laughed out loud at myself. "Of course not."

Santiago was right. I'd hyperventilated and fainted. End of story.

After the water cooled, I dried off, grimacing at my pile of dirty clothes. I didn't want to think of putting them back on. In the closet, I found a thick white robe begging to wrap itself around me.

It had grown dark and I was getting sleepy. Maybe a little rest would do me some good. I left the bathroom light on so he could find me when he finally returned and I crawled into bed.

If he returned. He'd been gone a really long time.

I bit my lip. What if he was having second thoughts about staying in the lodge with me? He'd acted pretty strangely after the kiss.

"Oh!" My voice echoed in the silent room. It was my turn to bolt up straight.

Maybe the kiss—the single most erotic experience I'd had in years—meant nothing to him. Did Spanish men kiss like Americans shook hands? *Nice to know ya, Erin*, nothing more.

I groaned, threw the sheet over my head. And quickly fell asleep.

CREO

Summer of 1495

Serena sits beside Clara in the antechamber of the *Sala del Trono*. The two girls are quietly working on their needlepoint while shamelessly eavesdropping on the conversation occurring in the throne room.

"It is done, Beatriz. The Austrians have finally agreed," Queen Isabel tells the Marquesa de Moya.

"It is settled? Princess Juana shall wed Felipe the

Handsome of Austria?"

Clara wiggles her eyebrows at the mention of the infamous Felipe, whom the ladies of the court think is beautiful beyond measure. Serena rolls her eyes up to the gilded ceiling.

"Praise be to the Virgin. I trust you will help me with the preparations?" The queen says.

"Of course. The wedding shall be here, in Segovia?"

"No. Felipe's family is adamant the matrimonial ceremony occur on Austrian soil. Still, we shall celebrate. My daughter needs to feel how much the people of Castile adore her. She is a bit shaken about sailing to a foreign land."

"We shall give her the grandest wedding ball ever," Beatriz announces. "Leave it to me. I shall invite everyone."

Clara tosses her head to the side as a gesture to sneak away. The two girls quietly tiptoe outside.

"Holy Madre! Did you hear that?" Clara turns in a circle and her skirts spin around her in a flash of pink. "A royal ball! I cannot wait."

"The marquesa will allow you to attend?"

"Did you not hear her? She said everyone. You, too, my friend." Clara claps her hands to her breast and spins around again.

"Me?" Serena's heart pounds. "I suppose noblemen shall be invited?"

Clara laughs. "*Sí*. All shapes and sizes. I shall dance with them all. Well, perhaps not the ugly ones, unless they are rich."

A knot twists in Serena's belly.

"Aya, you are pale, Serena. Do not fear. I shall teach you how a real lady collects a gentleman. And despite my aunt's admonishments, it has nothing to do with needlepoint and tapestries."

Serena's cheeks flame. "Do no such thing. I shall go to keep you company and watch the others."

"What fun is that? You shall dance."

"You are the lady-in-waiting noblemen will wish to dance with. I am a *señorita* with no dowry, remember?"

"How many times do you expect to be invited to a matrimonial ball? Enjoy the night for all it is worth. Besides, the noblemen will not know of your dowry unless you tell them. We will dress you in one of my fine gowns, or mayhap the seamstress will make you one for the occasion. Who knows, you could snare a wealthy nobleman after all."

"I shan't dance."

Clara shrugs. "Suit yourself. But do not expect me to hide in the corner with you. I shall be on the floor dancing with every handsome and rich nobleman in the place."

Cঽৎঙঀঌঌ

The news of a royal wedding is a lit torch setting the castle aflame with excitement. Each morn Serena wakes in her tiny loft smelling the aromas of exotic dishes wafting up from the kitchen below. Colorful decorations are scattered about as if dropped by unseen, kindly spirits. Perfumed breezes blow gently through the palace, whispering promises of hope and rebirth. Such a wind can breathe life into a girl's spirit.

The days tick off one after another until Serena thinks she might die from the excitement. Finally, the night of the wedded ball arrives.

Not wanting to miss a moment of the festivities, Serena dresses quickly and hurries to find Clara. Rapping lightly on the chamber door, she hears Clara's voice huffing from inside. "Holy Virgin! What is the matter with you? Can you not make this gown fit any better?"

"Sorry, my lady, your figure has bloomed since your last fitting," a maid explains.

"Consider it a blessing," another maid rushes on. "You should be happy to possess such womanly curves."

"Would you be happy if my gown were to split open in front of the king and queen? By the devil, stop pinching me so."

Serena knocks louder and then enters. "Can I assist?"

"Beloved saints, yes. Save me from this torture. Go on, you two."

Serena cinches the gown tightly while Clara lifts her heavy breasts and adjusts them into place.

"Count your blessings. You do not have to fret about popping out of your gown." Clara nods to the small mounds in

Serena's bodice. "It is a lovely gown, by the way. The head seamstress likes you. Never have I seen a more brilliant shade of blue. Your eyes sparkle brighter than sapphires."

"I feel like a princess."

"A princess would never wear her hair in that manner."

"My hair?" Serena's hand smoothes the long raven curls draping down her back.

"We need to lift it up as the maids have fixed mine. See?" Clara spins around and shows Serena the intricate updo. "Let me help you."

Serena's mouth drops. "I could never."

"Ah, I see." Clara squints. "You do not like the way my hair is done."

"No—I mean, yes, I do. It is beautiful. I must wear mine down."

Clara puts her hand on Serena's arm. "The scar is what bothers you?" Serena's hand cups her cheek in response. "Aya, Serena, no one cares one iota about a tiny line upon your countenance."

Serena frowns. "Hardly tiny."

"As you say, still, do you know what I see when I look at you?"

Serena shakes her head.

"A young lady with complexion the color of honey, full pink lips, a perfect straight nose, eyes as blue as the sky and long raven lashes. The ladies will have to shield their noblemen's eyes when you enter the hall."

"Me? You are the gorgeous one."

"True. So true. Together we shall make them salivate like dogs."

"That sounds truly awful. I am afraid of dogs."

Clara laughs. "May I fix your hair?"

CRØO

The festivities barely begin before Serena spots Andrés in the crowd. She marvels at how handsome he looks in his dark forest-green velvet doublet, hose and matching hat.

How can I escape without him seeing me? Holy Virgin, he comes this way.

She forgets entirely how to breathe when he strides up to her.

Pressing his hat to his chest, he bows. His deep voice washes over her. "What a vision. Serena de Avila, I am immensely pleased to see you here tonight."

He seems wider of shoulders and fuller across the chest than she recalled. In their last meeting a young man flustered her, here before her, making the heat rise to her cheeks, is no boy.

Mustering all the courage she can, she curtsies. "Pleasure."

"The lady speaks!" The brown eyes twinkle. "Will you honor me with a dance before the cock crows?"

She glances around the room at the beautifully dressed nobles moving gracefully to the music. Panic grips her. "I...I am afraid I cannot." She throws her hands over her face. "I do not know how to dance."

"Wonderful."

She moves a finger to peek through.

"It shall be my honor to teach you. Come, we shall find a quiet place to begin the lessons."

"Oh no. I do not think I can."

"Certainly you can. And you shall." He gently pulls her through the crowd to a secluded hallway. "This should do nicely. *Escuche*, we can hear the music, but no one shall be watching. Well?" His smile is radiant.

Why can she not stop shaking? It has been her secret desire to learn how to dance, yet she never dared hope her wish would come true. It is preposterous. And yet...

Blessed Saints! She imagines what it would be like to take his hand. A princess, a beautiful royal princess with her prince. Clara is right. When would she get this chance again?

"Son of the devil." He slaps his forehead. "My apologies, Serena. Did my mother forbid you to dance?"

She blinks, her hand presses hard against her side. "No."

"Ah, then I suppose you are only allowed to dance with men of your station?"

The truth stings like a slap across her face. She is no princess, no lady, simply a poor woman dressed up for one night. With no hope of ever being more to a nobleman like Andrés, her bottom lip quivers.

He slaps his thigh. "I have upset you. Again. I had hoped to make it up to you for my bad behavior the last time we met. What can I do?"

She swallows past the lump in her throat. "Your mother, the...the Marquesa de Moya, she—"

"I shall beg her not to be too strict with you. It is my fault you are here in the corridor with me. You shall not be punished on my account."

She blinks. "You misunderstand. The marquesa said I could enjoy the festivities."

He grins. "What good fortune for me."

"But as you have suggested, Marques, it is best I return to my station." Sadly, she turns on her heel.

He grabs her elbow. "No. Wait, please stay, Serena." His eyes have lost the amused sparkle. "I would be honored if you remained. Please?"

Her mouth drops. He really wants her to stay? She cannot fathom why.

"If it is your wish," Serena whispers.

"It is." He claps his hands together. "I promise this will be enjoyable. I shall teach you all the *baixas* and *ioyosos* I know.

Something inside her quivers. A want, akin to hunger, pulls in her lower belly and tingles in her back and legs. She has never experienced such a feeling.

"Do not fret." He smiles self-confidently. "They are easy."

"Why?" She asks.

"*Perdón?*" His brows furrow.

"Why spend time with me? There are many gorgeous noble ladies in the ballroom who already know how to dance."

The grin spreads and his dimples deepen. "I want to be with you, is that not reason enough? Come. Let us dance."

She takes a deep breath and places her hand in his.

"Dancing is not difficult," he explains. "Listen to the music. Feel it in your bones? Your blood?"

She nods. Is it the music making her blood run so hot and her mind spin?

"Just follow me. Do what I do."

To her delight, dancing is easier than she expected. The *baixas* he shows her are fun. Soon she is able to do them without tripping over her own feet.

"I think we are ready. Shall we?"

All she can do is nod and follow him onto the crowded dance floor. Andrés stands in front of her, holding her left hand while her right holds the hand of the person next to her. Long step, short step, long step again, all leading with the left foot, the dancers circle around the floor following the leader.

Andrés's voice lifts over the music. "You are doing well. Good, curtsy to the left, now the right. Terrific."

The dancers applaud once the music ends.

"Serena, you are a natural." Andrés bows to her. "Now it is time for the *ioyosos*. I shall understand if you do not wish to try them. They are a bit more intricate. The nobleman and his lady dance together without the group line."

"Yes, I would love to dance the *ioyosos* with you. That is—" she composes herself, "—if you desire it so."

When he smiles she feels a tightening in her belly—both painful and pleasurable. Her heart beats faster and she longs for him to smile at her again. He leads her to the middle of the dance floor where nobles are already moving to the music.

Many of the ladies wear long gloves. Serena is grateful her hands are bare. She likes feeling Andrés's hand in hers as they dip and sway toward one another. Her cheeks ache from smiling. She cannot take her eyes off the man grinning encouragement back at her.

A mist filters into the hall through the open doors. It creeps low across the dance floor like an evil presence. Menacing, dark, cold. The dancers keep moving, chopping the rising vapor with their feet. It grows thicker, undaunted.

Serena and Andrés do not take notice of the fog or the dancers rushing off the floor. They gaze into each other's eyes and fall in love.

The dance floor fades away. The ballroom disappears. It is just the two of them swaying slowly to the plucking of a lone harpsichord. The mist rises around them, growing thicker and thicker until they are completely enveloped.

And gone.

CRSO

With the end of the dream, I floated for a moment in the empty nothingness.

Who were the young lovers? What did it all mean?

Suddenly, the young woman stepped out of the fog. She came horrifyingly close, too close. I flinched and tried to turn away. But I couldn't move. Her eyes were like slate, cold and dead. I smelled decay on her breath. My stomach turned.

"Run! Fast!" she hissed. "Death is upon you."

Something grabbed my hand and I screamed like bloody murder.

Chapter Eleven

"Erin, you're safe." A gorgeous man caressed my hand.

The scream died in my throat. "Santiago," I gasped, rubbing my eyes with my knuckles, desperately trying to erase the image of her blue lips and dead eyes. "It was a dream."

"Must have been a bad one. Do you have nightmares often?"

"Only when I close my eyes," I joked, but I was lying. Lately, I was having them when my eyes were open too.

He gave my arm a little squeeze. "You're seeing a doctor about this?"

It sounded more like a statement than a question. I paused. Was this the time to tell the man I was falling in love with I was under a psychiatrist's care and addicted to sleeping pills? Oh, and also seeing dead people?

"Yes," I admitted. "They can't do much. Sleeping pills are my best bet."

He frowned. "I'll get you an appointment at a sleep clinic in Madrid. Maybe you're not going deep enough into sleep."

"Yeah, we'll see." I worried about getting stuck in one of those dreams and never coming out of it. *Can a person die for real in a dream?*

He smiled. "I like your robe."

I sat up, pulling the collar tighter over my breasts. "Think it's okay? I borrowed it from the closet."

"Better than okay." He grinned. "I brought you something."

"Let me guess, blood sausage?" I crinkled my nose in distaste.

"How'd you guess?" He winked. "Look in the bag."

"Which one?" Three rainbow-striped plastic bags were lined up by his feet.

"This one first." His face lit up like a kid on Christmas day.

I pulled out a candy-apple red two-piece bathing suit. "Ah, very pretty."

"There's a hot tub outside."

I turned the pieces over. They were pretty skimpy. "Took quite a risk, didn't you? You don't know my size."

"I asked the salesladies to model them all for me," he said straight-faced. "To be sure I got it right."

"What!" I hit him with the pillow. "You did not."

"No, I didn't. I admire your body. I knew this was right for you."

I blushed, probably brighter than the suit. Was Santiago Botello flirting?

"Next bag."

I reached in and pulled out a hot pink cashmere sweater. "Santiago. This is gorgeous. Ooh, so soft. Thank you."

"There's more, keep looking."

"Where did you find all this stuff?"

"One store in town had everything from clothes to gardening equipment. Next door was the deli." His chin lifted like Maria's does when she is proven supremely right about something.

Reaching in the bag, I pulled out a pair of jeans and matching hot pink socks. I was astonished. They were all my size, exactly my taste.

I pressed my hand to my heart. "I don't know what to say."

"Thought you would appreciate a change of clothes. But, I like this on you too." He rubbed his hand down the length of my robe sleeve, warming my skin beneath the material.

"Mmmm, feels so good," I purred. He really was flirting. "It's getting cold in here."

"Great."

"What? You really need to work on those hosting skills."

"I'll turn on the hot tub," he explained, already bounding out of the room.

"Okay, boy scout." As I put on the swimsuit I thought about my Get a Life Journal. Number 5 was definitely going to be: *No more nightmares, only sweet dreams from now on.*

When the water was hot, we carried out our snacks of Spanish wine, cheese, crackers and my favorite dried Spanish ham, *jamón serrano.* I wore my hot new swimsuit and he had on a pair of shorts he'd purchased, just as hot. We both covered up in white robes to block out the nippy air.

Lanterns hanging on wrought iron hooks lit our winding path. In the middle of a patch of dewy lawn, surrounded by a grove of pine trees, sat a dark-bottomed hot tub encircled by a redwood deck. The sharp, angled mountains loomed off in the distance like dark sleeping giants. Overhead the stars twinkled by the trillions.

Santiago stepped into the tub first, offering his hand for me to take while I eased into the hot water. His gaze traveled across my body. The hunger was unmistakable. "Careful, the tub's deep."

"You aren't kidding. Look, I'm standing on the last step and the water is up to here."

His gaze lingered on where the water lapped at my bikini cups. His hand squeezed mine. "I've got you. Come all the way in."

I floated over next to him, secretly thanking Maria for convincing me to purchase a small bottle of Carolina Herrera perfume. The little dab I'd rubbed behind my ears this morning was becoming revitalized in the steam. The sweet, musky scent with just a hint of pear from my bath wafted up and encircled us.

"Do you want bubbles? I can turn on the jets," he said.

"Can we keep them off? It's so nice and quiet. Hey, would you look at all those stars? I sure don't get a view like this in LA."

We both looked up. Silence settled over us like a cotton blanket. Everything was still until a screech owl screamed in a nearby branch. The sound reminded me of the ghost in the tower. I shivered in the hot water.

"You have chicken bumps on your skin," he said.

"Something stepped across my grave, I guess."

"What?"

"Just an expression."

"Are you feeling dizzy?" He peered closely into my pupils again as he had in the tower after I'd fainted. I was glad to see he had moved a bit closer. What could I do to convince him to stop being a medical professional and start playing doctor with me?

"No. I was thinking about the ghost in the tower," I said softly. "Could she have been pushed for some other reason? I mean, other than the ever-popular conspiracy theory?"

"The nursemaid? Possibly." He frowned. "What made you think about the tower ghost?"

"I had a dream about her. And her lover."

"You what?" If I had to draw a face of a man perfectly stunned, Santiago would be the model.

I winced. "I know it sounds insane, but it seemed so real. We were—they were dancing at some fancy ball."

"Oh Erin, the tower spooked you, that's all."

I wasn't about to tell him I'd dreamt about the ghost before I ever set foot in the tower. Some things were better left unsaid.

"I admit I got spooked. But there's something more." I took a breath. "I think she was trying to tell me something."

"You heard the ghost's voice in your head?" He had his clinical look on, the way, I assumed, doctors stare at the mentally ill.

I rushed on before I lost my nerve. "There was this palpable sense of danger even when she was dancing with the Marques de Moya—"

His hand gripped my arm. "How do you know that name?"

"Heard it." I scrunched up my face. He was really going to think I was nuts. "In my dream."

"I read about a man by that name. Beatriz's son? That Marques?"

"Beatriz? Oh yes." Hope did a little happy dance in my chest. "She was in charge of preparations for the ball. Some sort of special occasion." The memory rushed back like flood waters. "I got it. A matrimonial ball. Princess Juana was going to marry the handsome Felipe guy."

131

His mouth dropped open.

"Does any of this make sense to you?" I asked.

"You never knew these names before you dreamt them?"

"Nope." For the first time in weeks I was thinking I might not be crazy after all.

He ran his fingers through his damp hair. I had never seen anyone pace inside a hot tub before. "Is it possible?"

"What are you thinking?"

"Beatriz, the Marquesa de Moya, was Queen Isabel's dearest friend and confidant. She advised the queen to give Columbus a shot. Without Beatriz, Columbus would never have discovered America. She was *that* influential." His look was piercing. "What did she have to do with the tower ghost?"

"Maybe nothing." In a flash I could feel the Marques's hand in mine as we moved slowly to the soft stringing of a lone harpsichord. "But her son sure did."

"I don't know what it means, but I'm worried." He rubbed his cheek. "You didn't slap me, did you?"

"What? No. You thought I did?" Understanding dawned. "This afternoon."

"Something did. But I had your arms pinned. It couldn't have been you."

"So what are you saying? The tower ghost slapped you and then crawled into my dreams? How is that possible?"

He shook his head. "I don't know, *querida*. Let's do some research about this nursemaid. Maybe we can find out something about her in the history books back at the house." He hugged me. "Are you okay?"

Wrapped in his arms? "Couldn't be better."

He moved back. "You look good. I've been watching you for signs of...a relapse."

"You've been watching me?"

"You seem fine. Your pupils, your breathing, all normal."

I took his hand and pressed it over the hot red bikini top. "My heartbeat, my breathing, my eyes." I batted my lashes shamelessly. "Everything to your satisfaction?"

"Um, yes." His voice cracked, just a little.

I brought his hand up and kissed his palm. "Santiago,

there's something I want to clear up."

His Adam's apple bobbed as he swallowed hard.

"Earlier, on the couch—"

"I'm an idiot," he interrupted. "Can we just forget that I pinned a woman who had just been rendered unconscious?"

"Little hard to forget. It makes me wonder if—" I moved closer, "—you've ever been pinned by a girl in a hot tub?"

His mouth opened, but the time for talking was over.

Sensuously, slowly I kissed him. The kind of kiss designed to make a grown man weak. My tongue flicked at his lips. His mouth opened enough to let me in. When he sucked gently, I gasped with pleasure.

The air coming off the mountains was cold, but steam floated up from our bodies. We were cocooned in silence, the only beings on the planet. Under the water, his hands ran across my shoulders and down my back. I shuddered from his touch. Our tongues battled to taste more, our hands groping to feel more.

His hands moved up my back and my neck. Lifting my wet hair off my shoulders, his fingers gently twisted the dripping strands into a wild bun. I held on to his waist as the heat rushed through me. He deepened the kiss until I thought we might combust.

I let my hands drop lower until I held the most perfect butt cheeks God has ever made. He made a low, deep sound in his throat. He shifted his weight and I was able to feel the press of another perfect part of his anatomy.

The kiss on the couch had been no Spanish handshake. He wanted me, nearly as badly as I wanted him.

"Ow!" he yelped and pulled away from my lips with a loud smack. "Did you do that?"

"Kiss you?"

He wore the am-I-kissing-a-nutcase? look. "You didn't pinch my earlobe?"

I laughed. "Um, no. My hands were on your butt. Still are." I squeezed. "See?"

His eyes widened. "Something is in here. With. Us."

Chills rolled through me, lifting the hair on my skin. I felt it too. We were not alone.

"Get out!" he yelled, grabbing my arm and yanking me out of the hot tub.

It was too dark to see anything, so we snatched up our things and fast-walked back inside. He pulled the sliding glass door open, made room for me to pass and then lickety-split locked the door behind me. Flipping on all the outside lights he could find, he peered through the window. I hid behind his back and peeked around his arm.

"See anything?" I whispered.

"No. You?"

I let out the breath I was holding. "Did we imagine it?"

He turned to face me, wrapping me up in his strong arms. "I don't think so. I'm going to make a fire and then we'll try to figure this thing out."

I curled up in the robe watching Santiago while he lit the kindling and threw a couple logs into a massive fireplace.

"Now that's a fire." I was trying to play it cute and light. Inside my heart had a crack in it, splitting wider by the minute. I was on fire, why wasn't he stoking me? Our room had a lovely king-sized bed and stargazing ceiling. Why wasn't he carrying me down the hall? Every time we started to get close, something got between us. I wanted to cry.

He came and sat beside me. "Before we talk about anything else, I need to apologize for...for..."

"Thinking I'm a stark raving lunatic?"

"No." His gaze dropped. "I wouldn't say that."

"Of course not. I wouldn't blame you if you thought it. A little. Listen, Santiago, I know crazy. My family tree is loaded with nuts, from the odd to the committed." Not the kind of thing I wanted to reveal so early in our relationship, and yet, there it was. I rushed on. "I don't think I've lost my mind. Something...paranormal is at work here."

"I know." He looked at me sheepishly. "How can I make it up to you?" He picked up my legs and draped them over his lap. Then he did something no man has ever done to me.

"Ooooh," I sighed. Pleasure spread from where his fingers made slow, deep circles. "Keep it up and I will be your slave for life."

He grinned. "Really? What if I do this?" Those glorious hands kept rubbing deeper and deeper, probing, pressing.

My breathing picked up tempo. I could feel his fingers all over my skin. I rolled my head back onto the couch and closed my eyes. "I'm yours, master. Anything you want."

"Anything?" His voice was husky. "Just for a little bit of rubbing?"

I opened one eye and peeked at him. "Um-hmm. Rubbing is good." And I wasn't joking. Pleasure was fast becoming passion. If he kept going I would scream his name in ecstasy. "*Really* good."

"What if I touch you here?" He pressed his thumb against my most sensitive spot and made small delicious circles.

"Oooh, baby. Yes. Oh. My." A moan I rarely make escaped my lips.

"Harder?"

"Mmmm."

"Deeper?"

"Ohhh. Yes."

He laughed. "How about I massage the other foot now?"

"Yes, please." This was a man who *really* knew how to use his hands.

Squeezing the tips of my toes one by one he said, "What do you think it was? Out there."

I winced.

"Did I hurt you?"

"No. It's the answer that bites."

"The ghost from the tower?"

"Yep. Serena, the nursemaid, has been haunting me for days now. Before I ever set foot in the tower."

His fingers stopped kneading the arch of my foot.

"What I don't get is why she pulled your earlobe," I rushed on before he started thinking I was loony again.

"I have a theory," he said. "Here, pull your arms out of the robe and press them by your sides so I can tie you up."

"Sounds a bit kinky."

His grin was sly. "Just do it."

"Yes, master."

He cinched my sleeves tightly across my chest until I was all tied up. "There. Now kiss me."

I leaned forward and did as I was told. He took hold of my robe's collar, pulled me closer and kissed the daylights out of me. I never thought I'd enjoy feeling out of control. Dominated. It was a bit kinky, but wow, oh wow.

Just as I started to get into the whole scenario, losing myself completely to him, he made an "oof!" sound and doubled over as though he'd been kneed in the groin.

"Santiago! Are you all right?"

He made some unusual noises, trying to suck air into his lungs. After several moments he finally managed, "Theory proved."

"I don't get it."

He untied my sleeves. "That ghost is trying to protect you. From me."

"But, why? This man gives the best foot rub in the world," I yelled. "Leave him alone."

He didn't look into my eyes. "Maybe she knows about the darkness."

A sudden chill assaulted my skin, blowing across my neck, up my damp scalp. I remembered Rosa's warning—it could take anyone, anytime. "What...is it?"

The intensity glowing in his eyes could have burned my retinas. He gripped my shoulders in his strong hands. "Listen, Erin. There's something important I have to tell you."

The feeling of impending doom imbedded a lump in my throat. I gulped past it.

A ring interrupted us. He released me as a look of alarm flashed over his face. "My phone. Where is it?"

"Probably in our—my room. Next to the bags on the dresser."

"Sorry, I have to take this." He sprinted down the long hall. "Could be a patient. Dear God, I hope it's not..." I didn't catch the end of his statement. He was already gone.

The only sounds I could hear were the raspy, fast breaths coming from my open mouth. Anxiety burned hot in my stomach. No sane person would sit alone in the dark lobby of a vacant hotel on top of a quiet spooky mountain and do what I was about to do. Heck, even truly insane folks might turn and run. Fleeing was the rationale thing to do. The smart thing.

"Where are you?" I said quietly.

The fire threw long creepy shadow fingers up the walls and onto the ceiling. Each crack and pop made me jump. I squinted my eyes, trying to see her. There was no answer. No movement.

Had I imagined the whole thing? My heart sank. Maybe. The car crash had been pretty traumatic. Was the ghost just a figment of my post-traumatic stressed mind?

No, I can't believe it. I won't.

"I am not a lunatic, raving or otherwise. Come out."

Nothing. I closed my eyes, took some deep calming breaths and listened.

Did I hear...? Yes, there it was again, a sound softer than the whisper of the wind through long grass. But it was real.

Thank God.

"*Madre de Dios.* I am here." Serena waved her arms. "Do you see me? Erin?"

Holy cow, she said my name.

It was the only word I could decipher. Her voice hissed like static. I stared at the spot I thought she stood until tears dripped out of my eyes.

More movement. Good. Her shape was darker now, almost a shadow.

"I see you." I laughed. "Wow. I really do."

The static grew louder, as if someone had cranked up the volume but forgot to tune in the station. I thought I heard "say-on". I frowned. Why did that word sound so familiar?

"I can't understand you," I said slowly. "I'm sorry. Can you hear me?"

The shadow flickered. A nod?

"Good. I don't know why you're following me, but, and I mean this in the nicest way, will you please go away?"

She flickered again. Yes, she would go away, or yes, she

understood me?

Serena was overcome with joy. *She will help me go on. But how? She cannot understand me and barely sees me.*

An idea bloomed.

Serena backed up a little until the heat from the fire flashed up her backside, then ran as fast as she could toward the sofa where Erin sat. With as much force as she could muster, she threw herself upon the hapless woman, yelling her name as she did so.

"What the—? Ooh."

Something hit me, knocking me back against the sofa. I suddenly thought of the yellow lab I had as a kid. When I got home from school, he would race across the lawn and nine times out of ten knock me flat.

"Serena?" I croaked. "Was that you?"

"*I'm here,*" she said as clearly as if she were in my—

"Head?" I screeched. "Are you in my thoughts?"

"*I...I am not certain. It is dark in here.*"

"Don't strike any matches. It's supposed to be dark. Dear God, I'm certifiable. There's a dead girl in my head."

"*Dead...girl?*"

"Sorry. Do you prefer lady? Woman? Nursemaid?"

She made a tiny cry. "*Are you speaking of me?*"

Was she serious? "Um, yeah, you are Serena the Tower Ghost, right?"

"*Oh dear. Then it is true. I died in the tower.*"

I crinkled my eyebrows. "More than five hundred years ago. You didn't know?"

Her sigh was as heavy as sand sifting through my own cells. "*I have trouble remembering things.*"

"By 'things', you mean how you died?"

"*And how I lived.*"

"Wow. Bummer."

"*I could not recall a single moment until I met you.*" Her excitement rose and flushed my skin, "*The longer I stay with you, the more I remember. You shall save me.*"

"What? Um, no. That can't be right. I'm struggling to save myself from loonyville. Sorry, but you aren't helping me there. I'm probably bonkers already. Talking to ghosts in one's head is definitely not a good sign."

"It is my desire to help you."

"Ah good. Then you'll go away?"

"I cannot." Her depression sank deep into my bones. *"I do not know how."*

"Maybe you just forgot? If you think real hard, it might come to you."

"I shall stay with you. You help me to see my past."

I sighed. I couldn't shake her. *A ghost with a memory disorder. Great.* Just like Uncle Fred who kept forgetting where he lived and frequently crawled into bed with neighbors. Yep, sounded like someone I'd get saddled with.

"You see, Serena, I don't think I can help you. I've got my own issues to work out."

She grew frantic. *"No, you must help me find my one true love. I do not know how to go to him. Please."*

I narrowed my eyes at, well, thin air. "What about *my* true love? You kneed him in the groin, for cripes sake. You've got to leave him alone."

"I cannot. He is peligroso. *I am concerned for your wellbeing."*

"You're concerned? Then stop haunting me."

She fell silent.

"Sorry. I...I guess I don't mean it. I'll help you, if I can. Provided you leave Santiago alone. I don't expect you to understand, but I've been...ill. And he heals me." I smiled, hearing the truth ring in my words. I peeked down the hall to make sure he wasn't listening to the conversation.

Ha. What conversation? He would only hear me talking out loud to the voice inside my head. What would he make of that? My heart fell. His motorcycle would fly down the mountain faster than the speed of light and I'd never feel the good doctor's hands on my skin again.

"Every part of me springs to life when he looks into my eyes. I know as soon as I say this it's going to sound stupid, but here goes. He makes me feel like a goddess, like I am the most important person in the world. A feeling to die for."

"I will not let him kill you."

"Ow, jeesh, stop yelling, it's just an expression. He's not killing me, unless you count the moments my heart stops when he kisses me." Warmth pooled in my girlie parts just thinking about those lips. "You've got to stop hurting Santiago."

"Will you vow to help me find Andrés?"

"Your one true love? I will do everything I can to help, but— how can I put this?—you know he's dead, right? Buried five hundred years ago. How do you suppose we find him?"

She sighed and I felt the weight in my shoulders. *"I know not. Perhaps, when I remember—"* a shudder went through her and my entire body spasmed, *"—everything."*

A thought occurred to me. "You don't recall the moment you died, do you?"

She shook her head and mine shook too. Her fear made my heart thunder at a scared rabbit's pace. Suddenly, it occurred to me that Serena was repressing her memories. Something terrible had happened to her. Maybe Santiago was right in assuming she had been murdered.

"Post-traumatic stress disorder," I said.

"Perdón?"

"I think I understand why you can't remember. Maybe a little psychoanalysis—"

"He comes," she interrupted and ripped herself out of my brain.

Sure enough, I could see Santiago's dark shape coming down the hall.

"Remember your promise," I whispered. "Leave my man alone."

Chapter Twelve

I rose to meet him in the hall. "Everything all right?"

He exhaled deeply. "Come in here. We need to talk."

Oh. No. That didn't sound good.

I followed after him into our—my room. He sat heavily on the edge of the bed as if what he was about to say was really, really awful.

I sat next to him and rubbed his shoulder. "Who was it?"

"Maria. I missed the call and she didn't leave a message. I dialed back immediately and got the answering service. I called the house too. No one's picking up."

"She probably meant to call someone else and hit your speed-dial button by mistake. She does that to me all the time." I tried to sound reassuring. I knew he was worried about his mother.

"Maybe." Just then the cell beeped. "Text message from Maria." As he read the message his face pinched with worry.

"What does it say?" I was alarmed by the way his cheeks were losing color.

"911." He grabbed his helmet. "We've got to go. Now!"

"Hold on. It's not an emergency. It's code."

He gave me a dark look. "What do you mean?"

"Maria and I developed a text message code at work. '411' meant 'juicy office scuttlebutt' and '911' was used when one of the partners was heading down the hall. It was the code for 'Look out, danger coming your way'. But honestly, Santiago, I have no idea what she means by it right now. Do you?"

Instead of answering, he punched redial three more times.

His body became more and more tense when Maria didn't answer. Cursing, he turned his back to me and dialed again. This time he spoke to someone on the other end.

"What's going on there?" he demanded. "Go check. Make sure they're safe." He hung up and turned toward me.

"Who was that?" I asked.

"Protection."

"For who? From what...?" I was thinking about his mother. Maybe her situation was scarier than I thought.

"It's complicated," was all he'd say. His face was tired, and deeply sad.

I draped my arm over his shoulders. "I'm sure everything's okay. Maybe Maria was jerking us around, bummed because we didn't bring her along." I had an image of her as a little girl in pigtails covered with the snowball her brother had smashed over her head. Didn't she say she always got even? Sending a cryptic message in the early hours was her way of getting under her brother's skin.

The lines bunched up in his forehead told me he was still puzzling over some great dilemma. "Hope you're right."

I kissed his cheek. "I am right. And a little cold. Care to warm me up?"

Instead, he plopped back against the bed. Lacing his fingers behind his head, he stared at the ceiling as if trying to read answers written on the glass. "I'm not good at this."

I bent forward and kissed his neck. In his ear I whispered, "Oh yes, you are. Very...very...good."

He lifted my chin. "No, I'm not."

My heart sank. He was pulling away. Again.

"I didn't plan for any of this..." The sentence hung in the air. "Please understand," he started slowly, "I can't. We need to stop before someone gets hurt."

I took his hand in mine. "I'm not planning on hurting you." I nibbled on his thumb. "Much."

"This is serious."

I leaned over him, my hair draping his face, my eyes on his. "I'm a big girl, Santiago."

He lifted my hair and tucked it over my shoulder. "You

have no idea what you're getting into."

"I know what I want."

"It's safer if we remain friends."

The word "friends" stuck like an arrow in my heart. Did Helena have the same arrow in hers? "Sheesh, you Spaniards and your safety issues. Why don't you tell me what's going on?"

"There are things you don't know, about me, my family. It's too dangerous. I won't let you get mixed up in...my problems."

"Every family has a few skeletons in the closet." *Take me, for instance.* A white airbag popped into my mental picture. My stomach flopped. "So why don't you tell me about your problems? I told you about my ghost."

He exhaled and stood up. With his back to me he muttered, "I can't. I swore an oath."

"Uh-huh." I followed him. My blood pressure was skyrocketing, my cheeks aflame. "You know what I think your problem is? You like me, but you're just not that *into me.* Story of my life."

He groaned. "I'm not into you?"

"You swore an oath is the best you could come up with? And if you tell me the real reason, you'll have to kill me, right? Why do men think they can spout any old line and women will just buy it? None of you like to commit. I get it."

"It is not a line."

I blew through my lips in disgust.

"I'm telling the truth."

"You don't want to have sex with me, why don't you just say it? You don't want me—"

He rounded on me and slammed me against the wall. His hands cuffed my wrists and he held my arms over my head so tightly I couldn't move if I wanted to. Rock-hard chest, abs, thighs, held me captive. The heat from his body deliciously seared every inch of my skin. All that strong, unrelenting power made me weak.

My passion mounted, matching his fury. I arched my back and pressed my breasts against his muscled chest. Those wondrous hands still gripped my wrists, refusing to release me while his lips bruised mine. A truckload of frustration burned in that kiss.

I kissed him back, stealing air when I could. Breathing was highly overrated when his lips were on mine. I wanted him more than I had ever wanted anything in my life. Silently, I begged him to take me right there. Strip off my clothes and pound his hard self into me over and over...

When he pulled back, his breath was hot on my face. "We can't always have what we want."

As I struggled to catch my breath, he walked away, closing the door to the adjoining room behind him.

He flattened his back against the wall and yanked the phone out of his pocket. "Well?" he demanded.

"The house is quiet. Dark. They're asleep," the man reported.

"How can you tell?" Santiago pounded his forehead with his fist.

"I'm inside," the man whispered.

Santiago's eyes flew open. "Are you crazy? I told you how dangerous this is."

"I'm fully armed, Doctor Botello. Trust me, I know what I'm doing."

"No, you don't. None of us do."

"Relax. I'll call you if there's trouble."

"If there's trouble, you won't have time to dial. Watch your back. I can't be responsible for you too."

രുളൊ

It sounded like a party going on in the lobby. Dressing quickly, I went out to meet Rodrigo's family. Santiago came out of his room a moment after me, catching me in the hall. His hair was rumpled, his eyes dark. He stifled a yawn.

"Sleep much?" I asked.

"No," he admitted.

"Good."

"You think I'm an ass."

"Nope. Just a man." I walked as fast as I could to outpace

him to the kitchen where the voices were coming from.

"I didn't handle things well, I admit, but I had your best interests at heart. You must believe me." He sprinted to get in front of me and placed his hands on my shoulders.

Damn if his touch didn't send a little shiver of excitement through me. "Next time, please keep your hands off my *best interests*. I'm smart enough to make my own decisions."

"Of course you are. I didn't mean—"

"*Hola, bella,*" Rodrigo called from the front entrance. "You are here."

"Can we help you with those?" I wiggled around Santiago's formidable frame and rushed to take one of four grocery bags from Rodrigo's arms.

"Sure, there are others in the truck," Rodrigo said over his shoulder to Santiago.

Before Santiago headed outside he said to me, "I would like to have a word with you later."

I ignored him. "Jeez, Rodrigo, you feeding an army?"

"Worse—my family. They can out-eat any army. You will love the food."

I followed him into the kitchen. "If it's anything like the food at the restaurant, I know I will."

A short, round woman was putting pound after pound of meat into the sub-zero refrigerator. All I could see was her wide backside as she dipped and stretched to make room for the mass quantities of food lining the countertop.

"Marta, come here a minute," Rodrigo said. "I want you to meet someone."

To my surprise she threw her massive arms around me and planted a kiss on each of my cheeks. "Ereen, it is a pleasure."

I was dumbfounded. Who was this woman?

"Now Marta, give her air, for the sake of God. Erin, this is my beautiful wife of thirty-eight years." Rodrigo smiled.

"Lovely place you have here. Very kind of you to invite us."

"Where do you want these?" Santiago asked and then put his heavy load where Rodrigo pointed.

"Santiago!" Marta screeched, smothering him in her meaty arms before I had a chance to warn him.

I stifled a laugh at the surprised look on his face. "This is Marta, Rodrigo's wife."

"Ah," Santiago said after taking her kisses on his cheeks. "Nice to meet you."

"So glad you two could come. Rod has told me so much about you. Did you choose nice rooms? Oh my dears, there wasn't any food in the kitchen, you must be starving. I'll make you something straightaway."

"No, we made do," Santiago said. "Please don't trouble yourself."

"What trouble? How about a tortilla Española? Steak and eggs? American-style pancakes?"

"No, please, we are fine. We don't want to impose. Santiago bought some food in town."

"Bah. There are no decent restaurants in these mountain villages. You go, read one of the newspapers. I will make you a real breakfast."

"Better do as she says, or none of us will have any peace," Rodrigo teased.

"Hush, you." She swung a dishtowel at him. "I am just getting to know these nice folks. I do not want them listening to your nonsense."

"See? Just give in. It's safer." Rodrigo went back outside.

"Well, if you're sure," I said.

"Of course I am. Go now. Go. Go." She shooed us away.

As we walked down the hallway, Santiago tried to reach for me. I ducked and swerved away. "I'm going to take a shower, see you in a bit."

His mouth remained open, his hands shoved in his pockets as I closed my door.

"How can we possibly eat all this food?" I whispered to Santiago who was sitting on a barstool waiting for me.

"I don't know, but we better try."

"Sit down," Marta commanded from the hallway. "Enjoy your breakfast."

The plates were full of scrambled eggs, a vegetable frittata, bacon, sausage, pancakes and potatoes. Where to start?

"Oh my gosh, Marta. This frittata is amazing. How'd you do all this?"

"You are a dear. It is easy. I have been cooking longer than I can remember."

"At the restaurant?" Santiago asked.

"Some days. It used to be every day, until Rod started worrying about me being on my feet for so long. He tells me I am not a young girl anymore. I say sixty-nine is not old either. Still he worries. We have hired another cook. What do you think of the breakfast?"

"It's fantastic," I said.

Santiago nodded agreement with his mouth stuffed full.

She came and sat on the barstool next to us. "What do you do?"

"I'm on vacation. Santiago is a doctor—Internist, General Practitioner, Medical Director of the hospital in Salamanca. One man, so many talents." I grinned over my cup of coffee.

Something other than admiration flickered over her round face. "*Dios mío*. I was surprised Rod invited you to our party. He's not fond of doctors. But then I heard you were the one who operated on Diego Terrazas. Aya, I love that boy. And Daniela too. She is my goddaughter." She threw her arms around his neck and squeezed him so hard I thought he might turn blue. When she finally released him she fanned her eyes so as to keep the tears from flowing. "You are one of the family now. You and your beautiful *novia*."

"You're too kind," Santiago said softly.

I waited for him to clear up the misunderstanding. I was not his girlfriend, beautiful or otherwise. Last night, he had made it clear we would remain friends. Damn him.

Her face lit up with thought. "May I ask, doctor..."

"Santiago."

"Santiago," Marta repeated shyly. "Would you speak with Rodrigo about his weight? He will not listen to me. As you can see—" she patted her own large waistline, "—I am not one to speak. But he seems to be so tired and lately he is out of breath just walking to the car. I worry about him He is everything to me." Her eyes misted and she dabbed haphazardly at them with a napkin. "Oh, these eyes of mine. I never used to be so

147

sentimental."

Santiago patted her arm gently. "It is the least I can do to repay your generosity."

Her smile was more brilliant than the morning sun, "Thank you. It won't be easy. Hopefully he will listen to you better than he does his old wife. Now, hurry up you two. Everyone will arrive within the hour."

She waddled down the hallway in search of her husband.

"Thirty-eight years and she still loves him so much." I sighed.

Santiago took my hand and gently kissed my knuckles. "It's what you deserve, *querida*. A good man who will love you forever."

His pained eyes got me. "Why won't you tell me what's wrong? Maybe I can help."

We were interrupted by an invasion stampeding through the door. Santiago and I stared at each other in amazement. Our romantic, sleepy lodge had become a zoo. Everyone was hugging, kissing, snacking and laughing.

"Walk with me?" Santiago asked.

We passed through the kitchen hand-in-hand, stopping to be formally introduced to the ladies congregating around the snack-covered island. The dozen or so women seemed too well-dressed in their pantsuits and summer dresses to sit around watching bike riders on television. I figured the Tour watching was more of a social event than I'd anticipated. The hen party was just getting started.

Walking outside, we said our "*holas*" to the men gathering around a triangular pile of wood. Rodrigo was building the bonfire while the others tossed instructions like sticks on a fire. Poor Rodrigo neither wanted, nor needed, the advice and was quickly becoming hot under the collar.

"I know what I am doing," Rodrigo said. "I have cooked a *tostón* or two in my lifetime."

When a man who had a thinner, younger version of Rodrigo's face threw in his two cents, Rodrigo exploded, "Stefan, enough already. Tell me one more time how to roast this pig and you will be the one strung up over the fire."

"Oops, we better get while the getting is good," I whispered to Santiago.

He took my hand again. "We are going for a walk," Santiago called out, squeezing my hand in his.

"Do not be too long, the Tour starts soon," Rodrigo replied.

The man named Stefan had a loud voice. "For all the farts in the sea! If I had a woman like that one, I would not spend a minute watching anything but her."

The others laughed at his comment except Rodrigo who punched him in arm.

"Hey, why did you do that?" Stefan wailed.

"Someone has to, and since I am the only one in our family with any sense, it falls to me," Rodrigo replied.

They were still egging each other on as we rounded the bend and got ourselves lost in a secluded grove of Alpine trees.

Lacing his fingers through mine, Santiago pressed my hand to his heart. He had the sweetest boyish look on his face. "Are you still angry with me?"

"Last night I was ticked. Now I'm just sad. I know you've been hurt, badly. I have too. I wish you trusted me enough to give us a chance."

"I can't protect you."

"Okay, so we're back to poor, vulnerable Erin who needs protecting?"

"The thought has crossed my mind."

"Uncross it. Sure, I've had a few difficult months. Okay, a couple of bad years. I'm not the damsel in distress here. I have kicked asses all the way up the corporate ladder. Hell, I took on a ten-story building and won. Sort of."

He smiled and rubbed the tip of my chin with the pad of his thumb. "You sound tough. But you don't know what you're up against."

"Neither do you."

"It's dangerous to be with me, Erin. The thought of losing you scares me."

I was moved. "Isn't that what a relationship is? Risking it all, stepping off the edge of safety into the unknown? I have a new lease on life, Santiago. It's all about living to the fullest."

He placed his forehead against mine and closed his eyes.

"I've never met anyone like you."

I ran my fingers through his hair. "Probably not. That's a good thing, right?"

He exhaled softly. "Too good. I should send you as far away from me as possible, but I can't seem to let you go."

I sighed. "Yep, it's a good thing."

He pressed his lips to my forehead. "Give me time. I'll try to work through my problems and make it safe for us to be together. Can you do that?"

"I'm not going anywhere. Not now, anyway."

"Promise me something."

I didn't like the worry in his eyes. "Anything."

"If I determine your life is in danger, you will leave here and go back home. Immediately."

"Santiago—"

"I mean it, Erin. Promise me."

How could I ever leave him? "I know what this is about, Mr. Hurdles-Wrestler-Motorcycle Champion."

"If you did you wouldn't be smiling."

"You're afraid of the ghost, aren't you?"

"What?"

"Uh-huh." I nodded. "Worried a five hundred-year-old nursemaid is going to kick your ass. What would the Devils say of their coach?"

The sternness on his face slid sideways into a crooked grin. "Are you kidding? They'd tell me to run."

"From?"

"You." He tapped the tip of my nose. "Your ghost beats the hell out of me every time I try to get close to you."

I smiled. "See? I'm dangerous to be with too. But I think we're worth it, don't you?"

Before he had a chance to disagree, I grabbed his collar and kissed the stuffing out of him. He closed his eyes. Shifting his weight, he leaned into me, and crossed his arms around my waist.

"Wow," he breathed.

"Thank you."

"No, I meant I'm still alive. The ghost didn't touch me."

I laughed. "Nope, she and I have a deal. She promised not to bother you if I help her remember her past."

"And how do you plan on doing that?"

"I have no idea."

"You scare me. You know that?"

"Yeah. I know."

"Ereen, Santiago!" Marta's voice echoed down the canyon. "It's about to begin."

He wrapped me up in a hug. "I'd rather stay here with you. Now that I know I'll live through it, I plan on kissing you much, much more."

Chapter Thirteen

"Here, Santiago, up front," Rodrigo called. Santiago took the last chair close to the flatscreen. "Move over, you heathens," Rodrigo growled. "Where is Erin going to sit?"

"Not to worry." Santiago took my hand and pulled down me on top of his lap. "She has a seat right here."

"Not fair," Stefan whined. "My lap was available."

"Stefan." Rodrigo tossed a pillow at his brother's head.

"Hey, why did you do that?" Stefan rubbed his balding scalp. The whole group busted up laughing.

"Okay, quiet everyone. It's starting," Marta said.

I leaned over and whispered in Santiago's ear, "Might need a little help here. Can you clue me in about the race particulars? I'd hate to incite a riot with stupid questions."

He gently tucked my hair behind my ear. "The Tour de France is a grueling three-week endurance race. Twenty-something teams—"

"Twenty-two," Stefan interjected.

"Okay, twenty-two teams made of eight riders—"

"Nine," Stefan said.

"Who should be telling this story?" I teased.

Santiago ignored my comment. "They ride hundreds of kilometers each day. The toughest being the mountain stages, like the one today. The climbs into the Alps and the Pyrenees usually determine the final winner of the race."

"A three-week race? Insane."

A room full of eyes trained on me. It was unnerving to be such an oddball.

"Armstrong is riding again this year."

"I'm hopeful our Carlos Sastre will win. He's very good—" Marta started to explain.

"Sastre is adorable." One of the women joined in.

"Did you see the year when he won the stage and put the baby pacifier in his mouth as he crossed the line in honor of his—"

"Two-month-old baby. I hope he wins a stage again today." A clearly enamored young woman sighed.

"Impossible," Stefan said. "He's too old."

All the women jumped on him at once.

"Too old!"

"Look who's speaking."

"Don't listen to that old goat."

The young woman had the dreamy eyes of a groupie. "I wonder if Sastre carries the pacifier in his pocket for luck?"

"Sastre, Sastre." Stefan grumbled. "I want Peirero to win. He took it by default in 2006 when Landis tested positive for blood doping."

I raised my eyes at Santiago who simply said, "All a drama."

"Peirero, he's handsome too," a woman said.

They were off and running again until Rodrigo stood up. "Quiet, ladies, especially you, Stefan. The race has begun."

The room grew silent, for about a minute and a half and then the sideline commentary picked up again. I smiled at Santiago. It would be impossible to keep this bunch quiet for long.

"What are the riders putting inside their shirts?" I asked.

"Jerseys," Santiago corrected. "Newspaper against their skin keeps them warm as they fly down the mountains. They're going more than eighty kilometers an hour. A few years back a rider rode off the edge and died."

"No." Phobia fluttered in my chest. The fear of heights, again. Then I thought of Serena. Was I sensing her fear? Where was she hiding?

At commercial break pandemonium broke out. Arguing men tried to predict the outcome of the day and the women gossiped about the riders.

"I'm going to tend the fire," Rodrigo called out.

"Right. I need to stir the food on the stove as well." Marta rose and went the other direction.

"How long is this going to last?" I whispered to Santiago.

"I don't know, five or six hours."

"Five or six? Well, I better take a potty break now." I got off his lap.

"Whew, the air is returning to my lungs," he joked.

"Thanks a lot."

On the way back, I stopped by the kitchen. "Marta, can I help you with anything? It all smells delicious."

"Are you getting hungry? Have some of those snacks. Can you take this seasoning-salt to Rodrigo? He will need it for the *tostón*."

"Sure thing." I grabbed a handful of crackers and the salt and headed outside to where Rodrigo stood by the spit.

"Mmmm, Rodrigo, it smells good. How's it going out—?" I stopped abruptly. Something was wrong. He hadn't turned when I opened the door, or budged when I spoke to him.

"Rodrigo?" I tapped the back of his right shoulder. "Are you okay?"

His left hand grabbed mine, grinding it against his shoulder in a white-knuckled death grip.

"What's wrong?" I moved carefully under his tight grip.

His face was covered with sweat, his color ashen. "Chest...hurts...can't breathe." Then his body went slack. He fell into me, almost taking us both out.

"Santiago!" I slipped on the grass, barely holding Rodrigo's heavy, limp weight. "Someone! Help!"

Santiago was the first one on the scene. His long legs fairly flew across the lawn and he lifted Rodrigo off me. "What happened?" He laid the unconscious man down.

"His chest hurt and he couldn't breathe."

Santiago was already ripping Rodrigo's shirt open. Buttons flew off in every direction.

I backed up, trembling. "Oh God, he's not breathing." My voice sounded tinny and far away.

"Heart attack. Get the black box on the back of the bike." Santiago tipped Rodrigo's head back and began CPR.

I was frozen in horror. People were gathering around, murmuring, praying and asking me questions. I couldn't answer. I couldn't move. All I could do was watch Santiago blow breaths of life into Rodrigo's lungs and pound against his still chest.

"He is dead!" Serena screamed in my ear. Her terror mingled with mine.

And my own personal hell closed in. The panic attack struck hard. The grass tilted beneath my feet. My vision blurred and my breath came in fast gulps that couldn't quite fill up my lungs.

Santiago was stunned to see me still standing there. "You." He pointed to someone behind me. "Get the black box on the back of my motorcycle. Someone else call an ambulance. Quickly! Move!"

"Rodrigo!" Marta broke through the crowd. "Rodrigo, my darling, wake up." Her shrill voice echoed off the mountains and bounced back to stab me in the heart.

"Blessed Madre," Serena wailed. *"I do not want to see. I cannot see death."*

I wanted to scream at her to go away, but I couldn't catch my breath.

The women formed a protective circle around Marta in an effort to calm her and keep her from flinging herself on her dying husband's body.

"*Dios mío! Madre de Dios,* help us," Marta cried.

I fell back from the group, my gaze riveted to the scene before me. I was unable to do or say a thing. Serena had likewise fallen silent. I no longer felt her terror beside mine. Either she had flown the coop or fainted under the stress.

Santiago worked for what seemed an eternity until Rodrigo finally took a ragged breath and sputtered. He choked. His eyes were glassy, bewildered.

"Rodrigo, hold still." Santiago's steady voice rang with authority.

"By God, I found it," Stefan panted as he handed the black box to Santiago.

Reaching inside, Santiago produced some pills. "Here, Rodrigo. Put this under your tongue. Nitroglycerin will help keep your heart from arresting again."

"Rody." Marta could no longer be contained. Sobbing, she rushed to her husband's side, falling to her knees in the grass beside him. "You scared me, baby. Are you feeling okay now?"

Rodrigo smiled weakly. "No...*tostón*...today?"

"Do not worry, darling. Our dear friends and family will save us some. Won't you?" Her shattered eyes scanned over all of us, touching us with her grief. Mascara ran like muddy streams down her cheeks. "For now we need to go to the hospital."

"Yes," Rodrigo agreed, to everyone's surprise. "Hospital."

Sirens wailed from the valley below.

"They are on the way. You will be in good hands." Santiago's voice exuded comfort. "I will call later and check on your progress."

The ambulance arrived. Everyone followed the stretcher laden with Rodrigo's heavy body through the lodge to the ambulance waiting in the front drive.

I lagged behind, going instead to my room. Sitting on the edge of the bed, I wept.

"There you are."

"Oh, Santiago." I flew into his arms.

"Shh, shh," he crooned softly in my ear. Gently, he rubbed slow circles on my back.

"I was so scared. But you were brave. Santiago, you saved his life."

He held me, kissing my hair, until the trembling subsided. "Do you want to leave now?"

I nodded. We waited long enough for Santiago to call the hospital and speak with Rodrigo's attending physician. His eyes were on me as he discussed the details of Rodrigo's care. "Sounds fine. Yes, please call me if there is any change. You have my number." Hanging up, he put a hand on my shoulder. "He'll be okay. What do you Americans say? 'A wake-up call'? He and Marta will live healthier lives from now on."

"I hope so. They are such wonderful people."

We said our good-byes to the others. They all hugged us tearfully and made us promise to return next year. I had one final view of the La Querida de las Montañas before we rode down the mountain.

Who would have thought our romantic overnight would have ended as it did? Why was disaster constantly dogging me?

A strange feeling rolled through me. A voice hummed above the engine. I clung tightly to Santiago.

Serena was back.

⊗⊗

"Maria, we're here," Santiago called from the front door of the Botellos' house. "Maria?"

"It's about time." She came out of the kitchen. Her eyes were flashing.

He looked at me and shrugged. "Did you get my messages?"

"Got them. How were the mountains?"

"Beautiful. The lodge was different from the one we went to as kids. But you would have liked it—hey, what's bugging you?"

"Nada. Not one thing." Her put-on smile was as phony as the day was long.

I was baffled by the interchange. Something was going on between them, but what? I took a stab at clearing the air. "We lucked into this trip. Next time, you'll come with us. The lodge was really amazing."

"Yeah, sure." Her gaze was intensely focused on her brother. "Helena called. I didn't know what to tell her."

I almost fell over backwards. *Helena? I thought...I thought.* My eyes searched Santiago's for the truth.

He smiled weakly at me. "Uh, thank you. I'll call her."

Without saying a word, I walked briskly to my room. My cheeks were hot, my bottom lip quivering.

"Erin." He followed me. "Erin, wait."

I didn't stop until I was in my room, then I turned on him. "I thought it was over."

"Nothing to be over. I told you, Helena is my friend." Closing the door behind him, he stilled my quivering lip with his. "I don't love Helena. I swear."

I wanted to believe him. Oh God, I wanted it to be the truth.

I let him kiss me, the worry melting around the edges until it was nearly gone. Nearly.

"I don't want to, but I have to go." Keeping his eyes on me, he backed out the door. "I'll call you later."

"Leaving already?" Maria bumped into him in the hallway.

"Work to do." He rubbed his stubbled chin. "A shave would be good too."

He ruffled her hair. She muttered an obscenity, swatting at his hand. "I hate when you do that."

Winking at me, he kissed her cheek. "I know."

She rolled her eyes. "Be grateful you're an only child. So, how are you?"

"It was an adventurous weekend. Sit down and I'll tell you about the neatest couple."

ⱭⱰ

I opened my eyes to see *Señora* Botello's face inches from mine. This scared the heebie-jeebies out of me. I yelled, which started the *señora* screaming. We sounded like a bad horror flick until Maria ran into the room.

"Mama, what are you doing in here?"

"Oh Maria, I'm sorry. She startled me, that's all."

Maria shook her head, "It's not your fault. *Señora* Hernán!"

The nurse hustled into my room. "Sorry, I thought she was asleep."

"Help me." Maria took her mother by the arm and the nurse took her other one. The two of them propelled her out of the room, while she struggled to wiggle free.

All the way down the hallway I could hear *Señora* Botello screaming, "Die, die, die..."

My hair stood on end. I jumped out of bed, a little too afraid I might never wake up with the crazy old lady on the loose, and padded barefoot into the kitchen for a glass of water.

"How's you doin'?" Rosa asked.

I rubbed my neck. "Do you have any aspirin? Feels like

Serena is using my brain for a punching bag—" *I did not just say that.* "Um, nothing."

"Headache? Oh poors you." She placed two aspirins in my hand and went to pour me a glass of water. "Who take care of you when you head hurt in the U.S. of A.?"

"My mom." I smiled. "She made the greatest tea when I was a kid. She used her own secret recipe of flowers, spices, and orange essence. It always made me feel good. Loved."

"*Té,* I make me own *té también.* I go make for you."

"No. That's not necessary."

"I like to do it. I make you feel better."

"That's nice of you." I rolled my head from side to side, trying to ease the tightness building in my neck. "Rosa, I have to ask you a question."

Her face fell into an anxious frown.

I bent closer and whispered. "Does the darkness have anything to do with ghosts?"

Her eyes widened and she threw a worried look over her shoulder. "I tol' you, no speak of dat. It is *peligroso.*"

"Is it a spirit?"

She blinked at me in confusion. Then her face lit up. "*Sí.* You could say dat. Like in de Bible. You knows de story when Jesus drove dem spirits out of the man and de all went into pigs?"

It was my turn to blink. Vaguely, I recalled sitting next to my cousin Luke during Sunday school at Saint Mark's. When the teacher read the story about Jesus driving unclean spirits out of a possessed man and into a herd of swine, Luke teased me, "Maybe that's what's wrong with you, Erin. You're possessed. Let's go look for a pig to save you."

When I elbowed him in the gut, he'd squealed, and we both got thrown out of Sunday school.

At the time, I didn't understand what possession meant. Unfortunately, I did now. Panic disorder, fear of heights, and terror of failure had all taken possession of my senses. And now, I had Serena.

Rosa went on, "After dis we no more speak of de bad tings. People say you cannot catch evil like a cold, but I sees too much

159

of it. Evil is here, hiding for now, but it can come out at any time. Believe old Rosa, you no want a espirit catching you."

I gulped. "And if one does?"

"If a espirit gets inside you, you will be *loca*."

Crazy. Why doesn't that surprise me?

She shook her head, her eyes welling with tears. "Or you could be dead. Der is no stopping de dark thing." Surprising me again with her agility, she turned and was gone.

"That went well," I said to the empty kitchen.

As I downed the aspirin I wondered if there were any pills strong enough to get rid of a ghost. And the darkness, whatever the heck it was.

CR80

Early morning light peeked through the cracks in my blinds. I heard a noise. Quietly, I slipped out of bed, opened the door and peeked down the dark hallway. "Serena?"

A shadow moved toward me. "It's me. Did I scare you?"

"Santiago! Only three years off my life." I yanked him into my room, closed the door and slammed him up against it.

"You're going to make me pay, aren't you?"

"Oh, yeah."

We kissed as if we hadn't seen each other in months. My fingers wrapped around his neck. His fingers ran through my hair, catching on a few snarls.

"Oh." His class ring caught one of my tangles.

"Sorry, wait a moment. Let me try to—"

"Yow."

"There. Sorry," he laughed. "You have hair from the bed."

"It's bedhead. So, I tossed and turned a bit last night. I missed you."

"I missed you too." His hands roamed across my old, torn USC T-shirt. "Is this what you wear to bed?"

"You like? I'll come to your place and model my Victoria Secret collection. Some of it's really good."

His eyes locked with mine. "I can only imagine."

"Why imagine? You've got the real thing, right here."

He laughed. "Don't tempt me. I have patients to see."

"Oh, them. Can't they wait? I'm the one dying over here."

"Have dinner with me tonight. I'll ask Rosa to set a nice place for us on the veranda. Maria has a date, so it will just be the two of us."

"How can I refuse a lovely offer like that?"

"Good." He kissed me. "I'll come around eight o'clock."

I linked my arms around his waist. "Stay," I whispered in his ear.

"Tonight."

I had the rest of the day to dream about him.

Chapter Fourteen

Santiago, dressed in pleated khaki pants and a dark green short-sleeve silk shirt, had come complete with a bouquet of deep red roses and a bottle of Spanish wine. We sat on the veranda enjoying the meal while being serenaded by frogs in the pond.

I thought about the conversation I'd had with Maria on the plane. She was right. I was done with the toads. I had my prince sitting right there smiling his dashing smile.

"Delicious. I'm completely stuffed," I said, patting my full belly.

"Rosa's a great cook. I just wish you could have tasted *tostón.*"

"There's always next year."

The smile he flashed me would have knocked my socks off had I been wearing any. "Yes, there is." He scooted his chair out and pulled out my chair for me.

Chivalry to boot? I was dazzled.

"What about these? Let me bring them to the kitchen." I motioned to our dirty dishes.

"No, leave them. Rosa made me promise to let her do everything. She wanted this night to be special for us."

Sweet, romantic Rosa. I would give her a huge hug later. Maybe take her to lunch.

He took my hand. The night twinkled with thousands of bright stars and a half-smiling moon. The air smelled sweetly of gardenias and roses, a potent mixture bringing to mind indecent thoughts of warm skin on petal-covered sheets. My pulse raced. We walked slowly across the thick grass until we were out of sight.

He pulled me closer and draped his arm over my shoulder. "When I'm with you, the world feels...perfect."

I sighed. "You are perfect."

He stopped walking and turned to face me. "No. I'm not." Cupping my jaw in his hands, he said, "You deserve better. Oh God, you should run from me."

I looked into his tormented eyes. "I wouldn't go."

"Even if...if it meant life or death?"

I kissed his cupped palm. "I wasn't alive before I met you."

His face was hard-cold serious. "I mean it, Erin. You could be in real danger here."

"'Could' being the operative word."

He blew out a deep breath. "I'm trying to get a handle on the situation. But I wish you weren't so close to...the problem."

"So, maybe there's no trouble at all?"

His eyes were weary. "Maybe."

"I know there's a lot you can't, or won't tell me. But really, I'm not scared. I feel safe here with you."

"You aren't safe. I should throw you over my shoulder and put you on the next plane to LA until I'm sure."

"Why don't you?" I challenged.

His face was so sad that a lump filled my throat. "You're my drug, Erin. I'm addicted."

The kiss he planted on my lips melted my soul.

He pulled back. "The ghost hasn't punched me once tonight. Maybe she's gone back to her tower."

"She's here. Somewhere." I thought about Rosa's possession story and prayed to God Serena wasn't lurking somewhere inside of me. "You want I should call her? Have her throw a punch for old time's sake?"

"No. I can only handle one woman at a time."

"Darn tootin'. This woman would like you to handle her a bit more."

He laughed. Sexily he leaned into me, resting his triceps on my shoulders, crossing his arms at the wrists behind my head. His forehead touched mine. "What am I going to do with you?"

"I have some ideas."

"Do they involve Victoria Secret?"

I smiled wickedly. "Or not."

His crushing mouth shut me up. Our tongues met, urgently. Heat popped and exploded through my veins. His hands ran down my back and slowly up my sides. As if his fingers were amped with electricity, the trace of his touch lingered long afterwards. Every place he touched me was on fire.

He nibbled my chin and across my jawline. Whispering my name into my ear, he sucked on my lobe. When his tongue went into my ear, a deep moan escaped my lips. I swayed into him, hanging onto his belt loops to keep from losing my footing. When he cupped my breast, I gasped. Gently, he rolled my nipple between his thumb and fingers. I bit my lip.

The hardness pressed against the juncture between my legs was driving me to a sweet insanity.

"I want you," I said.

"Lift up your shirt." His voice was raspy.

I yanked it over my head. The cool air chilled my hot skin. He looked as if he had never seen breasts encased in black silk.

Slowly he lowered the strap off my shoulder. His warm, wet tongue combined with the night air on my skin was almost more than I could take. But then, when he gripped my butt with his hands and sucked my nipple...waves of ecstasy drove me to the brink of release.

He yanked on my short skirt, desperate to get it off. I wiggled my hips until the hem of the skirt was riding high on my thighs. Oh sweet heaven, his hand was inside my panties. I cried out with joy when his finger slid into me.

"So wet," he murmured against my neck. His finger dove deeper. The hardness in his jeans rubbed against my sensitive core.

Oh God, oh God...

I rode the tidal wave of pleasure. Kissing. Moaning. Crying out. Biting his shoulder before floating away into the liquid abyss.

I struggled to unbutton his pants. "I need you. Now."

"Wait." He stilled my hand. "Someone's coming."

A fast-moving car screeched into the drive at the front of the house. Santiago pulled my skirt back down.

"It's just Maria." I ached to pull him down into the grass, wanting nothing more than to feel him inside me.

Santiago kissed the tip of my nose and shoved his hands in his pockets. "I'd better go."

"What? Can't you stay the night?" I put my hand on his bulging zipper. "Please?"

He groaned and moved my hand. "One day. Soon."

My body was screaming all kinds of expletives. Desperate need pulsed through me, frantic for him. "Why?"

He grimaced. "I'll tell you everything when I have the answers. Please, Erin, just go inside."

Go inside, without him? My mind couldn't fathom the thought.

"Don't tell anyone about us. If the wrong person knew how much I care for you..." He didn't finish. Instead, he kissed me quickly on the cheek and sprinted to the side gate leading to the driveway.

Trembling in a pool of passion, I forced my boneless legs to carry me back inside.

Maria met me in the entryway. Before she huffed a single word I knew she was in a foul mood.

"Hi, Maria. How was your date?" It was an effort to make my voice sound normal.

She grimaced at me. "Horrible. But better than the guy I went out with the night you were gone. That dude was seriously deranged. What part of 'I need to go to the ladies room' means 'meet me in the stall to jump me fast and hard'?"

"No!"

"Yes. Don't worry, he's learned his lesson."

By the look on her face, he probably had. Maria had a black belt in Karate.

"Is that why you sent Santiago the 911 text message?"

She frowned. "What are you talking about?"

"You didn't send the message to Santiago when we were on

165

the mountain?" She was looking at me so strangely. "Never mind. Where'd you find deranged dude?"

"I was a little lonely when you and Santiago were gone. Sorry. I was, Erin. I wanted a little pick me up and found him in the coffee shop. Next time I'll stick to coffee. I sure know how to pick them."

I rubbed her shoulder. "I'm sorry we left you behind. It just...happened."

"I know."

"So, what about Jorge Lupes? He seemed totally into you."

Her face lit up. "He is. And what a great kisser he's become over the years. Yummy. He's out of town for a couple of weeks."

"Aw, too bad."

She thumbed over her shoulder toward the entryway. "I saw my brother leave. What'd he forget?"

"Forget?"

"When he came this morning for the mail."

"Mail?" *Didn't he say he came to see me?*

She cocked her head, wondering why I was echoing her. "I swear he got all the bills. I gave him the stack myself. Besides, I thought he and Helena were going out tonight."

For some reason, Santiago wasn't telling his sister about us.

"You all right?" Maria peered at me closely.

"Ah, yeah, fine." Pending disaster clutched at my throat. My mind raced. He said he was protecting me, but there was another reason for him to be secretive. *Helena.*

"You look like you might puke."

"It's just..." I bit my tongue. It stank, but until I knew what was going on, I had no choice. I had to keep our relationship a secret from my best friend. "Cramps."

"Do you need anything? Tylenol? Midol? Percocet? I've got a medicine cabinet upstairs stocked with every known drug to mankind."

"No, thank you." I rubbed my stomach, which really was killing me. "I'll just go to bed."

A shadow crossed her face. Suspicion, or my overactive imagination?

166

"I guess I'll go up too and read. Hang on, I forgot my book." She walked through the atrium right past the entrance to the veranda.

Don't look. With horror, I held my breath, and begged her thin legs to keep walking.

"Got it. This will keep my mind off—" it was barely a pause, but the corner of her eye had raked across the scene, "—men."

The burned-down candles, food-covered plates, empty wine bottle, red rose bouquet—she'd seen it all. The table was still romantically set for two.

 CRSO

"Maria? Want me to get that?" I was wrapping my wet hair in a towel when the phone rang.

When she didn't answer, I rushed down the hall just as the answering machine clicked.

"Maria, if you're there, please pick up. It's Martin. You know we need to talk. I'll be in my office and I expect to hear from you today." He hung up without so much as a good-bye.

Pushy. I wouldn't call any guy back who ordered me around like that. Was it deranged dude, or some other creepy male? Maria was right. She sure knew how to pick them.

"*Buenos días, bella,*" Rosa sang from the kitchen. "What can I make for you? Eggs? *Papas?*" She hummed a little while the eggs and potatoes sizzled in the pan.

"Yum. Looks great." I gave her a little squeeze. "Thank you for the wonderful dinner you made last night. Oh, and the tea? Better than Mom's."

The wise eyes crinkled around the corners as her face broke into a smile. "Aye, it is *fantástico,* but no is jus' *té* dat brings sunshine to your face."

"I don't know what you mean." I gave her my best coy smile. "Have you seen Maria this morning?"

"She is reading on de veranda."

Uh-oh.

The table and chairs had been put back in their proper places. All the dishes, silverware and even crumbs had been removed. It was as if nothing clandestine had happened the night before. As if I hadn't lied to her.

"Morning," I said, all sunshine and roses. "How are you today?"

Maria reclined on a lounge chair under a large umbrella. She didn't bother to pull her nose out of the book she was reading.

"Someone called." I plunked down on the lounge chair next to hers.

"I let it go on the machine. I'm in no mood to chitchat this morning." She waved her hand in a flicking-a-fly gesture.

"It was some guy. Martin?" I cocked my head at her.

"I especially don't want to talk to Martin."

"Don't blame you. He sounded a bit prima donna-ish."

She glared. "I don't want to talk *about* him either."

"Oh." I pretended I hadn't heard the bite in her tone. "I'm off to stretch my legs. Care to take a walk around town with me?"

"Not really." She turned a page in her book.

I frowned. *So that's how it is going to be?* "You sure? We can stop for some *jamón serrano*. I'm buying."

"Not this time." Little circles of red bloomed on her cheeks.

"Maria, you seem a little peeved. Can we talk about...things?"

I wasn't thrilled to see the sadness in her eyes. "I'm not peeved, I'm hurt. You could have told me you had a date with my brother. I hoped you two would hit it off. I mean, you're only staying for a few weeks, but I thought a little fun would do you both some good."

I was a steaming pile of manure. "I'm sorry."

I expected her to say, "Yes, yes you are," in her joking voice. What she said was far worse.

"Why do you do that? Keeping Jack a secret from me really hurt. Friends are supposed to share."

"I didn't mean to hide anything from you. I was..." *ashamed? guilty? stupid?* "...wrong. I wanted to tell you about Jack."

She waved the book through the air, shooing away the idea.

"Before, or after it was all over?"

"Before. I just couldn't."

"Couldn't what? Trust me?"

"I trust you."

"Really? Why don't you tell me about the car?" She crossed her arms. "The one you let everyone believe had an accelerator problem."

I stopped breathing.

"It didn't really malfunction, did it?"

Panic whooshed down on me like a falcon smelling the blood of its prey, picking and slashing my thoughts with its sharp talons.

"You had every intention of smashing the car full speed into the building. So what *was* that, Erin? A death wish?"

"No, I...I..." The hand of terror crushed my windpipe, cutting off my words.

Her voice was low. "Did you want to kill someone? Everyone?"

My heart constricted. The world closed in around me. "No. No, I don't...I didn't mean for any of it to happen. I..." *was confused, hurt, scared,* "...lost my mind."

"Because of the drugs? Don't look so surprised. I saw your supply in the bathroom drawer. Sleeping pills, antidepressants, muscle relaxants, anything else?"

I made a strange garbled noise, which in no way resembling human speech.

"Are you hooked on anything else?" she repeated firmly.

I shook my head.

She wrapped her arm around my shoulder. "Aw, Erin, why didn't you tell me? I can help you. I know good doctors and an unbelievable therapist in Los Angeles. We've got to get you clean before you get behind the wheel again."

My insides tore apart. Sweat poured down my cheeks, mixing with the tears. I covered my face with my hands and rocked forward, my forehead touching the lounge chair. "Oh God!" I cried out again. "It's all true."

She rubbed my back. "It's okay. Shhhh, you're all right. Breathe, Erin, breathe."

I was back inside the Buick again. "I barely remember starting the car. I was overcome with this—" I flapped my hands, "—blinding rage."

"I know." She rubbed circles on my back.

"What if I had... I could have...run over someone."

"But you didn't."

"I was out of my mind."

"Yes."

"I crashed the car into the posts at full speed. No sane woman would do that."

"No." She chuckled. "Quite a few of us were glad you did."

I blinked at her. "Huh?"

"DH&L was loaded with corrupt, evil men. You were our Great Female Leader. We were all pulling for you, even the scary chick in Accounting. You are our hero, Erin."

"I don't...understand."

"If you couldn't make partner, which, face it, wasn't going to happen after you professed undying love to Jack..." She made a face and patted my back sympathetically. "If you didn't make it to the top, then by God, creaming the building with their Buick was simply brilliant. You went down in flames. Great, big, beautiful flames. But you kept the power and showed them good. Now they'll be more careful to treat women with respect. You paved the way."

I shook my head. "I went nuts."

"Over the top, sure, but you should be proud of the effort you expended for that place. You gave it your all. Every last sleepless night."

I frowned. She couldn't possibly know about what really kept me up at night. "I made monumental mistakes. They'll haul me off to jail once the investigators figure out what happened."

"Nu-uh." Her smile was huge. "It's over. They're not pressing charges. I've kept my feelers out over there, listening in on the company meetings." She shook her head at the look on my face. "Don't you know the first rule in business? It always pays to make nice with the administrative assistants. The partners know the truth and they're letting it go."

"Why would they?"

"Fear, my friend, is a powerful motivator. The partners are afraid you'll countersue. You know, Mr. Big Shot overstepping his bounds with his employee, demanding sex for favors, in the office no less, and then giving the position to a far-less-qualified man. You would win. No question. The board of directors would be forced to fire everything in pants and you'd end up the only partner left. No, DH&L can't afford to let your story leak out. The insurance company has already provided a brand new Buick for some other chump to drive."

I blinked at her, letting her words sink in.

"It's over," she repeated. "Put it behind you."

"You knew what really happened?" I faced her. "All along?"

"Not all of it. I wanted you to come to terms with it on your own. You needed time. But I've grown tired of watching you punish yourself. We all make mistakes, Erin. Believe me, some of them more monumental than others. You've got to face life openly, honestly."

"I am—" hiccup, "—trying."

"Yes." She smiled lovingly. "I can see you are."

"I...am so...sorry."

She patted my head. "You don't need to be. We are friends, are we not?"

"The best."

"You relax, I'll get you something for those hiccups."

I slumped back into the lounge chair, heavy and hard. I was exhausted. Emotionally spent. It was good to finally release the pressure squeezing my heart. Things would be better now. I could move on.

"Oh, and Erin, there's one more thing I need you to do." She stopped with her hand on the handle of the sliding glass door.

"Sure, Maria." *Hiccup.* "Name it."

"Stay away from my brother."

"What?" I croaked. "I thought you wanted us to...get to know one another."

"I did, when it was all fun and games. Now I realize you are in the delicate process of inventing yourself. I've been there. I know how hard it is."

"No, you don't understand—"

"Listen, Erin, I'll help you in any way you need me to. But Santiago has enough problems right now. He needs fun, hot sex, no emotional ties. It's best if you stay away from him."

She closed the door, apparently not hearing my response. "What if I can't?"

Chapter Fifteen

"Here, drink." Maria returned with a mug. "Rosa says she made this tea special for you."

I drank it all, drowning the hiccups and wishing I could wash away Maria's words. It killed me that Maria thought I wasn't good enough for her brother. Her statement had stolen a little chunk out of my heart.

"I think you should take that walk. Get outside and clear your head."

"Let's talk more when I get back." I needed to get through to her, explain I wasn't crazy, or at least not too crazy. Santiago and I were good medicine for each other.

"Sure. I'll be here." Settled back on the lounge chair, she picked up the book. She seemed satisfied, no longer angry.

I tied my Reeboks and stepped outside into a furnace. The day was getting hotter by the minute. A steady, scorching breeze blew on my body, drying my sweat. Undaunted, I plugged on, down the long driveway overhung by ancient olive trees, trying to bring my heart rate up, burn some calories and leave my past woes behind me. It was time to reinvent Erin Carter in the right image.

How hard would it be to find a small house in Salamanca? I smiled. It could be done. I had no job or prospects in LA. There wasn't any real reason to stay, was there? Plus, and it was the *big* plus, Santiago was in Salamanca. We would put our past problems behind us and move forward. Together.

A dark car was parked on the road at the bottom of the

driveway. The man inside reading a newspaper startled when I walked past his window. He seemed familiar, but I couldn't place him. He lifted his paper higher to block his face.

Turning onto the main road, I tried to pick up speed, but the heat was a beast. I regretted not bringing a water bottle with me. Thoughts of buying a great big one *con gas* spurred me on.

My pocket vibrated. "Is this Erin Carter?" I could almost hear the woman's professional smile.

"Speaking," I huffed as I walked up a particularly steep hill.

"This is Pamela Lansing. How are you today?"

"Listen, whatever you're selling, I'm not buying." I turned the phone over to hit the "off" button. Rich laughter on the other end made me bring it back to my ear.

"Ms. Carter, someone would have to pay me a million dollars to sell crap by phone. No, I'm a headhunter, and your pretty head—I've seen photos—is in great demand."

"Huh?"

"Tell me you haven't signed a contract with any other firm yet."

"Forgive me, Ms.—"

"Lansing."

"Yes. Um, are you sure you've got the right girl?"

"Stockbroker extraordinaire for the folks at Warner Brothers, Sony, DreamWorks? Let's see." She ruffled through some papers. "A three-bedroom apartment in Palm Grove, speedwalks down Wilshire. Am I warm?"

"Jeez, who are you?"

"Pamela Lansing, Headhunter extraordinaire." She laughed. "My clients know a lot about you."

"This firm, does it have a name?"

"Not so fast. I can't divulge that information until we come to an agreement of sorts." Papers ruffled again all the way across the world. I imagined she was staring at my headshot. "So, you didn't answer the most important question. Have you signed on with another firm yet?"

I had to cover my mouth to keep the snort from escaping. "Ah, no. Not yet. You know those client lists belong to the firm, not the stockbroker."

"Of course the firm owns the lists. But we both know at least half the clients will jump ship of their own accord and follow you to our side. Probably more. I've checked around. Your clients worship you like a goddess, Ms. Carter."

I stopped walking. I didn't ask how she knew so much about my confidential client list or dispute her logic. Many of my past clients would follow me, *if* the firm proved to be a good one.

As if reading my mind, she said, "This firm is reputable. And that being said, you probably can guess who my clients are."

"Baker, Lynn and Taylor." The enemy. Up until the day I quit.

"Can I set up the meeting for tomorrow afternoon?" She pushed.

"Sorry. I'm out of the country."

"Lovely. How much distance did you have to put between yourself and those assholes?"

That time I did snort. "You do get right to the point, Ms. Lansing. I needed a vacation. Badly."

"Of course you did. Those old employers of yours need a good ass kicking, or maybe a substantial lawsuit. I can't imagine why they hadn't made you partner yet. Smacks of sexism to me. Are you ready to come home?"

I didn't answer. Instead I thought about Santiago. And those lips. Oh sweet heaven, those lips.

"Here's the deal. My clients want you. A partnership seat will come with this contract." She heard my gasp. "That's right. These guys need a fourth partner and love the idea of bringing in the 'feminine element'. They won't wait forever, however. How about you take a few more days to sightsee in...?"

"Spain."

"Nice. One more week running with the bulls then come in. Sound good?"

"It's rather sudden."

"Shouldn't be. A woman with your talents should be aware of her self-worth and be willing to fight for it."

A girl-to-girl slap.

"So? I'll set up the meeting for, um, July sixth and call later with the confirmation and directions. And Ms. Carter? Erin—" her voice dropped and for a moment she sounded like a friend, "—this is an offer of a lifetime. Do yourself a favor. Take it."

I dropped the cell back into my pocket. Now I had two directions to point my feet—the Spanish road with Santiago by my side, if he'd have me, or the lucrative partnership path I'd always dreamed of.

I sighed. Fate, life, love rested at the crossroads.

"And only one week to decide," I muttered.

I rounded a corner and found myself at the Plaza Mayor. Waves of steam rose up off the pavement. I kept as best as I could to the shadows alongside the buildings and searched for a place to order a drink. Finding a little café, I wandered in to escape the heat and sat at a table near the window. I downed the first bottle of water in about two seconds and ordered another.

Across the street was what could only be an apparition. When she tossed her hair over her shoulder, I jumped up from my chair, dropped a wad of bills on the table and ran out. In my rush to catch up, I smacked into a telephone pole. I glanced down fleetingly at the oily black tear in my T-shirt.

Dang it! My favorite Tommy Hilfiger. Another reason to curse the woman.

Mindful of the traffic, I crossed the street and tailed her for seven blocks to a tall apartment complex. Inside, the beautifully coifed Helena entered an elevator and told the attendant "*once*".

I gasped.

Santiago lived in one of the tallest apartment complexes downtown—on the eleventh floor. An apartment, I reminded myself, he had never invited me to.

Now, I knew why.

"Excuse me, sir, can you tell me which flat belongs to Doctor Botello?" I asked the elevator attendant in Spanish.

He pointed to the end apartment. He was too busy closing the doors in my face to hear my "thanks".

It wasn't courage or stupidity making me march myself

down the hallway and knock on the door. It was a deep psychological need to see for myself. If he was living with Helena, I had to know.

"Hello. Can I help you?" Helena asked.

Rendered speechless, I just stood there staring. Possibly even grimacing. Who knows, maybe I snarled.

"Oh, you are injured. Can I get you a bandage?" she asked.

I was startled to see dried blood from my run-in with the telephone pole.

"Bandage?" she asked again.

I shook my head.

"Is there something you want?" She tossed her hair from her eyes like a nervous tick. That fiery mane made my blood boil.

She doesn't know who I am. She must think I'm a lunatic. And at that moment, I probably was. "I want to speak with Santiago."

"I'll tell him you came by. You are?"

"A close friend," I said curtly. "Very close." We locked eyes. The silent tension hung thickly in the air. My hands clenched. My jaw tightened.

A light bulb went on. Her persona shape-shifted the moment she figured out who I was. "What's the message?"

I could feel the corners of my lips rise. "Tell him we need to discuss Victoria Secret."

"Is that some sort of code?"

"He knows what it means. Intimately."

I was down the hall before she could say more. It was good to make my presence known. Really good. I had thrown the gauntlet down at her feet and was willing to fight her for him.

With each step toward the Botello home, the bravado diminished and doubts began to creep in.

What if he chose her over me? Nice stable Helena with the tiny waist and perfect hair. Helena, the hospital volunteer, mommy material in the making. Helena, the one who lived here and would probably never leave. Helena, the one in his home, sharing his bed.

Damn it!

I stumbled and weaved like a drunkard down the street. Sweat dripped like a faucet down my face. I wiped my eyes with the corner of my shirt and pressed on, finally making it back to the long driveway. The dark car was gone. Heading up the walkway to the front door, my feet were heavy as bricks. The vow I had made myself to straighten things out with Maria seemed impossibly difficult at the moment. What I really needed was something to drink and a cool place to rest.

I found a cup of lukewarm tea on the table by my bed and drank it greedily. It was sweeter than the last time Rosa made it and had a slight tang, but it was delicious. Rubbing my forehead with the back of my hand, I was surprised to feel so much perspiration.

The inside of my mouth had turned to paper. I wiped the line of sweat from the top of my lip and drained the final swallow of tea from the cup. I ripped off the Tommy T-shirt plastered to my clammy skin and dropped it on the floor. My insides were cooking.

I sat on the end of the bed in my underwear. My ears rang. I planned to get up and splash water on my face when the room stopped behaving like a theme park ride.

I kicked off my shoes, lost my balance and nearly fell off the bed. "Whoa."

My bare foot stepped on something poking out from under the bed. It was Mrs. Botello's grisly doll in all its gruesomeness—missing eyes, nose, hacked-up hair—with one difference. The doll had a note pinned to her dress. I read it through the dancing spots projecting behind my eyes.

"What the—?"

My head felt like one of those snow-domes you shake up so that all the stuff flies around inside. Trying to ignore the horrible spinning, I concentrated on the note and whatever in the world it meant. I could almost picture the crazy lady, eyes ablaze, bending over the page and scrawling the big letters before me.

Leave or die! Leave or die! Leave or die! was scrawled in red crayon across the page.

Why was everyone trying to get rid of me? Rosa and Santiago had warned me. Serena told me to run, and now Mrs.

Botello? The dangerous Mrs. Botello.

"Carters don't scare that easy," I said to whomever might have been listening. I threw the battered doll across the room, where it hit the door with a thud. "Good, I hope I knocked your ugly head off."

Later I would talk to Maria about her brother, her mother, and whatever else needed clearing up. Now, I needed to cool my overheated body and rest. I lay back down and was immediately sucked into sleep.

∞

Spring, 1498, Segovia

Sneaking away from watchful eyes, Andrés has come like a thief in the night and stolen Serena away from her room.

Ah, but this thief I would gladly hand my heart and soul to, for he owns them anyway. How I long for him to lay claim to my body as well.

With her hand in his, Serena quietly follows him down the narrow stairway, out the kitchen and into the dark night. She barely breathes, knowing how dangerous it is to be together. The marquesa forbade them to see one another.

"Serena is a poor woman with no family. No dowry," the marquesa told Andrés months earlier. "I shall begin the search immediately for a suitable lady from a great noble family. It is high time you wed."

His mother refused to listen to his protests. Falling in love with Serena was silliness, or madness, whatever the case, it would not be tolerated.

Serena suspects the marquesa had a hand in King Fernando's decision to send Andrés away from the castle on one royal whim after another in an effort to clear Andrés's head. Of her.

In truth, he should have forgotten about a poor woman by now. And one with a scarred face?

He should never have loved me at all.

So many long months he was away. Imagining what he was doing during his absence tortured her. She dreamt of the beauties in Andrés's bed and fell into despair so deep there was no light, no life, and no hope. Her heart dried up, just as the rose he left months ago by her chamber door, the one she kept hidden in her drawer under the nightclothes. Serena longed for death to take away the never-ending grief.

And yet, miraculously, he is here now, stealing her away from her room and leading her into the rose garden.

His eyes are full of hurt. "I do not believe my ears."

"Shhh. Your mother might be looking for us."

"You believe I forgot you?"

"Why would you think about me?"

"Serena." He gently lifts her chin. "You were the one who kept me alive. When my enemies' swords measured four to my one, you gave me strength."

She shudders and he wraps his arms around her shoulders.

"Forget you? You are the very air I breathe."

The breath catches in her throat. He tosses his hair out of his face and she is swimming in those deep brown eyes.

Does he know my thoughts?

Darkness of night hides the blush on her cheeks, the parting of her lips. The gentle breeze caresses their skin like a thousand tiny fingers and strings a song of love across the tall grass.

She trembles with a startling need more urgent than hunger or thirst. Will she die from it? His hand is warm and strong in hers. His touch sears her blood. A feeling of wantonness swells from her belly, settling like an itch between her legs.

He tips his hat and places a slow kiss on her knuckles. "My rose of Avila," he whispers. "Please stop stalling and answer the question."

He kisses the tips of her fingers one by one.

Serena is afraid to blink. Is this a dream? She cannot seem to catch her breath. And his lips on her skin? *I would blissfully die for those.*

Even as joy races through her body, fear explodes in her chest. "It is no use. King Fernando wants you to marry another. You are the King's Chamberlain. How can you disobey him in this?"

"I shall speak with him again."

"No, my darling, it is madness. You must forget about me."

"How can I forget the fiber of my skin?" He cups my cheeks in his hands. "You are a part of me. All of me. I love you, Serena. Only you. Always have. Come with me."

"Flee into the night? The king's army will find us. And when they do..." A sob escapes. "It will mean your life."

"I led most of those men in battle. I know their weaknesses. Besides—" he smiles winningly, "—I am the best swordsman in Castile."

"Andrés—"

"Hush. Do you wish to marry me, or not?" His finger traces my cheek, down my chin.

"My darling, it is the only thing I have ever wanted."

"Then your answer is—?"

"Yes."

He lets out a joyful cry that she stifles with her hand.

"Do you want someone to hear? By now your mother has organized a search party to kill us both."

He lifts her into his arms and swings her around and around as the fragrance of rosebuds rise into the air. "I shall love you for all eternity." His deep voice promises. "No one can keep us apart."

In the tower window high above them a shadow moves.

Chapter Sixteen

Waking up was like trying to pull my dead body from the depths of the ocean to the surface. Prickly danger tugged at my innards. I was in trouble.

I swallowed hard and sputtered. Who put the sandy pebbles in my mouth? I coughed and choked myself awake.

"Erin, you're okay," a soothing voice said. The blinds were lifted and the morning sun rushed into my room. Santiago smiled down at me. "Here take a sip before you say anything."

I sat up and promptly threw up in a wastebasket beside the nightstand.

"Oh," I flopped back against the pillow, grabbing my pounding head.

"Maria! Rosa! Bring cool water and saltines. Quickly." He propped the pillows behind my back. "Sit up slowly."

"My head is killing me."

"Here, take these, they'll help." He handed me two large pills with the glass of water. "If you can keep them down, I'll remove the IV."

For the first time I noticed I was hooked up to a hanging bag.

"You needed to be hydrated."

I smiled weakly. "How long have I been out of it?"

He glanced at his watch. "Twenty-two hours."

"Are you serious? What's wrong with me?" My dry voice croaked.

He shook his head. "Not sure. I want to do some tests—" He was interrupted when Maria and Rosa appeared carrying crackers, cloths and a fresh pitcher of water.

"*Dios mío*, she's awake. Me Ereen is awake," Rosa lightly placed a cool cloth on my forehead.

"Thank God." Maria poured me another glass of water. "I am sorry, Erin, I can't help but feel this is my fault."

"Your fault?" I winced as another shooting pain tried to blow out my left temple.

"What do you mean?" Santiago frowned at Maria.

"I should have warned her about the Spanish heat. She's not used to these temperatures. It was much too hot to go walking. Poor thing had heatstroke."

"Heatstroke?" Santiago asked. "I'm not sure that's what it was."

"Of course it was." Maria nodded, her face serious.

"She's probably right. I've never been good in the heat." I was having trouble looking him in the eye. My mind was fuzzy, but I hadn't forgotten about Helena. When I had the chance I was going to ask him about the saucy hospital volunteer living in his flat.

"I am not convinced. First, the fainting and now this—"

"Wait. What fainting?" Maria asked.

"In the tower in Segovia. She was out for only a few seconds, but maybe it was symptomatic of an illness. I'd like to work up a blood panel to find out for sure."

"She's been complaining of stomach pains too. In Los Angeles. And actually you had cramps the night before last. Remember, Erin?"

Of course I remembered. I had just been caught lying about my date with Santiago. Those were guilt pains. Weren't they?

"Maybe she's got an ulcer." Maria's eyes were full of concern. "Can't you give her medication, Santiago?"

"Come on guys, I'm fine." All the worried faces in the room were staring at me. "Really."

Santiago and Maria exchanged glances I had trouble reading.

"I think I should take you to the hospital for tests," Santiago said again.

"No!" Maria and I both blurted at the same time.

I caught Maria's eye and sent her a silent message of "Help." She knew hospitals completely freaked me out. Uncle Harry, the only uncle I have who isn't crazy, went to a hospital for a routine procedure and nearly died from staph infection. My other relatives fear all medical institutions, for obvious reasons. Many go in and don't come back out.

"I'll take care of her." Maria put another cool cloth on my forehead. "You've got to stop the streetwalking."

"If my madam says so." I shrugged. "She runs this joint."

Santiago studied both of us quizzically. "Why can't I say 'no' to either one of you? Okay, one more day in bed. Get better, or it's the hospital, understand?"

"Understood," I said.

"Good." Gently he removed the IV. "Later tonight I'll return to check on you. Rest."

I was disappointed he was leaving before I had a chance to really talk to him. About us. About Helena. I sighed. It would all have to wait until tonight.

"I go make the *té* I promised. Sorry I no make it before," Rosa said.

"That's okay. I'd love some now."

"I will also make special dinner for all of you *esta noche*," she said as both she and Maria left the room.

I tried to remember what had happened before I had succumbed to heatstroke a whole day earlier. Everything was a bit disjointed, but something nipped at my craw. Something...something. I had to remember.

Whatever it was seemed important.

CR&O

That evening Santiago stopped in to see me just as he'd promised. I was feeling better. The vertigo was gone and the headache had diminished to a dull thumping against my brain—a vast improvement.

Softly, he closed the door and sat on the edge of my bed. "I was worried about you."

Holy hot tamales, his deep voice full of concern stirred the emotion in my belly. I reached for him. The bunching of his bicep under my fingertips surprised me. Did he flinch?

"Erin, I have to ask you something."

"Sure, anything, *querido*."

His smile flashed and fell off.

"What is it?" I asked.

"Why didn't you tell me about the man in LA?"

"Who?" *Jack? What had Maria told him?*

"You told me you weren't seeing anyone." A hot current surged through his words.

He was mad at me? "I'm not. I was dating someone, but it ended before I left. Actually, it was over long before that. You're one to talk, living with a woman who you claim is only your friend."

His eyes flew open in surprise.

"You didn't think I'd find out? I went to your apartment, Santiago. Helena was there." I jabbed my finger at his sternum.

His smile spread. "I wonder why she didn't tell me you stopped by?"

"Are you serious? Why would she tell you? Wait. Why are you grinning?"

"You're gorgeous when you glare at me."

"What is the matter with you?" I exploded.

"Calm down, *querida*, and listen to my words. I. Live. Alone."

"I saw her. Eleventh floor, apartment on the end."

He put a finger to my lips. "I'd forgotten a couple of medical files at home. Sometimes I go over the troubling cases at night. An old habit. I've never left them at home before. My mind seems to be on other things of late." He gave me a wicked look. "Helena volunteered to go to my apartment and pick them up for me. That's all."

"Oh."

"I told you. She's a friend."

I lifted his chin. "And what are we?"

"Much—" he kissed the tip of my nose, "—more."

Pressing my palms on his chest, I relished the heat radiating from his skin through the cotton of his shirt. I ran my hands along his collarbones and slowly outward over his shoulders and down his arms. A girl could lose herself in so much muscle and manliness. I splayed my fingertips to feel more all at once. I nibbled along his square jaw, wanting to gobble him up.

Being wrapped up in his glorious arms was heaven. His gentle kisses were like raindrops, rose petals, and chocolate syrup, all those things I adore.

I moaned. My body trembled. We were both breathing like marathon runners on the last mile. The room was flying around us, but I didn't mind this kind of vertigo. I held him as the great tide of emotion washed over me.

He ran his hands up my back and lifted my hair off my shoulders. "You are so beautiful. I have no right to keep you in my life. God help me, I want you."

"I want you too. Now, please."

Cupping my cheek with his gentle hands, he whispered, "What am I going to do with you?"

"Love me?"

He groaned. "I do, Erin. That's why this is so hard."

"Wait, you love me?"

His emerald eyes bored into my soul. "With all my heart."

He loves me? My head was going to either explode or implode at any second, yet it was still the happiest moment in my life.

"Erin," he murmured into my neck. "*Mi amor.*" He nibbled my earlobe. "*Corazón.*"

My scalp tingled, my blood boiled, my heart raced and his beeper went off.

Dang it, when were we going to catch a break? "I say we lose all cells and beepers." I hooked my finger through his belt loop and tugged him closer.

He gave me a lopsided grin while unsnapping the beeper from his waistband anyway. "Sorry, I'm on-call at the hospital."

"But I'm the one dying of kiss withdrawal." I pouted. "If I don't have your lips all over me in about two seconds I will shrivel up and...what's wrong?"

All the color drained from his face. He stared at the beeper as if he couldn't believe what he was reading on the miniature screen.

"Santiago?"

He glanced at me with features made of stone. His emotions were stuffed back inside, deep down where I couldn't see them. "In the mountains you made a promise to me. Do you remember it?"

My heart sank. He was shutting me out. Again.

His gaze lingered on the bottom lip I was stress-biting. "If I determined it's not safe for you to be with me, you promised you would go home. Immediately."

"I remember." It was a promise I had no intentions of keeping. Ever.

He exhaled deeply. Suddenly, he was very tired. "I should have put you on a plane days ago. Damn it!"

"What's it say?" I motioned toward the beeper.

"Call it a 911."

"Danger's coming?" I squeaked.

"I am afraid it's already here. I need to get you to safety. Quickly."

I scrambled to find a way out of this. "Uh, no way. I'm sick, remember? I can't fly home now. Besides, whatever it is, we can deal with it together."

"No. It's my problem."

Marveling at how his face had become so serious and hard, I rubbed his arm. How I longed to see the softness in his eyes again.

"Let me help you," I begged.

"Listen to me, go to the hospital. You can rest safely and get better while I am gone. When you're strong enough to travel, you will go home."

"That's ridiculous, I'm not going... Wait, where are you going?"

His gaze penetrated my soul. "We can't be together."

"What's happened?" I was more terrified of whatever was scaring him than any macho pronouncements.

"I can't explain, yet. Give me a few days to sort this out. Maybe a week."

My stomach flopped. "Are you in trouble?"

"Me? No." His eyes wouldn't meet mine. He was lying. "Please, trust me, this is the only way."

"If this is one of your top secret adventures, I have to say I'm not liking it. Can't you give me a clue?" I kneaded his shoulder. "A teensy-tiny one?"

"You'll be in my every thought. Always."

His words sounded like good-bye. "Will you call me tonight?"

"No. I won't involve you anymore."

I was stunned. *What the heck is going on?*

"Get ready. I'm taking you to the hospital now."

"No, Santiago. I'm going to rest here and wait for you to come back from wherever you're going."

"I can't protect you, Erin."

"We've been through this. I'm a big girl who doesn't need a man's protection."

He groaned. "Don't make this any harder than it is."

"I want to make it easier, but you won't tell me what *it* is."

He gave me a dark look. "If you want to help me, go to the hospital where I know you'll be taken care of."

I glared back. "No way, I'm staying here."

When he pinched the bridge of his nose, I knew I'd won the standoff. For now. "If you don't feel better in a day or so, go to the hospital. No *mentiras*, Erin. Just go. I'll leave instructions for my nurse, just in case. If the headache returns, take two of these pills every four to six hours. If the pain is bad, go immediately to the hospital. Don't wait."

"Yes doctor." I saluted him smartly. My feelings were stinging worse than my eyes.

"Promise me!"

"All right, I promise."

He ran his thumb down my cheek, his emerald eyes pouring over me. I had the terrifying feeling he was committing my face to memory.

"I will miss you." His voice choked with an unnamed emotion.

"Stay," I begged. If I weren't so weak I would have tackled

him and tied him to my bedpost.

Pressing his forehead to mine, he closed his eyes and whispered, "Be safe."

And he was gone.

CRSO

"Santiago, aren't you staying for dinner?" Maria caught him in the entryway.

"No. Why don't you walk me out? There are some things we need to discuss."

"What's up?" Maria asked, her hands on her hips.

"Do I need to be worried?"

"You? Not worry? That's a cold day in hell."

"Maria."

"What's got you going this time?"

He scrubbed his face with his hands. The women in this house were going to be the death of him. "I got an urgent message to call Martin. Have you spoken to him?"

"Of course. The man is a parasite. I can't shake him."

"You're not supposed to shake him. What does he say?"

"The sand is hot, the palm trees are swaying and the stars are all loaded. What else would he say?"

"I want the truth."

"I thought we weren't going to discuss this anymore."

He grabbed her shoulder. "Damn it, Maria. This is serious."

"Everything is always serious with you. Stop worrying, or your black hair is going to end up as white as Mama's."

He combed his fingers through it. She was right, of course, but what in the hell could he do? It was his job to protect his family—and now Erin too. But how?

Mierda, I don't even know if there is *a danger.*

He had to find the truth, but he dared not act rashly, or the people he loved would be destroyed. Then again, if he acted too slowly, someone could die. His choices were far worse than serious. They were life and death.

"I'm going to be gone for a few days to...take care of business. Call Martin immediately if there are problems."

"Business, huh? Why don't you take a sweet thing with you? I'd take two. No, make it three."

He made a face. "I'm telling you, brothers don't like to hear those things."

She laughed. "How about Helena, the volunteer with benefits?"

"Helena is more than a volunteer. She's a very special friend."

"Good, the rumors are true. I'm happy to hear you are having fun."

"What rumors?"

"Oh, you know, people like to talk, I like to listen. Don't frown at me. You haven't had a love interest in a while. People are bound to be happy for you."

His heart missed a beat. A love interest? He had no business falling in love with any woman. His love for Erin had put them all in danger. Now he had to end it.

"Yep, it's all over town Dr. Botello has a—here come the air-quotes—'special friend'. I guess the cat is out of the bag. So why don't you take her with you on this trip, have a little mind-blowing sweaty adventure? Call it fun."

He shook his head.

"I just want you to be happy," she said softly.

"That's why I have to go. To clear up my past mistakes so we all can have a shot at happiness."

"You sound like a man in love."

In the mountains Erin had asked him to step off the edge with her. Oh God, he'd fly to the moon with her if he could and love her every sweet day. "I'm ready to step off the edge." *If I can fix the mess we're in.*

She smiled. "And Helena?"

"Is staying behind."

He would've taken Erin with him in a heartbeat, if she were well enough to travel. She shouldn't suffer any more stress. And this was no pleasure trip. Every minute away from her would be torture. How would he sleep wondering how she was?

"What do I say to Erin?" Maria went on. "I've tried to dissuade her, but she's kind of sweet on you."

He snapped out of his reverie. "You have?"

"I love her, I do, but she's toting far too much baggage. Trust me on this, a smokin' redhead who has the hots for you is the better choice."

Smokin' hot? Had she seen Erin in her holey USC T-shirt and panties? Erin was the one he wanted. Now. Tomorrow. Forever. "Just take care of Erin while I'm gone, okay? She needs to get better so she can fly home."

She cocked her head. "She's going back to LA?"

"Yes." His heart was ripping to shreds. "The sooner the better."

After Maria had gone in, he sat on his bike a moment longer staring at the front door. He wanted to race back inside, snatch up the woman he loved, and run like hell. He didn't. *Not yet.* First, he had to know the truth. Besides, she was in no shape to travel.

Holy hell, she should be in the hospital, or as far from Spain as possible.

Despair swamped him. He knew deep down in his gut he wouldn't be able to get rid of the troubles plaguing his family. And if he couldn't put an end to the darkness, he'd have to give Erin up for good. He loved her too much to let her stay.

If I were a better man I'd have ended this already. Slamming his fist against his thigh, he cursed. *Why does everything have to be so hard?*

He was still sitting on his Harley when the front door opened and the love of his life stepped out. His heart plummeted. She was beauty and light, so frail, yet so brave. He knew what he had to do to save her.

I made it to the front porch, just barely. "Santiago! Wait."

The look on his face, so full of longing and despair, pierced my heart. I almost dropped to my knees right there on the front steps. I knew. Oh Lord, I knew.

"Erin." It was more a breath than a word.

"I'm never going to see you again, am I?"

His face twisted with pain. My knees swayed and I grabbed the railing beside me.

"Put me out of your mind, *querida*," he whispered. "Get on with your life."

He kicked the bike over and took off, spraying the drive with gravel.

Chapter Seventeen

Somehow I made it back inside the house.

"Erin, what are you doing out of bed?" Maria said.

"I had to...ask Santiago something."

"Well, come on. You look like you're about to keel over."

She was right. The air had been knocked out of my lungs. It was an effort to move my feet down the hall.

"There, now stay in bed. You were really sick. Delirium. Fever, chills, thrashing about. Really something to see. I only wish I caught it on tape," she joked, trying to make me smile.

I couldn't even muster the strength to roll my eyes.

"Seriously, Santiago wanted to take you to the hospital. I knew you wouldn't want to go, unless it was absolutely necessary. Besides, we had a Plan B."

It was hard to hang onto the thread of the conversation. I was weak. My heart ached.

"He thought you picked up a bad germ on the plane or something," she went on. "By law he couldn't draw your blood without consent. At the hospital, yes. Here at home, not so much." She lifted her arm to show me the band-aid. "Plan B— draw mine. You and I have been eating the same foods, doing the same things. If you're sick, it's quite possible I'm carrying the germ too, right?"

The corners of my lips rose. It was the best I could do.

"Besides, it always takes the lab too damn long to culture samples. This way, we should know quicker and get you the proper medication, if you are sick. Santiago did give you an IV drip to keep you hydrated. He never left your side."

There was a chair next to the bed. "He stayed the whole time?"

"Yep. He's quite a doctor."

"Yes, he is," I said softly.

"I, uh, didn't know if I should bring this up, but you said some things while you were unconscious." She scrunched up her face.

"What did I say?"

"Mostly gibberish. You did, uh, call out a name a few times." She frowned as if imparting bad news. "Andrés?"

"I don't know anyone by that name."

"Hmm." She shrugged.

"Unless... Oh. Santiago heard me?"

"Of course."

Now I understood why Santiago thought I had a lover in the States and why he'd been in an all-fire hurry to leave.

"You just rest. Santiago will kill me if I let you out of here too soon. I'm supposed to look after you for the next few days while he's...away."

Electricity shot through my veins. She knew something. "Is he going to a medical convention?"

"He called it business."

"You don't believe him."

"Come on Erin, I don't think I should be the one to tell you."

I gulped. "Is he in danger?"

She looked at me oddly. "Why on earth would you think that?"

"I feel it. Tell me."

"You have an active imagination. No. He's not in any danger. And I don't think I should say more."

"Spill it, or I'll put that New Year's Eve picture on Facebook."

"You said you tore it up."

"Maybe I did, maybe I kept copies, who knows?"

"You wouldn't dare."

"I'm tired, Maria. Please just tell me about the evil threatening your brother."

"Evil? Are you still delusional?"

I shot her a dirty look.

"I can see you won't let it go. I don't think you're going to like this."

Clenching the sheets in my fists, I steeled myself for the worst.

"Well, look, he admitted Helena is his special friend and he's stepping off the edge for love. It doesn't take a rocket scientist to figure it out, does it? My brother's going to ask Helena to marry him. And you, my friend, are going home."

My heart refused to beat properly. *Santiago and Helena.*

"How...? This is not..." *happening. I'm dreaming. Wake up. Wake up!*

"I'm sorry, Erin. I really am. Truly this is the best for everyone. I know there was an attraction there, but you two aren't right for each other. Just let it go. Santiago said he'd buy your return airline ticket home and you can cash in the one you purchased. He feels bad, I guess."

I fell back on the pillow, completely, utterly weak.

She fanned herself with her hand. "It's so damn hot. Can I get you something to drink?"

I gaped at her. *He doesn't love me?*

"Erin?" She rubbed my shoulder. "You okay?"

I blinked, unable to focus.

"Oh, no. Do *not* lapse into a coma on me. Breathe, Erin. I'll be right back with some nice cold water, okay? Maybe some crackers? Don't move."

I was hopelessly alone. Reality crept in. The plans we were making—correct that, the plans *I* was making were never going to happen. His choice was clear. He wanted the woman close at hand, who was not career-obsessed, not crazy, not possessed. He chose *her*, not me.

My heart exploded like a live grenade inside my chest. The panic attack was avalanching.

I've got to get out of here.

I laced up my running shoes.

What happened? He said he loved me, he said... But no, he wants to marry her. He wants her. She is safe.

My footfall was fast and furious down the lane. My shoes pounded the concrete, tears flew out of my eyes, my arms pumped violently. I would outrun the pain or drop dead from exertion. My piston legs were going faster than ever before when I hit the bump in the road. Like love, I never saw it coming.

I fell head over appetite into the street. Landing hard on my shoulder, I tumbled over and over, my skin scraping over rocks and black asphalt. My head bumped once or twice against the unforgiving road.

"*Señorita*?" A man in a dark car pulled up beside me. "Are you all right?"

Ignoring him, I pulled myself up and examined the damage. I was going to live. Goody for me.

"Can I take you back?" he said.

"Hey, you're that guy. The security guard at the airport and the guy who's been parked in front of the house."

He cast a nervous eye at the pedestrians who were beginning to stare. "Keep it down."

"Stop following me. Tell whoever hired you I'll go back to the States when I'm ready. And if I see you again? I'll call the cops." That, of course, was a bluff. For all I knew, this guy was a cop.

He opened his car door and reached out to grab me. "Get in the car."

I jumped back. "Stay away from me, or I'll scream."

"Sweet Madre! Do as you want. You are not part of the job." He slammed the door and drove away.

Ignoring the honking cars, and the blood on my hands and knees, I walked aimlessly. I had nowhere to go. No one to run to.

"Get out of the way!" a female driver hollered at me. "Use the sidewalk."

"Yeah, yeah." I waved over my shoulder, not altering my path. I had landed in the street, the street was where I was going to stay. More cars honked, obscenities were yelled. I ignored them all. Pressure was building in my head like a headband squeezing too tight. Sanity was slipping from my grasp. Again.

Finally I came to a stoplight. I had fleeting thoughts about walking into the middle of oncoming traffic. *That would show him. The bastard.*

Strength came to me like a lightning bolt out of nowhere.

"Stop this madness," she said.

I whipped around. I was standing alone in a gutter. "Serena?"

"Sí."

I tipped my head sideways and pounded as if to get water out of my ear. "Get out."

"I am not leaving you."

"Why not? What is it, torture Erin day?"

"I want to save you."

"Too late for that, ghostie. I'm past saving. Just leave me alone."

"Do not be idiotic. I tried to stop his feelings for you, but they were too strong. He loves you. You two are meant to be together, just as Andrés and I are. It is fate."

"What in the hell are you talking about?" I yelled.

An old woman passing on the street gave me a wide berth.

"He loves you, Erin. There is no escaping now. You must fight."

"Fight for what? He wants to put me on the next plane home."

"For love. For him. It is the only way to stop the evil."

"The only evil I know is named Helena. And how can I stop her? She's already won."

"Hush," Serena ordered. *"She shall not win unless you let her."*

"Oh, please. Why should I listen to a ghost with memory disorder? You forgot you were dead."

"As I witness your pain, I taste the bitterness of my own. Come, I shall show you why you have to put an end to this once and for all."

In a flash I saw a vision of another red-haired beauty at the end of a long hallway. She was petite with the air of a queen and an ugly red mouth. I hated her the moment I laid eyes on her.

"Do you see her?" Serena whispered in my head.

"Who is she?"

"She is Andrés' intended as I met her for the first time."

"Intended? I thought he loved you."

"He did, but his mother and King Fernando wanted him to marry Lady Mara, the governor's daughter. Andrés had no choice in the matter."

I couldn't fathom how awful it was for her to stand by and witness her beloved's engagement to such a horrid woman.

As Serena would have it, I was soon to find out.

CRSO

Summer 1498, Segovia

Serena hustles down the corridor, searching for Clara to see what she has heard. Rumor has it a noble lady is visiting the castle, someone of high distinction. All the servants were put on notice to cater to the lady's every wish.

Surely, Clara knows who the lady is. Serena rounds the corner and nearly smashes into her friend.

"Serena," Clara says. "Are you being hunted by demons? Where are you going in such a hurry?"

"To find you. I wanted to ask you about the visiting lady."

"Sssh." Clara grabs Serena by the arm. "They approach. You should not be here."

The marquesa and a lady are coming down the corridor. Serena gulps. There is nowhere to hide and it is too late to run. Clara shoots her an apologetic look. Bracing themselves, they stand shoulder-to-shoulder to greet the marquesa and the visiting lady.

Serena's legs begin to shake. Until this moment, she has done her utmost to avoid the marquesa. It is no secret the marquesa sees her as no more than a bucket of dirty water to be tossed over the castle wall.

Should I run? she asks Clara with her eyes.

Clara gives a short shake of the head and pats Serena's clenched hand with her fingertips. They both curtsey.

"Clara, dear," the marquesa says, not even looking at

Serena. "So good you are here. Let me introduce a dear friend of mine. Lady Lucia Mara, this is my niece. Clara, will you please see to her needs? I must go, as Queen Isabel beckons."

"Of course, Aunt Beatriz," Clara says with a smile not reaching her eyes. "Welcome, Lady Mara. We have met before."

The young lady moves forward to take Clara's hand and her gown, as beautiful as spun gold, makes an exquisite swooshing sound. "At the Governor's ball no doubt."

Serena stands motionless, taking the scene in as if she were a painting on the wall. The lady's striking beauty mesmerizes her. Lady Mara's blue eyes sparkle against skin as fair as moonlight. Her pale brows all but disappear under the face powder. The woman's lips are too thin to be so brightly painted and her cheeks too heavily rouged for Serena's liking, still the effect is breathtaking. It is not until Serena notices the tomato-colored hair piled high upon the lady's head that she stops short.

Sweet Mother. How in the world has she ended up here, blinking at Andrés's intended?

"And you are?" Lady Mara's blue eyes rake over Serena.

Clara gives Serena a quick shake of her head, warning her not to speak. "This is Serena Muñoz who is just leaving, right Serena?" She flashes Serena a look saying, "Go now!"

"*Sí.* I must be...going," Serena mumbles and nearly trips over her own feet to get away.

"Wait. You seem familiar." Lady Mara turns to Clara. "Where have I seen her before?"

"I know not, my lady," Clara lies. "Let us go. There is much more of the castle to show you."

Serena blushes furiously, knowing exactly where Lady Mara saw her last—holding Andrés's arm on the dance floor at Princess Juana's matrimonial ball. She hides her scarred cheek against her shoulder and longs to escape.

Lady Mara taps a pale, thin finger against her temple. "Wait. Oh, this is a bother. I am going to be haunted until I remember why Serena looks so familiar. Were you at the Governor's Ball last spring?"

Serena longs to melt into the tiles like candle wax. "No, my lady."

"Hmm. The one in fall?"

Serena shook her head.

"What other balls have you attended?"

"Only one, my lady. Here."

"Ah, Princess Juana's matrimonial ball. You know, she looks a bit like..." Lady Mara's blue eyes fly open in amazement. It seems she has remembered after all.

Clara clears her throat. "Continue on, shall we?"

"Not so fast, Clara. The Marquesa de Moya said all my needs would be provided for, did she not?"

"Of course."

"Then I shall have Serena as my lady-in-waiting while I am here."

"Surely, you would rather have one of our best maids assist you." Clara refuses to meet Serena's eyes.

"No. I want Serena."

Serena's mouth falls open. What evil trick of fates is this? How can she be required to assist Andrés's betrothed? To brush the lady's hair until it shines even more, to rub lotions into her beautiful skin, to fix her beautiful gowns so she is even more pleasing to his eye?

Clara's face is flushed with the same shock rushing through Serena's veins. "But Serena is awful as a lady-in-waiting. Trust me, simply horrible."

Lady Mara puts her hands on her hips. "Hmm. Perhaps I shall speak to the marquesa about this."

"No, if it is Serena you desire—"

"It is. No worries, if she is so unskilled, I shall teach her properly," Lady Mara says with a gleam in her eye.

"It will be a pleasure, my lady." Serena's whisper sounds like a groan.

"Finish the important duty you were doing before we interrupted you, Serena. Then go to Lady Mara's chambers." Clara's face is full of sympathy.

Serena walks on numb legs up the stairs to her room. There is no important duty she must do. Clara is trying to give her time to compose herself before returning to Lady Mara's chambers. *Ha, as if there will ever be enough time in the world to do that.*

Flopping on her bed, she tries not to think about the redheaded lady from Madrid. It is impossible.

She is a real lady. When he sees her, he shall soon forget me.

CR&O

The vision ended as quickly as it had come. To my surprise, I found myself standing at the Botellos' front door. A redheaded vixen had plagued Serena too. I suspected hers had been the death of her.

"You had to serve her?" I asked. "Did she know about you and Andrés?"

"She knew. I was her lady-in-waiting, but she treated me worse than the lowliest of servants. She beat me at every chance, hoping to carve more scars upon my face. I was terrified she would kill me in my sleep."

"Andrés let her hurt you?"

"Oh no," she sighed. *"My love was far away from the castle, searching for spies, being the king's emissary, protecting the crown. He had no inkling the worst threat of all was poised to strike him in the Alcázar. Your love does not know what harm awaits him either. You must stop Helena to save him."*

"All right, Serena," I whispered to thin air. "I'll fight."

Chapter Eighteen

The ancient stone cathedral was locked. Damn, I'd hoped for a little quiet time. My body was feeling much better, surprisingly normal, but my heart was broken. It had been a while since I'd been to church, but the spiritual pull was enticing. I needed a sanctuary. I reread the posted times and sure enough the doors were supposed to be open.

"Even God doesn't want me around."

I walked to the side of the building to a curio shop loaded with all sorts of touristy trinkets. A man in a brown robe was sitting behind the counter.

"*Bueno*," he called out cheerily. "Come in."

"Can you tell me when the cathedral will open again?"

He rose quickly. "Apologies. Sister Julia is on a break. I locked up to assist her in the store." He chuckled. "No one has come in since she left, though. I fear I am better at tending His flock than selling to them. Care for a prayer card? Today's the memorial for Saint Bridget of Sweden."

I took it, glancing at the picture of the patron saint in a green dress with an open book and pen in hand. "She looks young."

"Most martyrs did not live long. Occupational hazard."

Joking? Do priests do that?

"Should I come back later? I really wanted to go inside the cathedral."

He lifted a circular gold keychain off a hook nailed on the wall behind the counter. It reminded me of the keys used for prison doors in westerns. "No worries. I'll lock the store and open the cathedral doors for you. I'm sure the Lord would prefer it."

"Thank you, father—"

"Father Roberto Vargas."

I shook the hand he offered. "Erin Carter."

"American? In that case, call me Father Bob."

Father Bob? I cringed. *That's like calling my gynecologist "Frank".*

In his forties, starting to bald, of medium height and build, he was average looking, except for those eyes. Deep brown and warm, his eyes seemed so familiar. They reminded me of someone I cared for. But who? Jack's were blue. Santiago's green. Who had sensitive, knowing eyes the color of brownies fresh out of the oven? It was going to drive me crazy.

The lock clicked and the tall wooden doors creaked open. I gasped when Father Bob flipped the light switch. The cathedral was beautiful, much bigger inside than it seemed from the outside and full of intimate alcoves.

The walls were splattered with very old, probably famous paintings. The carved wood beams were painted a beautiful sage green and the chandeliers were bursting with electric tapered candles. Sunlight glinted through multicolored windowpanes, a work of art in their own right. Lattice made of gold framed the altar. Statues of Christ and his mother came alive in the flickering candlelight. The musty air was still, heavy, sacred.

"Welcome," Father Bob said cheerily, motioning for me to step over the threshold.

I wasn't sure I could lift my foot. I felt so small, unworthy and pitiful.

"You did want to come inside?"

He was looking at me with those warm eyes and I suddenly couldn't swallow past the lump in my throat.

"Does something trouble you, Ms. Carter?"

My laughter echoed off the walls. It was a cold, humorless sound. "I am troubled, yes." Hell, I mean, heck, I should be locked away in a sanitarium.

"Would you like to step into my office?" He pointed to the

confessional.

"Oh, I couldn't. I'm not Catholic."

Little lines crinkled around his eyes, deep commas framed his smiling mouth. "A pew then? We can just talk. Think of me as a counselor, a free one. Or better yet, a friend?"

I thought about the lies I'd told Maria and grimaced. "I haven't been very nice to my friends lately."

His brow furrowed, but he said nothing.

"All right. It would probably do me some good. To talk." Pushing back the needling fear, I went in and sat in the last wooden pew.

He genuflected toward the altar and sat lightly beside me.

"How do I...where do I start?"

"Wherever you'd like."

So I told him my own personal soap opera of soul-stealing obsession, relinquishing my body to a coldhearted bastard in the hopes of furthering my career and lying to everyone at the office, including myself. And about the blinding rage, the likes of which can drive a person into concrete posts.

"Was it an act of intention?" he asked. "To crash the company car?"

"I wish I knew. Sometimes I think I did it on purpose, other times it seems like an evil force overcame me. For a few seconds I actually think I passed out in the car before it crashed. So the truth is, it was not entirely intentional, but part of me was happy to do it. Horrible, right?"

"I'd say it is truthful."

I sighed. "Truth can be illusive."

His eyebrows hitched.

Then I told him about how falling in love with Santiago had changed me. How I was suddenly getting a glimpse of the person I wanted to be, was supposed to be. How we were making plans to be together when the floor was yanked out from under my feet.

"You had thoughts about ending your life, Erin? When you walked into the street?"

I liked the way we'd progressed to my first name. "For a minute or two. That's all."

"You must not think that way. God gave you the gift of life. He would be hurt if you threw it away."

"Don't worry, my MO is to kill *things*—cars and plants—not people. Not myself."

He sat back in his chair, looking relieved. "That is good."

"There is something more, but you're going to think I'm crazy." I kneaded the back of my neck. "I think I'm crazy."

"You don't seem so. Believe me, I've seen my share."

So have I. I took a deep breath.

He sat forward, listening to my every word. I told him about the dreams, the weird sensations, and my connection to the tower ghost. He was holding his breath by the time I got to the part where she could take over my mind whenever she pleased.

"The truth is, losing my job, the dreams, the ghost, all seem a part of some great plan. Like a divine hand has been guiding me here, to Spain."

"To love?"

"Maybe," I said quietly. "But why? Why would God get me here and then take it all away?"

"We can't know His plan, Erin. Sometimes it seems clear, as bright as the shining sun. Many days it's cloudy, unclear to our simple minds. We need Jesus to be our light, our guide through the darkness."

"Did you say 'darkness'?"

"Yes. There is evil all around. Put your hand in Christ's. Place your trust in Him, Erin. He will guide you toward the right path."

I wasn't sure I liked his answer. It seemed like no answer at all.

Father Bob's face was serious. "You doubt, I see." He touched my hand. "Life is rarely easy, but it is always better with divinity on your side. Trust."

"I will try."

"Good. It is all I ask."

"No Hail Marys, or some sort of punishment, for partially intentionally crashing the car and for the—" I had trouble even saying the word, "—lying?"

"Isn't the sorrow you feel punishment enough?"

"I thought it was called guilt." I grinned.

"Indeed. It's called many things. You feel it, no?"

"Yes, I feel it."

"Then you will make amends when you get back to the United States regarding the car. Even if the insurance has already paid for it, I am sure there is something you can do to improve matters. And you must make things right with your friend. Maria, is it?"

I nodded. Today when I met Maria at lunch, I would tell her the truth. All of it. "And Santiago? How do I get him back?"

"He asked for a week, give it to him."

"What if he chooses someone else?"

"You can't force a person to love you, no matter how hard you try. Give him his time, Erin, be patient. That's all you can do."

"I hate that answer," I grumbled.

"Sorry. I'm not paid to lie to you."

I sat a long, quiet moment staring at the frayed burgundy carpet between my shoes. Big drops of sadness rolled down my cheeks.

"What about the rest?" I whispered. "You know, the ghost. Am I crazy?"

He steepled his fingertips. "There are spirits, angels and saints, all around us, Erin. They are our ancestors, our family, who have traveled on before us. Like Saint Bridget of Sweden." He pointed to the prayer card on my lap. "We ask them to pray for us, guide our footsteps."

"I don't know this Serena. As far as I know, she's not a relative and she lived over five hundred years ago, for gosh sakes."

His face was grave, his fingers worrying the tassel on his belt. "It is a long time ago, I agree. God must have a reason."

"She thinks I'm the only one who can help her move on. But how's that possible? My mom made me perform a séance once. It was all baloney. I had no idea what I was doing. As if a kid would even know what a séance—" My mouth remained open, but the words stopped short.

"You were saying?"

"'Say-on'."

"Are you all right? You've grown pale."

"That's it." I clapped my hands together. "The ghost wants me to perform a séance to help her move on. She doesn't know how to do it herself because of the post-traumatic stress."

"Do you know how to do this?"

"I have no idea."

"Hmm." He rubbed his chin. "What would happen if you do not succeed in this task?"

"I...I hadn't thought of that. She'd go haunt someone else?"

"Perhaps. Then again, she may get angry. I would keep my eyes open if I were you, Erin. And be careful. I will pray the Lord will keep you safe."

Seeing the worry in his eyes gave me pause. "Am I in danger?"

The flicker of fear across his face said more than his words. "I will pray for your safety."

Now, why didn't that make me feel any better?

CRO

Luigi's Italian Restaurant was packed, with a line snaking out the door. Luckily, Maria was already seated and waving to me through the window.

Father Bob had helped to ease my spirit. I was ready to clear the air with Maria. I had a lot of atoning to do.

"Hey. I already ordered for us. Linguini is the daily special, but we need the breaded calamari too. It's to die for. Did you like the cathedral?" Her voice was soft, obviously treading lightly over the subject.

"I really did. I spent the whole time talking to Father Roberto Vargas. Do you know him?"

Her eyebrows rose as she shook her head. "You converted to Catholicism in the last three hours?"

"Nope, but he did let me unburden myself. And to that end, I owe you a huge apology. I wasn't straight with you about—"

"Your feelings for my brother." She silenced me with a raised hand. "I know."

"I'm sorry. I don't even have a good explanation. As it turns out I'm an utter jackass and a total idiot."

"Yes, yes you are." The old sparkle glinted in her eyes.

"I deserve it. But do you have to be so gleeful while I grovel?"

"*Yo?*" She pressed her hand to her chest. "I'm just glad we're friends again. I missed you."

I smiled. "All's forgiven?"

"Oh, babe, I always forgive, never forget."

My smile matched hers. "So, we're okay?" I made an air circle between us.

"Better than okay. We're sisters." She raised her glass. "To the end."

I raised my water glass and clinked with hers. "To the end."

Maria nodded to the waiter who brought the pasta and bread. "So tell me about this Father Roberto Vargas. Was he cute?"

"He's a priest."

"So? Men leave the priesthood for women all the time."

"Ah yeah. That's sure to improve things in my life." I pointed my water glass at her. "Entice a man to leave God? No. I've got enough issues. Besides, Father Bob was nice-looking, but I don't normally go for men in robes."

Suddenly a flashback of Santiago wrapped in a white robe walking down a winding path carrying wine out to the Jacuzzi rushed through my brain. The knot of sorrow twisted tighter around my heart. "Even if I did, I've sworn off men. Possibly forever."

"Too bad." She spun her linguini in her spoon. "They can be such fun when they're not being monsters." She smiled wickedly. "Then again, some monsters are loads of fun."

"So how about you? Did you find a present for your friend? What is it, a birthday?"

"No. More of a special event sort of thing." She patted a wrapped gift. "Erin, I have a favor to ask. I've invited my friend over to dinner. Someone I'd like to get to know a little better. I was wondering if maybe you wouldn't mind eating out?" Her eyes pleaded.

"Ah-ha. This sounds promising." I winked. "I'm feeling pretty much myself now and would love to get out of the house for an evening. How about I go to dinner, maybe take in a movie, and then slip in late tonight so you and your friend can have a long visit?"

This was a good thing. The time away from the house would give me a chance to talk to Santiago. Father Bob had suggested waiting, patience, giving Santiago space, blah, blah. But I couldn't wait. In less than a week I was supposed to be in LA interviewing for a new partnership. I couldn't leave without knowing the truth. Did he love me? Could he let me go?

"Very nice." Her shoulders visibly relaxed. "Thanks."

"Is that all you're going to say on the subject?"

"Isn't the food good here?"

I laughed. "Spoilsport. What's the matter, you don't want to jinx your mystery date? I just told you I've given up men. How can I live vicariously through you, if you won't share?"

She sipped her wine.

"You're terrible." I broke a piece of steaming bread and dipped it into the balsamic vinegar and olive oil mixture. "It's nice to feel like eating again."

"Poor baby, you've had such a rough time here."

"Rough? I've been the sick guest from hell. I'm sure you'll never invite me again."

She patted my arm. "Well, I haven't been the best hostess either. I don't know if you've noticed, but I've been just a tad grumpy. And I haven't been totally straight with you."

I glanced up from my salad. Was she finally going to tell me what happened to her five years ago?

"I didn't want to talk about it before." She played with her fork, dragging it through the marinara sauce. "There was a reason why I had to leave Salamanca."

"What happened?"

"I was hurt. Badly." Her eyes didn't reach mine.

"Abused?"

Her head shook. "Only my heart. You go along, living your life, building this little world around you. It's fragile, not great, but at least it's comfortable. Safe. Yours. You know?"

"Yes."

Her face contorted in agony. "Then this bitch comes along and takes it all. Your life. Everything. All gone. He swears he'll always be there for you the day before he stops taking your calls. You want to scratch out her eyeballs, make him come back—" her voice dropped, "—but there's nothing you can do. Your mind feels like it's melting, poison dripping into your veins..."

People were staring. Her mouth clamped shut, her eyes glowing with emotion.

"Oh, Maria. I'm so sorry."

"I spent five years in therapy sorting out those feelings. Putting them behind me."

"I had no idea." I was shocked she had kept such an important secret from me. "And you're okay now?"

"Yes. No. Sometimes I feel like I'm coming apart at the seams."

I recognized the symptoms. "Anything I can do?"

"Yes," she said softly. "Stay here with me until I feel strong again. Be my friend."

Maria had lost her father, mother, and a man she loved all before she was thirty. Who wouldn't have a breakdown under the circumstances?

"Well, I..." I started to mention the job offer. I was scheduled to fly back to Los Angeles and start my new career. But seeing her so fragile and scared, I said, "I'm always here for you. We're quite a pair aren't we?"

I rounded the table and hugged her. The black clouds we had been holding against each other evaporated like steam.

Chapter Nineteen

Opening my bedroom door gave me a shock. Something was wiggling under my comforter.

"*Señora* Hernán?" I called softly.

The nurse came running with Maria right behind her.

"Not again. Mama, I told you before. Stop bothering Erin."

"She's not really bothering me."

"Hey, what's this under your shirt? Mama, give it to me. Did you take something that belongs to Erin?"

The two struggled. Mrs. Botello refused to return what she had clutched against her belly. Mrs. Hernán shot me a worried look.

"Whatever it is, Maria, let her keep it," I said.

"No," Maria said sternly, "She has to learn to leave other people's things alone." She reached under her mother's shirt and pulled out a teacup. "This is Erin's, Mama. Not yours. Where's your doll?"

"Um, here it is." I picked up the heap I'd thrown against the door.

"Thanks. Señora Hernán will take you back to your room. Erin wants some peace and quiet."

I tried, but a little voice in the back of my mind was whispering a warning. Something important had to be pieced together. What was it?

I ventured into the den. It was warm and cozy and smelled of rich leather and dark mahogany. It reminded me of the lodge. I swiped at the tear dripping down my cheek.

Enough of that. I'm here to do research.

I let my eyes drift across the book bindings from shelf to shelf until something popped out at me. *The Castles and the Crown*, by Townsend Miller, sounded like a good place to start.

Curled up in a big reddish-brown leather chair, I tucked my sock-covered feet under me and began to read about the lives and times of Queen Isabel and her family. I could understand why Santiago liked this period in Spain's history. It was fascinating.

I was just getting to the part about the birth of Prince Miguel, the tiny prince Serena took care of who died, when a sharp pain came out of nowhere like a horse's kick to the side of my head. The jolt burst through my brain. The screech accompanying the pain in no way resembled my own voice. But it was. I grabbed my temples, pressing as hard as I could. The book fell to the floor with a thud so loud it shook the house.

"Stop," I begged. I fell to my knees on the hardwood. "No! Make it stop."

The room went dark. The pain left as quickly as it had come. I pressed my forehead to the floor and wept. I had never been so grateful in my life. When I was able to crawl back into the chair, my legs were shaking, my body weak.

My head fuzzed as if I'd taken a strong dose of cold medicine. I plopped back into the chair and pulled my legs up. Closing my eyes, I rested my clammy forehead on my knees. Before I knew what was happening, I wasn't sitting in the leather chair anymore.

Summer, 1498, Saragosa

She stands in the hallway outside a room full of frantic women. Her head throbs.

"Serena, hurry, bring the towels," a maid orders, her face pink and shiny with exertion. "The babe is coming."

"How is she?" Serena's gaze travels toward the woman whimpering inside the room.

"Horrible. The baby is stuck. Princess Isabel has lost so much blood. Oh, dear Lord. So much blood..." The nursemaid runs back into the room clutching a rosary tightly against her breast.

"I have towels and water." Serena's voice is lost amidst the commotion. Stepping further into the room, she hands the towels to Clara, who nods grimly. Several servants, nursemaids and midwives bump into each other within the confines of Princess Isabel's chambers.

Serena shudders. *Why does the princess thrash about like that? She will surely fall off the mattress onto the floor.*

Queen Isabel clutches her daughter's hand, shouting words of encouragement over the din. "Bella-Rosa, you are doing fine. Do not worry, my angel." Over her shoulder she pins the two midwives with her terror-filled eyes. "Do something!"

"Hurry, there is not much time left," one midwife, who is up to her elbows inside the princess, yells to the other. A glance passes between them.

Then, to Serena's shock, the other midwife climbs atop the princess's rounded belly. Using her own weight, the midwife pushes down with great force.

"Get off! You are killing her!" bellows the queen.

Trying desperately to maintain her balance atop the thrashing princess, the midwife ignores the screams of pain and the queen's interference. Heaving, she continues pushing down as hard as she can.

Serena cannot bear to look, but does.

After long, excruciating minutes, both midwives come to the inevitable conclusion that all is lost. Thrice they tried to turn the little one. Thrice they failed. The delivery of the small babe is in God's hands now. With bloodstained fingers, they make the sign of the cross over her large belly.

Serena drops to her knees, her fingers moving rapidly across the rosary beads. She recites the prayer she learned as a child. "Hail Mary Mother of God, pray for us sinners now and at the hour of our death. Amen." The princess's screams makes her start the rosary again, her lips praying faster and faster. Her eyes are shut tight. The smell of blood fills her nostrils.

"The baby," someone cries, "I can see the head."

Serena opens her eyes.

"Oh dear God," says another.

"A boy! Thank you, Blessed Mother!"

A baby's cry fills the room. Joyful cheering erupts.

"Mother..." Princess Isabel moans. Of all the cries she has uttered, this one is the most tragic. It is her last.

"Bella-Rosa? Bella-Rosa!" the queen shrieks.

The princess is dead. The whole world shakes apart.

"He is your charge now, Serena," a maid says, and places the baby, dripping in blood, into her arms. "The queen will trust no mere nursemaid to look after the prince. Lord help you if anything should happen to the royal heir."

"Stop it," I hissed. I wanted Serena's vision to end. Now.

"Take him and guard him with your life. Many would rather see him dead," the marquesa says in a faint voice. "Do not let anything happen to him, or it shall be your head."

Serena understands why she has been chosen for this task. She is no nursemaid, but the duty will keep her locked far away from Andrés and Lady Mara. In the nursery, she will be forgotten. And if she fails in her task, she shall be killed.

"No! Make it stop, Serena."

"All of Spain rests in your arms. Do not fail us," Queen Isabel herself commands.

"That's it." I pressed my temples with my palms. "Get out of my head and leave me the hell alone."

The vision cleared and I was sitting once again on the leather chair in the den. Gasping, I clutched my splitting head. "I can't take this anymore. Serena! Show yourself. Right. Now."

Her figure wavered before me. "I am sorry."

"What was that? You can't just force one of your memories on me without asking. That's...that's rude."

"Forgive me. I had no control. It just appeared and I could not stop it."

"It better not happen again."

"That one was scary. I was terrified to become the nursemaid. What did I know of babies?"

"You're right. It was scary." I started to get excited. "I bet it was one of your repressed memories."

"*Perdón?*"

"I have a theory. I think your mind has blocked the really bad things that happened to you. To protect yourself, these memories have been pushed down really, really far in your subconscious. Now that you are trying to remember, the repressed memories might just pop up without any warning."

Her face fell. "And if I do remember them, will I feel the pain again? The sorrow?"

Her fear and sadness shook my heart. "Maybe. But hey, I'm here, right? You don't have to go through this alone."

"Thank you, Erin. You are a true friend."

"Yeah, well, just try not to drive me insane in the process. That was pretty intense. I'm putting the history away for a while." I jumped out of the chair and shoved the book back into the bookcase. The movement made my head hurt and a hiss escaped my lips.

"What is it, Erin?"

"My head, it hurts really bad. Are you doing that?"

"What? Oh dear, no. I do not think so."

"Oh...it's killing me."

"Who is killing you?"

"Yikes, keep it down, screaming doesn't help. It's just an expression. Oops."

Clutching my head, I stumbled back to the chair and accidentally bumped into a round table. The lamp on the table shook and a teacup jostled in its saucer. I stared at the cup a long moment until the puzzle piece I'd been missing turned in my brain and clicked into place.

"Oh...my...God."

Staring at the still-shaking cup, the image of *Señora* Botello's hands wrapped around my teacup came to mind. And visualizing that triggered another memory. Days ago Rosa had apologized for not making tea and yet I remembered very clearly drinking a full cup of tea before I lapsed into a twenty-two hour slumber. I was beginning to draw some nasty conclusions.

I hustled back to my room. Grabbing the teacup, I turned it over in my hands, wishing it could speak. I sniffed it. I ran my finger around the inside of the cup, feeling for any residue. Like I would know if I found any.

Had I been poisoned? If so, by whom and why?

"Rosa?" I was covered with goose bumps as I crept into the kitchen. "Where are you?" I called in a voice barely resembling my own.

Maria came up behind me. "Looking for someone?"

"Yes, I, uh..." Looking down at the teacup in my hands I found the excuse. "Wanted to see if Rosa would make some of her special tea for me. Love that stuff."

"Didn't I tell you? She left this afternoon."

"Left?" I could barely contain the tremor in my voice.

"Her sister is ill. I gave her as much time off as she needs. I'll try to find some temporary help, but in the meantime, it's just us chickens."

More like sitting ducks. "Rosa didn't say anything about her sister this morning."

"Knowing how badly you've been feeling, she probably didn't want to bother you. Besides, I think this came up rather suddenly. It's bad timing for me, though. Guess I'll have to whip something up tonight."

"Tonight?"

"Remember?" she replied patiently. "My company?"

"Oh, that's right, your friend is coming to dinner."

"Around six. Just so you know."

"Yeah sure, I'll be out of the way. Uh, Maria, can I have Santiago's cell phone number?"

She slit her eyes at me. "Why?"

"I have a medical question."

"He told me not to call him." She wiggled her fingers at me like she was casting a spell. "He's gone dark."

"What?"

"He doesn't want to be disturbed. If you call his office, the nurse can refer you to the on-call doctor. I'm sure he can address any of your medical questions."

"Yeah, all right. Oh, look at the time, I better go clean up, it's getting late already."

All during my shower I had an eerie feeling crawling up my

spine. Now more than ever I wanted to talk to Santiago to tell him my suspicions. Plus, I needed to clear the air between us. If he really didn't want me, I would go back home, settle into my career life and all would be normal. Not happy. Just normal.

Grabbing my purse and a light jacket I bounded out of my room, fifteen minutes too late. Voices came from the sitting room.

6:15? Maria's going to kill me.

Well, not much to do about it, I couldn't really sneak out the door without them seeing me. I'd say hello and then hit the road, leaving the lovebirds alone.

"Sorry to interrupt. I'm Erin Carter and I'm leaving."

The person sitting on the couch next to Maria started to rise at my entrance then froze, neither fully up, nor down.

A wave of horror washed across Maria's face. Her hand clutched her crucifix. The silence in the room crackled with electricity.

Maria cleared her throat. "Yes, you are. And this is Helena Blanca."

Somehow I found my voice. "Helena." I bobbed my head slightly, acknowledging her presence. *This* was Maria's dinner date?

"Pleasure." Her head bob was even slighter than mine. "I hear you are going back to LA soon."

Nice try. "Soon? I don't know. I might hang around all summer. Maybe longer." The last part was catty, but I couldn't help it. She didn't have to know I would be gone in less than a week.

"Oh. Well. You should see Barcelona. Lovely this time of year." She turned away, clearly dismissing me. "Maria dear, do you have any wine? I'm dreadfully parched."

"Coming right up," Maria sang a bit too cheerfully as she went out of the room leaving me alone with Helena.

I was still standing in the archway. Helena sat back down on the couch. Neither one of us moved or spoke for a long moment.

"Well, as fun as this is, I'm out of here." I headed to the door.

Without warning, she jumped up and shoved her size-four frame in my face. "Good, because you have overstayed your welcome. Santiago and Maria are too nice to ask you to leave, but I'm not. Get out of this house and leave Santiago alone."

"Excuse me?"

"I know influential people, who don't care what your passport says. I can have you followed. If you keep harassing the Botellos—" she shifted her weight, "—you'll wish you hadn't."

That scared me. I hated to admit. Trash talking is probably part of the game, but having never been in a catfight and after receiving my share of recent death threats, I was leery. "I'm not harassing anyone. Maria asked me to come to Spain. Santiago asked me to stay."

The last bit made her blink in surprise. "Well, I'm sure he just felt sorry for you because of your...condition."

"What?"

She crossed her arms. "Santiago is a good man. He's already stretched to the limit with his job and taking care of his mother. He doesn't need another woman in the house with a mental illness."

"I don't know what you've heard—" I dropped my voice, realizing that Maria could probably hear us in the kitchen, "—but I'm not crazy."

"Why don't you let an expert be the judge of that? I'm sure you can find a good psychiatrist in LA."

I flinched. That one hit too close to home. "Look, I don't really care what you think about me. It's Santiago I'm worried about. Tell me where he is. He might be in danger."

"You're the only danger around here." Her hands fisted.

I grabbed her wrists. "Do you know what's after him? Tell me, so I can save him."

"Let go of me!"

"What is the darkness?"

She struggled out of my grasp and fell backward several steps, her tush hitting the armrest of the loveseat. "You're insane! If you come one step closer, I'll...I'll call the authorities. You need to be locked up."

"Don't get your panties in a bunch. I'm leaving."

"Good." She moved behind the loveseat.

She was petrified. And that *was* good.

At the door I turned. "If Santiago wants to be with me, how will you stop him?"

She was stammering when I closed the door.

Chapter Twenty

The next morning I got up early to track him down. I had a map and phone book. I would comb the entire city for him and even file a missing person's report at the police station if I had to. With each passing moment he was gone, I suspected the worst. He was in trouble. I knew it.

I had only four days left before it was time to cut my losses and head for home. If, after I found him, he told me he was going to marry Helena, then I would bow out gracefully. Even though sticking around simply to torment Helena with my presence sounded appealing, the healthier thing would be to get the heck out of Dodge.

Especially if someone was trying to kill me. There were sure enough people who wanted to. Did I really need to have a near-death experience before taking the hint?

Before I left the Botello home, I wrote an entry in my Get a Life Journal: *6) Find Santiago before it's too late.*

I found the address in the phone directory and stopped at a store for directions. After checking my nerves and lipstick in the mirror of the car I had rented, I took a deep breath and went inside.

The waiting room was empty. A plump woman behind the counter startled when I walked up. "Sorry, I wasn't expecting to see any patients in here today. Can I help you?" she asked, hand over her heart.

"Yes," I said, fighting the quiver in my voice. "I'm here to see Dr. Botello."

"Do you have an appointment?"

"No."

"I see. I'm sorry to tell you, but Dr. Botello is indisposed until next week. Can I recommend Dr. Virgilio? Just down the hall." She pointed with her pen.

"I really need to see Dr. Botello. Is there some way he can be reached?"

She shook her head, "Sorry, *señorita*, I cannot say."

"Can't, or won't say?"

She frowned. "I have my instructions."

"Please, it's a matter of life or death."

"Oh dear, then I'll call Dr. Virgilio." She lifted the phone. "You may have a seat in the waiting room."

I walked out the door.

Next thing I knew I was taking that elevator up to the eleventh floor of his apartment building and knocking on the door with more gusto than I felt. My heart was in my throat as I waited for the door to open.

No answer.

I knocked again several times, harder and harder each time. A few days ago, all I wanted was to pound my fists against his chest and bloody his nose. Now, I just wanted to hold him. Sorrow flooded my heart.

I'll never see him again.

I sobbed with my forehead against the wood.

"*Señorita*, no one is home." An ancient lady with cataract eyes peeked out from behind her door. "Do you wish to come in? Have something to eat? You look a bit...unstable."

Haphazardly I wiped my cheeks. "No, thank you. I need to see the doctor. Do you know when he'll return?"

"I'm not sure it will be today. When he left he was carrying a suitcase. Please come in. A little meat on your bones would do you some good."

"I should be going. If you see him, can you tell Dr. Botello I came by? Here's my card. It has my cell number on it."

"I see." Watery eyes squinted at the card and then back at me. "American, hmm?"

"Yes, I'm going home in a few days. I wanted to say good-by to Santiago, uh, Dr. Botello. Thank you again for your kindness."

Her thin and gnarled arthritic hand grabbed at my wrist like an old bird claw. "How can you leave with the airlines on strike? Didn't you hear about it on the news? No planes leaving today, tomorrow, for who knows how long." She patted my arm. "Looks like you are not going anywhere."

Story of my life.

I thanked the old woman and drove to the police station.

A harried officer with a thick black moustache leaned over the counter at me. "You wish to file a Missing Person's Report?"

"Yes. My doctor friend is in trouble."

"So you say, but he has only been gone for one day?"

I sighed, knowing what was coming next. "Yes, but the circumstances are unusual."

"Really?" His dark eyes bored into mine. "What are the circumstances?"

"I'm...I'm not sure. What if you suspect someone is in danger, but they won't tell you exactly what it is?"

He shook his head in a now-I've-heard-it-all fashion. "Hold on." He raised a finger and dialed a number. As he spoke on the phone, he kept glancing my direction, a frown spreading under that black moustache. When he finished the conversation he was fuming.

"Do you know how dangerous it is to lie to a police officer, *señorita*? Why do you want to waste my time?"

"I'm not lying."

"Doctor Botello is not missing. I just spoke to his nurse. She knows exactly where he is."

"Good. Then you can call him for me to make sure he's all right."

"I will not call a doctor who clearly does not wish to speak to you. Maybe you should see another doctor. You look feverish to me."

I threw my hands up in disgust. "How am I going to find him?"

"*Señorita*, sometimes men do not wish to be found."

CRED

"Maria, you here?" I called.

I didn't know what the darkness was, but it closed in all around me, crushing my lungs, blackening my thoughts.

Maybe he didn't want me to find him. Maybe he just wanted me to go home. *Stop it,* I chastised myself. *What if he's in trouble and no one helps him?*

"On the veranda," Maria answered.

I slid the glass door open. "Hey, how I can get in touch with Rosa?"

"Why?" Something flickered in her eyes.

"To see if there's anything I can do. You know, with her sister being ill and all? Maybe she needs something I can bring to her."

"That's nice of you, Erin. I don't know where her sister lives."

I sat on the lounge chair next to hers. "You don't have an address? Phone number? Anything?"

"No."

"Relatives of hers I can call?"

"Nope."

"That seems strange to me. I can't believe you don't have any emergency contacts."

"What's the emergency?"

"Um..."

"Exactly. Rosa is a private person. She doesn't want any of us meddling in her personal affairs."

"I'm not meddling. It's just odd. How do you know when she'll return?"

She shrugged her shoulders. "When I see her little round face, otherwise, we don't bug her."

"I see."

"Look, while we are on the subject of harassing people, there's something we need to discuss." Angry circles formed on Maria's cheeks. "Helena said you went to Santiago's apartment, his office, and the police station looking for him."

"How'd she know?"

"Come on, are you saying Helena's lying? Of all the people I know, *she* doesn't lie."

Helena had me followed.

"No, she's not lying." I squeezed the tension building in my neck with my fingers. "But it's not like that."

"Aww, sweetie, you need to leave them alone. He's made his choice. I'm sorry you're hurting. You've got to see that you're making matters worse."

"I know," I whispered, pressure building behind my eyeballs.

She sighed. "I love you, you know that, right? I'm sorry to just come out and say this, but someone needs to intervene. You're sick, Erin. You should really see a professional."

My heart sank.

Her lips were set firmly, her hands on her hips. "Crashing the car, stalking people, talking about evil and such?" She sighed again. "I'm sorry, so sorry. You need help."

I smiled weakly. She didn't even know about the ghost business. "As soon as this strike lifts, I'll fly home."

CRSO

Dangling my feet off the edge of my bed, I rested my chin on folded hands. How had everything gone so wrong? I wanted to pull my hair out. Insanity made the most sense of all. But I knew I wasn't crazy. Or did all crazy people feel they were perfectly sane?

The shrill ring of the phone made me jump. Quietly, I moved down the hall.

Maria answered it in her room. "Santiago."

Eavesdropping is not normally the kind of thing I'd do, but desperate times call for desperate measures. I held my breath outside her bedroom door and listened for all I was worth.

"Where are you?" she was saying. There was a significant pause. "Top secret, huh? You can trust me. I won't spill anything to Helena. Oh all right, spoilsport."

I leaned into the wall.

"Oh, she's just fine. Back to normal," Maria said.

He asked about me at least. Where are you Santiago?

"No. I don't need to anymore. Everything's fine." There was silence as she listened to him. "No. I told you, no more pills."

Whaaa? Pills?

"Santiago, will you stop? There's nothing to worry about." Her tone sounded as if one of them was worried. "Why are we talking about this? Concentrate on making those future plans. I'll take care of Erin and send her on her way."

I didn't like the way *that* sounded.

I tiptoed down the hall to the kitchen, not a moment too soon. I was standing in front of the refrigerator replaying what I had just heard when she came in the kitchen.

"Hi," I called out cheerfully. "Was that Rosa on the phone?"

Her brows drew together in a frown. "No, some telemarketer. I swear they get worse all the time."

"Wow, you've got them in Spain too? What was he selling?"

"Hmmm? Oh I don't know, who listens to them?" she said a bit tersely. "I was in the middle of making us lunch and now it looks like I'm out of time."

Four pieces of bread, lunch meat, sliced cheese and a jar of mayo were lined up on the cutting board.

"You going somewhere?"

"Doctor's appointment." She grimaced. "Yeast infection. It's bad."

"Eeew. Those are awful. Why don't you talk to Santiago about it?"

She shot me a look. "Go see my *brother* about a feminine problem?"

"No, I mean, can't he just prescribe the pills you need so you can start taking them right away? What's his number?" I took my cell out of my pocket. "I'll call him for you if you feel funny about it."

"No! I mean, no, I don't want to bother him with this. It's kind of embarrassing. I already have this appointment, I might as well just bite the bullet and go."

"Are you sure?" I placed the phone on the counter in front of her. "You can call him, I'll step away."

"No." She turned her back on my phone and helped herself to a Coke out of the refrigerator. "I hate to bother him with all my shit. It's time I grew up and took care of myself. See you later."

I frowned. My little trick hadn't worked. I desperately wanted his number on my cell so I could call him after she left. Well, at least I knew he was alive. For now.

I went ahead and used the fixings she'd left to make my old standby, a turkey sandwich with mayo on a wheat roll. My appetite had returned in full force and I was starving. Leaning over the counter, I wolfed down the sandwich and chugged down a Coke. It was good to enjoy eating again. The illness or heatstroke that had upset my system was completely gone.

"One good thing on a perfectly horrible day," I said to the empty kitchen.

Half an hour later, I was dying.

Slumped on the cold bathroom floor, knees drawn up to my chest, I rested my heavy head on the toilet seat. Consciousness was an elusive state, fluttering in and out of my grasp. I was coming to for the moment and the terrifying situation became real.

"Maria," I called as loudly as I could for the hundredth time, but my voice was feeble and hoarse. "*Señora* Hernán? Anyone here? Please...help."

No one answered. I was alone in that huge house. Alone and dying.

For all my efforts I was rewarded with another wave of nausea. I had lost the strength to drag myself back to bed. Walking was impossible. My muscles knotted and ached. I could barely lift my head. The spasms in my stomach threatened to go on forever. The strength required to stand and walk had seeped out of my body.

How long had I been draped over the toilet? It was growing dark. Could that be? I turned my face toward the window and felt the warmth from the sun on my cheeks.

I'm blind.

"Maria! *Señora* Hernán!"

All the muscles in my stomach convulsed. I lay there for a few moments, trying to catch my breath. Then slowly I began to crawl out of the bathroom.

"Help! Please, someone."

From somewhere far away a shrill noise was scraping against my eardrums. I willed it to stop. Begged it to stop. I was tired. So spent. A heavy hand shook my shoulder. I opened my eyes. Or at least I thought they were open. I was still blind.

"What can I do?" Serena asked inside my thoughts.

"The phone..." I whispered. "Call for help."

"The what?"

"Help me...to the phone."

I started to crawl. It was a painstaking effort. I grunted, I groaned in monosyllabic curses, dragging my body a few feet at a time before I had to stop, panting and retching.

I am so cold. My teeth chattered. *My head...oh, God, my head.*

"Keep going," Serena crooned softly. *"You can do it. You have to."*

The phone was only fifteen feet down the hall, but it might as well have been in another country. I wasn't sure where I had left my cell phone. In the kitchen? I couldn't waste time crawling in the wrong direction for it. Relying on my hands to guide me, I dragged myself like a blind inchworm.

The shrill sound started again. The phone was ringing. I had to get to it and tell the person on the line to call for an ambulance. I inched on.

The ringing stopped and the machine picked up. "Santiago, it's Martin," a deep voice said in English. "Pick up. This is important." He blew out a breath. "The results are back from the blood sample you gave me. It's not good. Hell, I'm not going to downplay this, it's what you feared—it's returned."

Patting the wall, my palm hit a doorframe. I tried to recall. Three steps? Four, to the table with the phone?

"Are you hearing this?" the man shouted into the phone. "You're all in danger. Let the authorities take care of...things. I know your usual modus operandi, but you can't intervene, not this time." His voice lowered. "I'm sorry buddy. I tried. We all gave it our best shot."

My hand hit a table leg.

"Holy shit!" Horror zinged into the man's voice. "I'm in

trouble too, aren't I, by association? Santiago, get out of there. Get out now."

The line went dead.

My heart stopped for a fraction of a second. The image of Santiago's face came into my view so perfectly I thought he was really standing there, arms outstretched and a beautiful smile on his face. My heart lurched and did a couple of fast beats.

Resting back against the cold wall, I sucked in huge gulps of air. Then I reached for the receiver. I was light-headed and delirious. I wasn't sure I could dial 911. "Serena, help me."

She didn't answer.

"Serena?"

She was gone. I was alone. Cold panic flopped in my gut. When the onslaught passed, I pressed the 0.

"*Buenos días,*" the operator said.

The room was dark except for the shooting lights zinging past my eyes. I was going to pass out soon. "Help, I need help."

"*Hola?*" She hadn't heard me.

I tried again, but was forced instead to swallow hard in an attempt not to vomit. I wasn't successful. The incensed operator's curse words were new to me.

"No! Please..." I cried to the dial tone. The phone slipped out of my hand and crashed to the floor.

For a few moments I lay there and sobbed. I was dying. Part of me prayed it would be over soon. I had never been in so much agony. Every part of me was rebelling at once.

The room was pitch black, or rather, my sight was. I groped around on the floor for the phone. When I finally found it, I touched each button. Maria liked to store frequently called numbers. I hoped beyond hope I would find a button to connect me to someone. Anyone. I didn't want to die alone.

Thank God. The phone was ringing. It rang and rang and rang.

Sweet Jesus, no one's going to answer.

"*Bueno?*"

"Please...help...me," I whispered and swirled away into oblivion.

Chapter Twenty-One

Someone was trying to lift me off the hard tiled floor.

Squinting through the watery slits of my eyes, I tried to focus on the comical face. "Handsome dream."

"Shh, Erin, don't talk," Santiago lifted me with surprising ease and carried me outside. "I've given you an injection to stop the vomiting and relax your muscles. You'll feel better soon."

"I...hurt...am...so sick." I groaned.

"I know, *querida*. I'll make you well again." His face was full of agonizing fear.

Tears of relief rolled down my cheeks.

"Please don't cry," he said with choked emotion. "I won't leave you."

My limbs were warm and heavy. He placed me gently inside the car. My head felt like a pumpkin when it flopped back against the headrest.

When he reached across to buckle my safety belt, I lifted my hand and placed my palm against his cheek. The stubble tickled. His smile swirled lazily before my eyes.

"It's the medicine. Be a good girl and close your eyes."

"I'm not crazy anymore," I slurred.

When he shook his head, the movement was disjointed and as choppy as an old silent movie. A strange white halo shadowed his head and his green eyes bored into mine. "You never were, *querida*. Rest, now. You're safe with me."

Safe. The Spanish buzzword. For the first time in my life I understood, deep into my core, what the word meant.

I smiled and drifted into a drug-induced dream. Something about finding love in a palace rose garden.

CR&O

"Maria hasn't come today?" I worried she was still angry with me.

"No one is allowed to disturb your rest, *Señorita* Carter," the nurse explained. "Doctor Botello's orders."

I was mighty tired. Chewed-up-by-a-dog-and-dragged—through-the-mud kind of tired. And the pain? I couldn't even talk about that.

"You are very sick and need to sleep."

Sleep. Sleep is good...

Hours later, a light tug on my arm woke me.

"*Señorita*?" the nurse said quietly. "There is a phone call for you."

"What?" Full of pain medication and muscle relaxants, it took a while before my eyes peeled open.

She held up the phone so I could see it.

"'Kay." I knew it wasn't the headhunter. The nurse had called her for me and told her I needed to reschedule the meeting. I didn't really care if they gave the position to someone else. My heart belonged here. With Santiago.

The nurse placed the phone on the pillow next to my ear. I listened for a moment, trying to shake the cobwebs from my brain.

"Hello? Anyone there?" a woman's voice said. "Oh nuts, I've been disconnected."

"Mom?"

"Erin! Are you okay?"

"Guess so." My tongue was thick enough to belong to a cow. "I'm in a hospital."

"I know, sugar, how're ya doin'?"

"Better. I'll be...out...here soon."

"She says she's better." Mom was talking to someone next to her. "You sure, Erin? Is that what the doctor said?"

"Yeah."

"Maria called and said you were real sick. Your father and I want to get ya. Bring you on home."

"Maria...called...you?"

"She says the doctor's gonna release her," she was still talking to someone else. "Yes, all right, here."

"Honey, how're ya feelin'?"

"Okay...Dad."

"Oh, sugarplum, you sound terrible. Mom and I are catchin' the next flight from Zimbabwe. The Peace Corps can survive without us for a while."

"Fine...really."

"Are ya sure? You sound funny."

"Medication."

"Oh. Mom's trying to yank the phone from my fingers. Take care, sugarplum. We'll call again soon."

"Sugar?" Mom was back on. "There's a huge line here to use the public phone. We've gotta go. You sure you're all right?"

"Sure." The cloud was getting thicker and thicker in my head. My eyes were already closed.

"We'll call you soon—"

The line went dead. And I was already asleep.

෬෪෨

"You're looking good," Santiago smiled at me while checking my pulse.

"Are you planning on getting your eyes checked anytime soon?"

"I'm serious. Your color is better. Pupils normal."

I reached for his hand and placed it on my chest. "My heart feels better too."

He pulled his hand back and tucked it into his pocket. "You probably have questions."

Questions? I was filled up to my eyeballs with them, but with Santiago looking at me with those loving green eyes and throwing compliments my way, did I really want to know the answers to such things as, "Did you and Helena tie the knot yet?"

Denial? Call it rose-colored shades. Besides, he wore no wedding band, so hope flickered brightly in my little corner of the universe.

"Yes. I do." Panic bubbled in my chest and hope turned down a watt or two.

"When I get the final test results back from the lab today, I should have all the answers for you. I'm sorry it's taken so long. I wanted to be...had to be sure."

I reached for him, relishing the warmth of his forearm radiating beneath the white coat. "I'm not just talking about my health."

Staring at my hand, a shadow crossed his face. "I know." His voice was quiet as he patted my hand. "Please. A little longer. I'll explain everything. Soon."

The nurse walked in smiling. "Doctor Botello says you will probably be able to leave the hospital today."

"Really? Great news. No offense, Eva. This hospital saved my life, but wowie, will I be glad to walk through those front doors."

"Will you go back to the *Estados Unidos*?"

I looked at Santiago. "I'm not sure yet."

His face was grim when he turned to go. "I'll be back later."

"This is the last bag for you." The nurse adjusted the IV drip. "It has been nice taking care of you. Stay safe, okay."

I rolled my eyes. "When I figure out how to do that, I'll let you know." I lifted my arm, complete with the dangling IV tube accessory and we shook.

Sitting up, I dropped my legs over the edge of the bed. I had to move slowly, dragging the stupid IV pole beside me, but could now go to the restroom by myself. It's amazing how we take those little luxuries for granted. I cleaned up and applied a little makeup to my pale face. My hair was a disaster, but perked up a bit after I brushed it. After returning to bed, I was surprised to find a note on my pillow.

When I picked it up, a familiar wave of vertigo swooshed through me. I smiled. "Serena? Are you here?"

"*Sí.*"

"I thought you left me for good back at the house." I

shuddered, not wanting to relive the terrifying memory.

"Aya, no. I simply went to find your love. To bring him to you."

My mouth fell open. "You went to get Santiago?"

"You were trying to find him with that odd machine. What did you call it, the fon? I wish it were that easy for me to reach Andrés." Her eyes were misty.

"But how did you find Santiago?"

"Ah, you helped me. Your thoughts about him were so clear. I concentrated on his face as well and suddenly I was there. He was coming down a long hallway with his keys in his hands. I encouraged him to hurry."

"You saved my life."

"*Claro que sí.* Now, come. While you were here in the infirmary, I found another memory. It... I do not know why, but this one...aya, Erin, I am frightened."

Was this it? The death memory? "Maybe this is something you really need to see. To move on."

"I believe you are right. The truth is just out of my reach." She took a stuttering breath. "But I fear we are almost there."

ᏣᎬᎦ

Summer, 1500, Segovia

Staring at her reflection, Serena smoothes the wrinkles out of her best gown. Her eyes are ringed with fatigue. Happily the bruise on her cheek is gone. She smiles, grateful for one good thing about her new duties—in the nursery she is safe from Lady Mara.

Turning, she notices how different she looks from the day Andrés first met her in the gardens. *Will he like my womanly curves? Or will his eyes be only for Lady Mara, the woman soon to share his bed?*

"Serena? Are you in here?" Clara whispers.

Serena swipes at her eyes. "Yes. Enter."

"Holy Madre! You are going tonight? Why?"

Serena swallows the lump still lodged in her throat. "Lady Mara demanded I come."

"Then it is a trap."

Serena is silent.

"Listen to me, no good can come from this. She must be planning to humiliate you before all those guests. You mustn't go, Serena. Please. Stay here where you are safe from her sharp claws."

"Do you not see? It may be my last chance to see Andrés before he marries—" The sob catches in her throat.

"Oh dear." Clara pats Serena's head. "Do not cry. I hate to see you like this. I promise you, one day soon, Lucia the she-devil will get her just desserts."

The ballroom is full of noblemen and ladies. Music lifts into the air, mingling with laughter. Serena's heart hurts. As hard as she tries, she cannot forget the last time she was here, dancing with her beloved.

Where is he?

She stands up on her toes to look over the crowd. A long table is set at the front of the hall complete with gold-stitched tapestry, tapered candles and the finest cutlery. The marquesa sits at the head of the table next to Lady Mara.

Serena ducks down and slips through the guests. She wants to put distance between herself and the ladies who despise her.

I cannot let them find me before I speak to— She stops short. She would recognize that broad back anywhere.

Andrés scans the crowded ballroom. Is he looking for her?

"Hey, there you are, old man." Don Ricardo slaps him on the shoulder. "Quite a gathering."

Serena steps back, blending into the crowd.

"Smells like an ambush, does it not?" says Andrés.

"Indeed. And you, my friend, are the target."

"Any idea what my mother has arranged? She claims it is a celebration of my becoming Head Chamberlain. That news is long in the tooth. What is she really up to?"

"What man could profess to understand the thoughts of women?" He drapes his arm across Santiago's back. "Let us enjoy. Your mother and intended have organized a splendid get-together."

"By hell's name, Lady Mara is not... Do not call her that."

Ricardo raises his eyebrows, "No? But your mother said—"

"I do not intend to marry her, no matter what the great marquesa says."

"You shan't be put upon then, if your best friend dances with the lady?"

He slits his eyes. "Who says you are my best friend? Dance the whole night if it pleases you. Keep her out of my hair."

"I shall." Ricardo pounds his shoulder and strides away toward Lucia Mara.

As Andrés walks, people pat his shoulder and linger to wish him well. He smiles and makes polite conversation while his eyes race across each face in the crowd, searching...searching.

For me? Serena hopes. "Andrés?"

"Serena! You are here."

"I should not be."

His gaze pours over her face. "You are more beautiful than I remembered."

"Are you well?"

She is concerned by what she sees in his face. He is battle-bruised and worn thin. His brown eyes are ringed from lack of sleep, but more than that, they appear...haunted.

What torture has he endured?

"I am better now that you are here."

A bolt of electricity arcs through her when he brings her hand up to his lips and kisses her knuckles.

"Andrés, don't." She pulls away. "Not here where everyone can see."

"What do I care of them? I see only you—"

"There you are, Andrés," Don Ricardo interrupts. "Your mother and *querida*—I mean, the Lady Mara, have asked me to hunt you down and send you their way. Something about a toast."

"I cannot leave you again, Serena."

She lets him see the love in her eyes. "Go, Andrés, this is a special night for you. We shall speak later."

"More than that. We shall dance."

"I count on it, Chamberlain."

He strides off toward his mother's table. Serena cringes when Lady Mara rushes to take his arm.

"There you are. Everyone waits for us to dance the first *Ioyoso*," Lady Mara says.

"Dance? Not toast?" His voice is angry.

Lady Mara pouts. "No one will set foot on the floor until I dance with my intended. We cannot spoil their fun."

"Dance, son, there is all night for toasts," Beatriz calls out.

He pauses for a long moment before tapping his hat and allowing Lady Mara to drag him toward the group of dancers.

Serena goes to join Clara, who is eyeing the eligible noblemen.

"So you came after all. I warn you, she is up to no good," Clara whispers.

"I know. "

Clara elbows Serena. "I hate to admit it, but they look good together."

"Beside Andrés, a sow looks attractive," Serena says.

Clara laughs. "*Sí*. He looks extremely handsome tonight. I swear, I cannot remember the last time he smiled like that. Oh, *lo siento*, Serena, perhaps it is the festivities, not Lady Mara who makes him happy."

A male's voice comes from behind them, "Bless me, two of the most gorgeous women in Castile standing idle while the music plays?"

Clara and Serena turn to see the wolfish grin on Don Ricardo's face. His reputation with the ladies is known far and wide.

A pink blush fans out across Clara's bosom and up her neck. "It is difficult to dance without a partner."

"No? I shall rectify this outrageous situation immediately."

"*Bueno*." Clara lifts her hand for him to take.

Don Ricardo smiles and offers his arm to Serena. "How about the next one, Lady Clara?"

Clara's mouth falls open.

"Don Ricardo, I beg of you, take Clara in my stead. I do not feel like dancing."

"You will once you have taken the arm of the best dancer in all of Castile."

Serena's salmon-colored gown swishes and twirls about her ankles as he pulls her towards the floor. She dares not look back at Clara.

"You are my choice," he whispers in her ear. "Tonight I shall not ask any other to dance."

"Don Ricardo, do not say that." Serena is horrified, remembering what Clara told her after the last ball. "Noblewomen take great offense when they are not asked to dance."

His smile is genuine. "They will clamor to dance with the best. I shall not need to ask a one. Mark my words."

"Oh, you are incorrigible." Her hearty laugh breaks over the music. When Andrés's head swings toward the sound, she catches the look of love in his eyes. She tries to ignore the murderous look in Lady Mara's.

"Andrés, perhaps it is time for that toast. Let us sit," Lady Mara says loudly.

He walks away with her, but his gaze remains stubbornly locked on Serena.

"Ah well. It seems the music halts, for now. Shall we take our seats over there?" Ricardo points to two seats at the back of the hall.

Serena frowns. "Surely you jest. Those are too far away."

"Trust me, we shall hear better than those sitting beside Andrés. And we shan't have to strain our necks to see over the heads of others."

Skeptical, she follows him, casting glances over her shoulder toward Andrés's back.

"Are you sure we will be able to hear from here? Mayhap we should go closer." She points. "I see two empty chairs."

"Nonsense. Besides, I doubt Lady Mara will want you seated so close to...the head table."

She sighs. He is right.

"I am more than happy to keep you company." He moves his chair closer. When his leg brushes against hers, his eyes shimmer. "You are so beautiful."

The intensity in those black eyes makes Serena uneasy. She shifts in her chair.

"I have known Andrés since we were three and have never seen him gaze at a woman as he does you. You must be special, indeed."

"Very kind of you to say, Don Ricardo." She looks down at her hands in her lap. Nervousness flutters in her stomach.

"I do not mean to be kind. I wish to learn for myself what makes him desire you." He grabs one of her hands and brings it to his lips.

At the sound of clanking glasses, she turns her head from him, squirming in her seat to see.

"Time to make a toast." The marquesa's voice rings out.

Ricardo whispers. "To sleep in a nobleman's bed is surely better than a poor woman's cot."

She presses a thin finger to her lips, motioning for his silence.

Ricardo rubs Serena's arm, his hand hot on her sleeve. "No lady has ever refused me. And all have been well-satisfied."

"Please, Don Ricardo." She pulls her arm away. "I cannot hear."

"First of all, we say welcome home, Andrés," says the marquesa. "We have all missed you. For those of you who do not know, King Fernando has appointed Andrés his Head Chamberlain."

Cheers fill the room. Serena strains to see Andrés's face and does not notice when Ricardo's arm slides around her shoulders.

"Raise your glasses," Beatriz continues once the cheers die down, "to my son's happiness."

"*Salud!*" the crowd cheers.

Andrés smiles at his mother, mouthing the words, "Thank you."

"And there is more..." the marquesa rushes on.

In the back of the room, Ricardo yanks Serena closer. The pit in her stomach turns to fear when the black-eyed devil grins like a wolf.

"Four days hence my son and Lady Mara shall be married."

Deafening cheers explode off the walls. *Four days?* Serena blinks at Ricardo in astonishment. Her lips part, but no words come forth.

Ricardo seizes the moment and crushes her mouth with his own.

She is shocked still, her mind reeling. Unlike the sweet kiss Andrés first gave her, this kiss is an attack. Violent. Punishing. Like a serpent, his tongue forces its way in, probing, violating. Serena tries to scream, but cannot. Rough fingers grope her breasts, painfully squeezing her nipples. Hot panic surges through her body as she struggles to break free. She fights, but is no match for his strength. She cannot breathe, cannot move.

The crowd is on its feet cheering so loudly no one notices her plight at the back of the hall.

In a flash of instinct, she bites down as hard as she can, her teeth grinding against the foreign object violating her mouth. Ricardo's tongue is nearly severed. He screams out in agony, releasing her. Her screams join his as she scrambles away from him.

A murmur goes up through the crowd.

Andrés bolts up, toppling his chair. "Serena!"

"Andrés, you must toast your intended," his mother says.

He is already pushing through to the back of the crowd. "Serena! Where are you?"

"Do not go. Stay with me." Lady Mara runs after him, clutching his arm.

"Release me." He flings her off. Lady Mara topples over backwards, landing hard on her backside.

"Andrés!" Beatriz's voice is shrill with shock.

"Serena!" He lunges into the crowd, knocking over everyone in his path, shoving his way to the back of the crowded hall. "Are you hurt?" He tips her chin up to look at her face. "Answer me."

"You—"

"What is it?" he demands, his body trembling. "Speak to me."

"You are...married...four...days?"

"For all that is holy." He curses. "Come with me." Swiftly, he maneuvers her through the chaotic crowd, not stopping until they are outside.

Chapter Twenty-Two

Serena tried to jerk her arm free from Andres's grip and my hand knocked the TV remote onto the floor. The loud clatter brought me back to the hospital room.

"Wow. That memory was...intense. I'm so sorry, Serena. What that man, Ricardo, did to you, is unforgivable."

My head nodded with her response.

"But the real pain was believing Andrés was finally going to marry the horror-show Lucia, right?"

"I always thought we would be together. Somehow."

Her depression was dragging me under. It felt like drowning. "Well, maybe there's more to this story. We aren't to the end, right?" Of course not, the end was her death. I shuddered, not sure how I was going to face that.

She sighed. *"You are right. We shall just have to hope. What is that on the table?"*

I picked up a note and read it out loud.

Sorry I can't discharge you in person. I'm in surgery all morning. We need to talk, privately. In the top dresser drawer you will find money for cab fare. After I'm finished here, I'll meet you at Rodrigo's restaurant in Segovia. It's too dangerous to go to the house, or my apartment.

Be safe, Querida. I will be there soon.

Signed with a giant scrawling *S.*

"Do not go," Serena whispered in my ear. *"Segovia is a place of death."*

Your death, I didn't say. "You don't have to go with me, if you don't want to."

She didn't answer.

"I could visualize some beautiful place like Hawaii, for instance, and you could vacation on a warm beach for a while."

Nothing.

"Serena? Do you hear me?"

She squeaked. *"Oh. No. I do not wish to remember this."*

But it was too late. The memory took us both.

CRSO

Andrés guides her at a fast clip through the palace and onto the patio. They are alone at last.

"Unhand me, Andrés." She shakes his grip off her arm.

"What is the matter with you?"

"With me? You are the one marrying in a few days." She tries to step away from him. He pulls her all the closer.

"Serena, listen."

"I had hoped, prayed." She shakes her head. "I cannot believe you are doing this."

"Serena." Gently, he touches her arm.

"Do not touch me." She pushes against his chest with all her might.

He grabs her around the waist and lifts her feet off the ground. As if she were no more than a sack of grain, he drapes her over his shoulders.

"Put me down." She kicks furiously, trying to break free of his strong arms.

"Not until you have quieted. I need you to listen. I am taking you somewhere where we can talk."

Wriggling wildly, she pounds her fists against his back. "Put me down, I say!"

"All right then, I shall, but only if you will be still."

She blows the hair from her eyes and notices they are in the rose garden. Their garden. She stops fighting. Slowly, he lowers her feet to the ground, keeping his hands firmly on her tiny waist.

To her surprise, he kisses a tear from her cheek. "Foolishly, I believed time would take away the pain." He kisses the tip of her nose. "And that my need for you, deep and raw like an open wound, would stop burning." He looks into her eyes. "See me now. Without you, I die."

Her body trembles in his hands. "I have been dying too."

"Forgive what I did to you. To us." With one finger he traces the scar meandering down her cheek. "And marry me."

"But I thought...Heaven's Glory! What of your wedding this Sunday?"

"Do you refer to the announcement made in the hall? My mother and Lucia Mara view me as a witless ox to be yanked about by my nose. I shall have none of it. Besides..." His hands run gently up her arms. "I love you."

"What of your family? Your honor? The king expects you to marry her."

"None of it matters."

"Andrés, I will do anything to be with you. Even if you must...marry her."

Her breath sucks in sharply when he roughly takes hold of her shoulders. "No. I would rather die than have the woman I love treated like a whore, our sons to be bastards."

"Oh, Andrés," she cries. "You see, there is no way for us."

He pulls her into his arms, against his hard chest. "You are wrong, my love. We shall disappear. As long as we are together, we will be happy. Forever."

They both know the dangers facing them. How can they flee the king's army?

Finally she answers. "All right. Whatever it takes, I will be with you. It is the only thing I have ever wanted."

He kisses her soundly, lips, cheeks, down her jawline.

"I will convince our king," he murmurs against her neck. "There must be a way."

"What of Lady Mara?" Serena shudders.

"Surely Lucia shall understand. She deserves better than I can give her."

"Be careful, my darling." She bites her lower lip, choosing her words slowly. "She is pure evil."

"What evil can touch our love?" Andrés smiles.

Serena smiles too and squeezes his hand.

"Wait for me in your chambers. If the king is unfavorable to our union, we shall leave here in secret tonight."

She entwines her fingers around his neck, pulling him closer. They melt into one another. Their kisses burn hot in the dark.

Reluctantly he pulls away. "*Dios mío*, I could kiss you all night, but I must go." Smoothing her soft hair with his fingers, he loses himself briefly in her gray eyes.

She watches him gather his strength and go inside. Where will they go? She knows nothing of the world outside the palace walls. But she trusts Andrés. He will protect her.

Her thoughts wander to little Prince Miguel. She will miss him the most. He is as much her child now as he is the queen's. She says a silent prayer for his health and wellbeing and wishes once again he had not been taken so far away. Queen Isabel had been adamant about presenting Miguel as her heir to the Council of Cortez.

She worries more about royal duty than the nasty cough wheezing in Miguel's chest.

As she turns to go inside, a strange feeling overcomes her. The hairs prickle on the back of her neck. Was someone watching? The sky is as black as Don Ricardo's eyes. Scanning the darkness around her, she sees no one. She listens. Not a sound. She hugs herself and goes inside.

In the tower, high above the garden, a figure silently moves away from the window.

CR℘

Rodrigo opened the door for me and kissed my cheek. "Bella! Wonderful to see you again. Aya, but you look pale. Come inside the restaurant and sit down. Marta is coming over too. She cannot wait to see you."

CR℘

Serena packs her things and awaits for word from Andrés. It has been a long exciting day. Starting to doze, she is awakened by a rustling sound.

Throwing her nightdress over her clothes, she creeps to her chamber door. Something crinkles under her shoe. A note has been slipped under her door. Lifting it up to the candlelight, she reads:

Serena,

Meet me at the East Tower. Do not let anyone see you go.

Short and to the point, she knows what the letter means—she and Andrés will run away together tonight. Looking around the room, she realizes she might never see it again. The castle has become her home. She will miss it and all its occupants. She wipes her eyes. From now on, she will be with Andrés.

We will make a new home. Together.

She cinches the drawstring on her satchel, closing up all her personal belongings. Just as she is about to leave, she hears footsteps coming up the stairs to her room.

Her chamber door is thrown open wide.

"Ha!" Lady Mara rushes in, her eyes blazing. "Caught you." Her flaming hair flies wildly behind her.

"What are you doing here?"

"That letter you are holding like a babe against your breast, is from him, is it not?"

Serena makes two movements at once—she steps in front of her satchel and crinkles the letter into a ball in her fist.

Lucia does not see the hidden bag. She wants the letter. "Give it to me." She snatches Serena's thin wrist, squeezing as hard as she can.

"You cannot have it."

"I shall teach you a lesson about stealing a woman's husband." Lucia's sharp nails dig into Serena's flesh, drawing blood. "Open your fingers."

"He is not your husband. And never will be."

"Filthy rotten whore! I shall have you flogged. Beaten within an inch of your life." Rage blazes like fire through Lucia's eyes. Her nails cut deeper. "And I will report your insolence to the marquesa."

Something inside Serena shifts. She suspects the change has been coming on for some time now, but feels its full force with Lady Mara's threatening words. She is no longer a child without any family to care for her, but a woman with a man who loves her. A coil of strength unfolds within her. Confidence she has never before possessed turns up the corners of her lips.

"Have the letter." Serena throws it. The balled up paper ricochets off Lucia's nose and lands on the floor.

Lucia gapes in amazement. Her countenance rages purple with anger. She releases Serena's arm and snatches a handful of her wavy locks.

Dragging Serena by the hair to where the letter landed, she snarls, "Pick that up."

"Release me." Serena tries to break free of the clutches of a madwoman.

Lucia's pretty face contorts into a hideous grin. "Did you not hear me? I gave you a command."

Anger burns hot in Serena's chest. For the last few months she has silently endured Lady Mara's commandments and savage beatings, knowing the madwoman was doing her best to kill her. In truth, Serena was so broken with grief, she did nothing to protect herself. If Lucia killed her then the pain would end, her shattered heart would finally stop beating. But now that Andrés has come back to claim her, she will never allow Lucia to hurt her again.

Serena spins and fists Lucia's red hair. "Never again will I do what you say."

"Owww!" Lucia's scream bounces off the chamber walls. Long dark curls slip freely through her fingers. "Oww oww oww, let go," a voice much smaller demands.

Serena does, of her own accord.

"Who do you think you are?" Lucia asks, rubbing her scalp, the fight expended from her voice.

"I am Andrés's intended. The next marquesa. Be gone," Serena says firmly. "Do not enter my chambers again."

"You're mad. Wait until the marquesa hears about this. You will be thrown out of the castle like the filthy rubbish you are." Bending over quickly, as if fearing a swift kick, Lucia snatches up the crumpled letter and flees from the room.

Serena smiles. She fought her personal demon and won. It may not be the last time she encounters the horrible woman, but for now, she is not afraid. With Andrés by her side she will never be fearful again.

She thinks about the crumpled letter in Lucia's clutches and is spurred into action. Gathering her belongings, she tiptoes quietly down the stairway, through the kitchen and out the back door into the garden. Nerves and excitement constrict in her chest, yet she believes without question they are doing the right thing.

We will be together forever. She races to the tower to meet him.

છજ

"I worry about you," Marta said. "You've lost too much weight." She was sitting across from me, heaping another scoop of paella onto my plate. She had been force-feeding me for the last hour.

"Please, Marta. I can't eat another bite. Besides, Santiago should be here soon."

"I hope so. You look tired. Maybe you should go lie down in the back. There's a bed back there."

"Excuse me," the hostess said, approaching our table. "There is a message for *Señorita* Carter."

"That's me." I took the yellow sticky note from her hand and read it.

"Is it bad news?" Marta asked, "You look like you might be ill."

I gulped. "It says meet me at the tower. There is something you must see."

"The tower of the Alcázar? Why? I do not like the idea of you going there so close to dark."

I didn't either. Not one bit. But I would walk off the end of the earth for him, no question about it. So I took another cab and paid the driver extra to break the speed limits to get me to the castle.

I was devastated to find out I was too late.

"What do you mean I can't go in?" I asked the young girl at the ticket counter who refused to sell me a ticket.

"The Alcázar closes in fifteen minutes." She handed me a

brochure with the printed times on it.

"I won't be more than fifteen minutes. I promise."

She popped her gum and closed her ticket window in my face. The Alcázar was officially closed.

Sometimes in a girl's life, she does stupid things for love. This was one of those times. I went around the ticket booth and hopped the fence.

CRSO

Serena is disappointed to find herself all alone at the base of the tower.

Never mind. I have waited this long, a few more minutes shall not matter.

She climbs the narrow stairway. Looking out the window for his familiar figure, she studies every shadow. The wind howls through the opening and circles about her. Long strands of her black hair lift and dance with each gust. The candle she holds flickers. Shadows move menacingly across the dark walls. A shiver runs up her spine. Her senses prick up, alert.

What was that?

Standing very still, she listens. Hearing only the wind, she laughs to herself. *Andrés would surely think me silly. Scared of my own shadow and the howl of the wind.*

She leans over the window ledge slightly, longing to glimpse his powerful stride moving across the grass toward the tower. She sighs, content. One day soon they will be married. Pressing her hand to her heart, she feels the racing beat in her chest. The corner of her eye catches a wisp of movement, barely more than the fluttering of a moth behind her. She turns.

Too slowly.

A large rock, meant to crush her skull, smashes between her shoulder blades. Air explodes out of her lungs from the blow. Flying forward, she lands with a heavy crash on her right hip.

She lies where she fell, shocked, gasping for air, not understanding. Nothing makes sense. And then she hears the voice from the shadows.

CR⬥SO

Lying on my right hip, gulping for air, I couldn't believe what just happened. I was five seconds behind starting to comprehend. This wasn't one of Serena's memories, it was a nightmare all my own.

I've been attacked.

My back and hip hurt so badly. Did I break any bones?

My eyes strained to see my attacker. It was so dark in the tower it was hard to see anything. The flashlight Marta had given me had been knocked out of my hand and clattered across the floor.

How did I let this happen? I mentally kicked myself. Images of robbery, rape and worse flashed through my head. Why had I come up into this tower alone? I was trapped. The familiar panic started to pop and snap in my chest. I had to focus my thoughts to get out of this alive. Ignoring my bruised hip, I forced myself into a crouched position, squinting to see.

There was only one way out—well, two if you counted the gaping window. That was not an option. My attacker blocked the only viable escape route. I had to think of something—and fast.

The dark figure stood still. Watching me. Waiting for something. But what? Keeping my eyes on the silhouette, I squatted down, groping for the flashlight. I touched it.

"You are such a monumental bitch," a voice sneered.

I couldn't believe my ears. I actually recognized the horrifically altered voice. When the laughter echoed off the stone walls, I fell back on my butt.

Mierda, this was bad.

Chapter Twenty-Three

"Hey, Marta! How are you?" Santiago walked into the restaurant and kissed her on the cheek.

"Santiago, what are you doing here?" She blinked in surprise.

"I'm here to eat dinner with my girl at our favorite restaurant." He scanned all the crowded tables and frowned. "Where's Erin?"

"She left."

"What do you mean? She was supposed to wait for me."

Marta clutched her breastbones. "She got a message to go to the tower. It wasn't from you?"

The floor fell out from under Santiago. And his heart stopped.

"Oh, dear," Marta said. "I warned her not to go. She seemed so frail. I didn't want her hiking up into the dark tower. They don't have good lighting in there."

Santiago didn't stick around to hear more. Dying a thousand deaths, he raced back out the restaurant doors and jumped on his bike.

As he sped through the darkening streets, his mind screamed.

Why is this happening again?

He'd never been so powerless. So utterly bereft. He saved lives every day, but the one woman he loved more than life itself was in danger because of him. He'd broken his promise never to leave her alone. Foolishly, he believed she would be safe if he got her away from Salamanca. He was wrong. Dead wrong.

He knew now, beyond any doubt, the darkness was gunning for the women he loved.

First Cristina and now...

No. He wouldn't allow the thought to materialize. Erin would be all right. She had to be. Dear God, he couldn't lose her.

Tears flew out of his eyes as he weaved around cars. He was topping a hundred on crowded streets, ignoring the angry car horns blaring all around him. Adrenaline shot through his veins. Griping his gut was a sickening feeling he wasn't going to make it. Too much time had passed. Opening the throttle, he sped on toward the Alcázar.

Dear God, no, he pleaded over the whine of his motorcycle, *I can't be too late.*

03♥80

Inside the tower, Serena picks up the candle. Miraculously, it is still lit. She rises to her feet and faces her attacker. "You hit me?" Her voice cracks.

"You have no right to speak."

"I do not understand."

"I am not surprised. Stupid sows are good for only one thing." A large knife was waved in the air. "To be slaughtered."

Serena's blood turns cold when the candlelight flickers off the sharp blade. She backs up until her shoulders graze the wall. There is nowhere to escape. She has no weapon, only a candle, the light of which plays across a menacing face.

Serena gasps. The features she knows so well distort with rage and madness.

03♥80

Oh, Lord, it's a knife.

My little flashlight was not going to be much good against that frightful thing. But maybe...

I began to formulate a plan. A flimsy plan, which had to work. Closer and closer danger crept. Not too slow, or fast. I readied my weapon, took aim and shined the flashlight in the eyes of my assailant. A millisecond later, I threw my "weapon" at the startled face and made a run for it.

I almost made it, until a foot shot out and tripped me. Just as I was falling to the floor yet again, the blade slashed upwards, ripping through my left arm.

I cried out in agony.

It was the most extreme pain I'd ever experienced. I screamed again and again. I'd have screamed for days until a sharp kick to my temple banged my head against the floor. The last cry strangled in my throat.

As I clutched desperately to consciousness, I fantasized it was all a dream. Nothing like this could possibly be happening. The vision of the assailant's face flashed through my head like a poster from a horror movie.

I knew who it was.

C880

Serena is surprised her leg is no longer hurting. When she tried to flee, the blade caught her, slashing from her knee to her hip. Even though her leg bled profusely, it has become strangely numb. Dead. She falls back on her side, unable to stand.

She has to stop this madness. Yelling for help does no good. The music from the ball below is far too loud for anyone to hear her. Leave it to the marquesa to continue an engagement party sans the man-of-honor. Serena's only hope is for Andrés to reach her in time. Yet she hugs her knees to her chest and prays he will never come. Above all else, she does not want him hurt.

"What are you doing? Praying for my forgiveness?"

"Why are you doing this?" Serena asks.

"By my witness, you should have known the truth long ago."

"What truth?" Serena's body grows lighter. She has to get help quickly. "Please. I am badly injured."

"You do not deserve the Marques de Moya."

"Andrés?" Serena's heart surges. "What about him? Tell me! Have you hurt him?"

252

"Hurt him? How can you be such an idiot?"

"You are angry. Let us bandage my leg and speak later of these things." Serena's eyelids grow heavy. She closes them just a moment...to...rest.

"No. You must die. For all you have done to me."

Serena's eyes open. "What have I done to *you*?"

"You have robbed me of my heart's desire," the figure snarls.

Serena takes a breath of relief. "This is a mistake. I do not know what you have been told, but I have not robbed you, or anyone, of a thing."

"You imbecile, you stole my love. My title. My life. Andrés would be in my arms this very moment, dancing at our beautiful engagement party, if not for you." She blows air forcefully through her lips. "With you gone, Andrés will be mine."

"You love him?"

Suddenly, things make sense to Serena. When she was a girl facing a difficult problem, Mother Catarina would tell her to look at the situation from a different angle. Sometimes turning puzzle pieces upside down made them fit. At that moment, some very disturbing pieces came together.

"Are you forgetting Lady Mara? If I am...gone, Andrés will marry her," Serena says through quivering lips.

"That stupid burro? Andrés will never marry her. She is moments away from being thrown out of the castle on her fat arse." She laughs at the funny image in her own mind. "No one can stand her. I myself have despised Lucia Mara for years. Which is why I recommended her to Aunt Beatriz as the perfect bride."

"It was your idea for Lady Mara to wed Andrés?"

"A few well-placed comments here and there. It was the perfect arrangement. Aunt Beatriz thought so too. She had her own reasons. Mine were pure. It was the only way, do you still not see?"

Serena stares in disbelief.

"I shall make it simple for you. Lucia was the shield to protect my beloved from those gray eyes of yours. You bewitched his heart. If Andrés and Lucia were engaged, you would no longer be a problem. Simple as that. Then once he threw her out like the refuse she is, he would be free to love me." She raises the blade. "I am the only one for Andrés."

∞

I couldn't believe my ears.

It's shock, I thought to myself. *I'm going into shock.*

I'd lost too much blood. My limbs were heavy. My head was spinning. The desire to close my eyes was more powerful than PMS chocolate cravings.

She squatted in front of me. "Santiago and I are a team. Just the two of us. No one else allowed."

I was sickened by the way she turned the knife over and over slowly, mesmerized by the sight of my blood dripping down the tip of the blade.

"He protects me. I protect him." She shot an accusing look my way. "I would never leave him. Or stop loving him."

"You think I'd hurt him?"

"Let me see." She tapped the knife handle to her temple. "Um, *yes*. Name 'Jack' ring any bells? How about the other guy—Andrés—you are always moaning about in your sleep?"

"Look, I don't really know Andrés—"

"Shut up! I'm sick to here with your lies." She waved her hand over her head. "You can't have him, you'll break his heart. And turn him against me."

"I wouldn't."

She rocked on her haunches. "Just like Cristina, the tramp. Why don't you look her up, she's probably saved you a nice little spot in hell."

"You killed her?"

An ugly grating laugh exploded from her lips. "Let's just say she got what was coming to her."

"Santiago sent you away—" my heart broke with the weight of my thoughts, "because he knew?"

"No. He understood I had some sort of breakdown, true enough. He sent me to the quacktor Martin Lawrence at UCLA."

Dr. Martin Lawrence. He was the renowned psychiatrist Dr. Stapleton was always gushing about. He had developed some new medicine to help with schizophrenia. He was also the Martin who left the message to run. Now I knew why.

She was truly insane. And deadly. Why hadn't I seen it earlier? Was I so wrapped up in my own problems I couldn't see hers?

My head seemed to be floating off my shoulders. I needed to do something quickly, or I'd die listening to the ravings of a madwoman.

"Martin and his pills," she said with disgust. "Always trying to get rid of the darkness. But I like the darkness. The power. You felt it." Her eyes flared through the blackness like an animal's. "When you drove the car into the building, the power overtook you, right? I thought we had that in common."

"Maria, help me. I'm hurting—"

Her hand shot up. "Don't call me that. Maria was your friend. She wanted to bring you to the power. But you're not worthy. You lied and stabbed her in the back."

"Come on, Maria, please—"

"No! I am a goddess now. The Goddess of Death. Here to exact my revenge."

❦

Serena awakes when someone lifts her off the floor. Strong hands grasp her by her armpits, dragging her away. A sense of relief washes over her battered body. She is saved.

"Andrés," she sighs dreamily.

Hiccupping laughter, like the braying of an ass, awakens Serena fully.

"What...are you doing?" Serena whispers, her thin voice almost gone.

"Pushing you out the window," Clara says.

❦

Maria droned on while I bled all over the place. "Helena is no threat. He doesn't love her, so she can't hurt him. No one would break up the team. I'd thought of everything. Until you came along." She spit venomously at me. "You ruined it all."

"Please, I need help." I was running out of time. "I'll do anything you want, just help me out of here. Take me to a hospital."

"Nu-uh." She wiggled her finger. "You don't like hospitals."

"Today I'll make an exception. Help me." I reached my good arm toward her.

She slapped it away. "Don't touch me."

"Sorry, please—"

"No. It's your day of reckoning. Time to pay for your lies and the pain you've caused. Today, Erin, you die."

My ears rang with her pronouncement. Fuzziness filling my head deadened the prickly terror racing through my veins. I knew I was passing out a split second before it happened.

As the cotton smothered my senses, a voice mimicked the Big Bad Wolf of children's nursery rhymes. "Good. All the better to throw you out the window, my dear."

The laugh was the last thing I could hear before the lights inside my head were snuffed out.

CR&SO

Serena fights with every drop of life left inside her. She screams, kicks out, tries to scratch and bite. All her efforts are in vain. Her foe is much stronger and not bleeding to death. Exhausted, she feels herself being dragged closer to the window.

"Might as well not fight me. It is long over."

In a tiny voice Serena says, "I loved you like a sister."

Clara's face bends over Serena's. Long strands of golden hair fall forward onto Serena's cheeks. "I am sorry. Truly I am. But you see, do you not? You cannot live. Even if you went away, Andrés would find you. He has succumbed to your spell, disobeying his mother and even the king for you."

"I beg you," she pleads. "Do not do this."

"There is no other way."

Clara yanks her toward the window again. She is

dangerously close to the gaping hole.

"I told you. My mother sent me here to marry a nobleman with a title. There is no title greater than the Marques de Moya. Andrés's father was King Fernando's confidant, as his mother is the queen's.

"My mother taught me to set my sights high, so I aimed them at Andrés's heart. I was the little girl who gave him rolls snatched from the kitchen. Cook was furious when she caught me. The only thing that mattered was that Andrés knew I loved him. I cheered for him when the boys had mock-sword fights. I chased after him when he and Prince Juan raced their ponies in the fields. I was there, skipping along behind, begging to be seen.

"I would have snared the nobleman of my dreams if an orphan from the convent had not struck him blind. I ripened into a woman before Andrés's very eyes, but he could not see me. To him I was still the young girl, the baby sister he never had. You were the woman he desired.

"You destroyed my plans, my everything. Now I shall destroy you."

CRSO

I was having the strangest dream. Something was tugging on me, hard. I didn't care. I was too exhausted to care, so I dove deeper into sleep.

Serena waved her arms wildly. Somehow she was sharper, more brilliant in this dream than she'd been before, almost alive. Except for her coloring. Everything about her—clothing, skin, lips, all except the jet-black hair—was a pale shade of blue. The opening and closing of her mouth reminded me of the fish Dad and I used to catch off the Santa Monica Pier. I hated to see the poor things flopping on the deck, their mouths ineffectively sucking in air. I cried until Dad threw them all back in.

What was she trying to say? The wind blew her long hair and ruffled her gown. Suddenly, her beautiful eyes enlarged. The whites were whiter than blue. Pointing at something behind, she mutely screamed.

I still couldn't hear her.

She took a few steps backward and then ran straight at me. I would have fallen over with the impact if something weren't pushing me up from behind.

"Wake up!" Serena screamed so loudly I would have gone deaf if she were actually yelling in my ear and not my brain.

My eyes flickered open just in time to see my worst fear-of-heights nightmare coming true. I was being shoved out the window.

"No!" I pushed back, stopping the forward momentum.

Moving my sluggish body around, I wrestled with the Goddess of Death. I was badly outmatched with my wounded arm and low blood levels, but I fought because my life depended on it. My only chance in hell was to fight dirty.

Wrapping my fingers around a big hunk of Maria's hair, I yanked as hard as I could. She screamed out in pain, trying to shake me off. I wouldn't let go.

I worried about the knife until I saw she'd dropped it in her efforts to drag me. I fought with every ounce of strength I could muster. She was hell-bent on pushing me to my death. I smashed my body against her, pulling her hair all the while.

Dear Lord, it was no use. My feet were slipping out from under me. To my horror, I was being shoved closer and closer toward oblivion. Just like my nightmares.

Somewhere in my head I could hear Serena's excited voice. *"He's coming,"* she said. *"Do not give up."*

During all the commotion, none of us had heard the motorcycle busting through the closed gates below.

CR&SO

"Have mercy, I beseech you," Serena pleads. Her blood coats both of them, her strength ebbs away with its flow. "By all that is good and holy in you, do not do this."

"I do not have goodness—or holiness—in me. The truth is, killing you is my only chance to win Andrés's love. It is all I have left."

Picturing Andrés's handsome face, Serena hears his deep voice whispering eternal love in her ear. Love rushes through

Catch Me in Castile

her body, and with it she finds grace and dignity. She smiles. She will not die alone, nor end life without love.

Facing Clara, she pulls her shoulders back and lifts her chin. Her soft voice is firm and unwavering when she says, "I shall speak the truth. Andrés loves only me. Our love shall never die."

Clara's rage explodes, bellowing across the palace compound. Guests leaving Andres's engagement ball hear the scream and rush toward the tower.

All agree it sounded like death.

⊗⊗

I still had a hunk of her hair, but that was about all I had on her. Maria snarled and cursed at me and fought like a wild animal.

"Help, someone help me!" I yelled.

She laughed. "Everything's closed. Shut up, you're busting my eardrum."

This only made me yell louder, until she punched me hard in the gut, knocking the wind out of me. I lost my grip on her hair and fell to the ground in a crumpled pile of bloodied uselessness.

I sucked hard to get some air into my lungs and she doubled over, trying to catch her own breath. Her shoulders heaved up and down from the violent struggle. I hoped her craziness had been expended and reason would return, until I remembered Aunt Lulu.

Sweet Lord, don't let her turn into Aunt Lulu.

I couldn't lift myself up anymore. How much blood had I lost? I was starting not to care. My eyes closed.

Somewhere far away a ghost of a voice said, *"Erin. You must open your eyes."*

I ignored her. It was too hard.

"Erin!" the voice said louder. *"You have to fight. It is our only chance."*

When I opened my eyes, I was confused. How could I be bent forward at the waist, seeing the ground a hundred miles below? Clarity slapped so hard, my eyes watered.

"Help me." I struggled to lift my body off the window ledge. Terror, exhaustion, and loss of blood made it difficult to move.

"Erin! Don't move, I'm coming," a male voice tried to reassure me. "Maria, let go of her. Now!"

"No!" It was the bellow of a lunatic pushing me even further out the window. "I'll use the knife."

My strength gave way. I fell forward, teetering on the edge of life and death.

"Stop!" said the man again, and I knew. Santiago had come to save me.

Dear God, Santiago was fighting the crazy knife-wielding Goddess of Death and there was nothing I could do. All I could see was the dark ground, far, far away and swimming up toward me.

"Hold on," Serena said.

Clutching the ledge with slippery, bloody hands, I did the best I could. I knew those jagged rocks were down there, waiting to peel the flesh from my bones.

"Let her go," Santiago demanded. "It's over."

"It is for her," Maria snarled.

"Listen to me, you're sick. You don't know what you're doing. Move her away from the window."

"Get back," she threatened. "She's going to die."

"No!" we all yelled at once—Santiago, Serena, and me.

There was a violent struggle behind me. Someone slammed into my back, violently. I lost my grip on the window ledge and rocketed out the gaping hole. By some miracle, I stopped short when my hips banged into the ledge.

Bent like a *V*, my upper body dangled out the window. I kicked behind me, trying to reach the floor with my feet and wiggle back inside the tower. I couldn't reach. It seemed impossible. I was stuck, upside down, the last few drops of my blood rushing to my head. It was only a matter of minutes. I couldn't hold on with my legs for long. I was going to fall to my death.

"Help!" My cry was pathetic. Resigned.

Serena shoved herself even deeper into my brain. It was

like diving into a pool, the warm water lapping over my skin, the sounds muffled, the colors light blue when Serena took over.

I don't know how she did it, but Serena was there, moving my body as if it were her own. Gripping the ledge with strong fingers, she hung on, saving my life. And as she did, her memories flooded my brain.

"Do you see?" Serena said.

And I did. All of it. Visions of Andrés atop his charcoal steed, holding Serena's hand, dancing at a great ball, kissing her passionately in a beautiful rose garden. I saw it all and experienced the strongest love a person could ever know. If only I could love like that, I'd die a happy woman.

"You shall not die today if I have any say in the matter."

A bloodcurdling scream filled my ears. I couldn't see what happened next. Something heavy bumped into me as it flew over and out the window. The tremendous weight hit me hard. My forehead smacked into the stone wall, knocking me senseless.

As I lost consciousness, my body sailed down…down…down. The bone-crunching impact waited at the bottom.

Instead of dying, I was hoisted up by two strong arms.

Serena sang, *"Holy Madre, Erin. I remember!"*

Chapter Twenty-Four

Serena's spirit hovers over her dead body. A blinding light sings to her, pulling her like a great current. She hesitates. She desires to see Andrés's face one last time before she moves on.

Is he coming? No, she sighs. Someone else runs toward her.

Hearing Clara's horrible scream, Beatriz gathers her long skirts up to free her legs and rushes to the tower. The light from her candle splays out across the gruesome scene with long, delicate fingers. She bends over Serena's body, wincing at the sight. Serena herself cannot look.

Beatriz glances up to the gaping window in the tower and sees the figure moving away from the window. "Your secret is safe with me, Clara. I am grateful."

Shortly thereafter the guests from the ball surround her. "What happened?" They all want to know.

"Glorious Saints! It is a woman, is it not?" a nobleman asks.

"Oh, marquesa, who is she?" one of the ladies whispers.

Beatriz takes a stuttering breath. "Serena, Prince Miguel's nursemaid."

Collectively, all eyes travel up toward the tower. Few can look upon the bloodied body.

"Why?" a nobleman asks with a shudder. "I remember her from Princess Juana's ball. A beautiful *señorita*. Why would she take her life?"

Beatriz does not bat an eye. "She must have heard the news."

"News?"

"Yes, my dear friends, I am sad to tell you that Prince Miguel has died."

There is a collective gasp. The royal heir to the throne is dead?

They do not have time to ponder the implications before the marquesa continues, "The messenger arrived a few moments ago. Serena must have overheard..." She motions to the body. "She loved him deeply. Poor girl. Her grief I understand, but to commit a mortal sin?" She shakes her head. "I would not have wished it upon her."

Serena glares at the lying woman. "Andrés will never believe you. If it takes an eternity," she vows, "he shall know the truth about my murder and how you sought to cover it up."

And with that vow, Serena steps away from the blinding light.

ભજ

"Wake up, Erin. I remember it all," someone said in my...ear? Head?

"Erin? Open your eyes, *querida*," a deeper voice said. "It's all over."

I was flat on my back inside a small room with medical supplies all around. My arm hurt like a son-of-a-gun and there was a lump on my head. "Where am I?"

"An ambulance. I'm taking you back to the hospital."

"Hospital?" My thoughts were jumbled. Why was his face so sad? What happened? Why—oh God, suddenly I remembered. "Maria."

When he bent over and kissed my cheek, his tears mixed with mine. "Fell...out the window...didn't make it."

With my good arm, I pulled him toward me. He sobbed against my neck while I held on tight. The ambulance guy closed the door and left us that way, tangled up together in misery. The cot shook slightly with the rumble of the engine.

We had at least a half an hour in the back the ambulance to piece the story together. When we both stopped crying, I held his cheeks in my hands. "Tell me."

"I did everything I could to heal her." His eyes were

bloodshot and tormented. "After the problems with Mama, I sensed Maria was heading for a breakdown too, but I couldn't be sure. She hid her emotions. Buried them deep. It's something we both learned too well.

"The day Cristina disappeared, I was distraught, angry, confused. Maria looked me in the eye and said, 'Let the darkness take over. It's easy. Sometimes the lights just go out and there is nothing left but power and rage. I can kill with my bare hands when the darkness takes over.'

"I was terrified. Had Cristina run off? Or had the darkness taken her and my baby sister with it?

"I sent Maria to UCLA the next day for extensive testing. What was the darkness and could it be destroyed for good? After five years of the best medicines and therapy, Dr. Martin Lawrence, the number one psychiatrist in the world, assured me she was well. But I couldn't be sure. Some things you feel in here." He pressed his hand to his stomach.

"She seemed so...normal," I said. "But then again, I might not be the best judge of normal."

"Yes. Most of the time she acted fine. But there were flashes... It scared me. I wondered if she was taking her pills. I sent one of her blood samples to Martin to find out."

"Right, after my heatstroke incident you drew her blood. She thought you were trying to determine if she and I had been exposed to a germ on the plane."

"It would have broken Maria's heart, or pushed her over the edge, to know I was checking up on her. I had to know the truth. It was killing me, thinking you might be in danger. I flew to LA to speak to Martin and study the results myself. It was the hardest thing in the world to leave you behind, Erin. I couldn't sleep or eat." He tucked the hair behind my ear. "I can't breathe when I'm away from you."

I cupped his cheek. "Me too, big guy."

"I hired a man to follow Maria and keep an eye on you while I was gone."

"The guy at the airport and parked outside."

His eyes widened. "You saw him?"

"Yeah, but Maria didn't believe me when I told her we were being followed."

He took a stuttering breath. "Her perception of reality wasn't always accurate."

"But she worked, had friends, lovers. I had no idea she was sick. It's a real testament to how strong she was, Santiago. No one knew."

"I should have known. And saved her."

"How? Force-fed her the pills? The best doctors in the world couldn't save her because deep down she liked the darkness. The power thrilled her. She didn't want to give it up."

"If I had known, I'd never have put you at risk. I love you, Erin. More than I have ever loved anyone. I would have sent you to Mars to keep you safe."

I smiled. "Newsflash—I love you too much to leave you. Ever."

"But you promised you'd go home if things got too dangerous."

I kissed him on the nose. "I lied. It was the last time, I promise. I am so done with secrets and lies."

"Not telling you the whole truth almost got you killed. And Maria..." A wave of sorrow surged through him, filling his eyes. "I lost my sister."

I laced my fingers with his. "Above all else, she wanted you to be happy. I hope you will let me have that job. I will make your life so sweet."

"After all this, you want to stay with me?"

"Only forever. Now, lie back down here with me and rest. We'll get through this. Together." I scooted over a little, trying not to jostle my arm.

"I love you, Erin Carter." Mindful of my injuries, he curled himself around me.

I sighed. I was tired, beat up, and emotionally whooped, but those five little words had healing power. They were dark chocolate for my soul.

"I love you too, Santiago Botello."

"*Mi amor, mi corazón, mi vida...*" He kissed me as the ambulance drove on.

Epilogue

Four years later, Salamanca, Spain

I pulled two cute little bodies out of the tub and wrapped them in heavy cotton towels. They were warm and sweet smelling, like milk and honey.

"I could just eat you up." I kissed the closest pudgy tummy.

"Mama!" My daughter giggled. "That tickles."

"Get me too, Mama." My son thrust his belly in my face.

"Oh, I'm gonna get you." I laughed and blew zerberts on his bellybutton. The giggles were deafening.

"There, all dry. Now off to your room. Rosa's bringing your PJs from the dryer. See, there she is. Uh-oh, looks like she's winning."

Squeals of delight echoed off the walls as the twins raced to beat Rosa to their shared bedroom.

"*Dios mío*, me old bones," Rosa exclaimed as the two-and-a-half-year-old forces of nature ran past, almost knocking her off her feet.

I laughed and thanked God all over again for my good fortune. I had the love of my life and two treasures flying buck naked down the hall. I owed it all to Serena. She saved my life in the tower and together we found her memories. The good, the bad, and the beautiful.

She came to me one last time in the hospital. I didn't need to open my eyes to know she was there.

"You came back," I whispered.

"*Sí*, to say *adios*."

"What? Why? We haven't done the séance yet. I promised I

would find someone who really knows how to send you on."

"I know. But I have been thinking. Do you suppose other ghosts are here?"

I scrunched my eyes at her. "I suppose so. People say they see ghosts all the time. Why?"

"What if an evil person like Clara were to die? Would her spirit remain evil?"

"I...I really don't know."

"And if such a bad spirit were to enter living persons as I did to you? What then?"

I thought about Rosa's warning about becoming possessed. I also thought of Aunt Lulu who claimed a person was talking inside her head all the time. "It would be bad."

"Exactly."

"What are you saying?"

"I must do everything in my power to stop Clara from hurting others. And then find a way to send her spirit straight to hell."

"Ah, okay. But what if she isn't here? What if she's cooking her toes as we speak?"

"Then I shall find someone else to send me on. You gave me back my memories of Andrés. You have done more than enough."

"I'll miss you."

"I shall miss you as well. Be safe, my friend." And she was gone.

I would always be grateful and wished I could thank her somehow.

The opportunity presented itself in two small packages. When I told Santiago the names I had chosen for the twins, he smiled and nodded. "Serena and Andrés Botello? Perfect."

I bought a new notebook and wrote down the love story of Serena and Andrés. One day, when the twins were old enough to allow a ghost story into their lives, I would read it to them. I had a feeling these two munchkins would enjoy hearing about their namesakes, provided I left out some of the lovey-dovey stuff.

An hour after I had put the kids to bed, a tired Santiago

came through the door.

"Hi babe." I kissed him soundly. "Long day?"

"Not the longest, but close. How was yours?" he mumbled into my collarbone. His breath sent a shimmy of warm delight across my skin.

"Not boring." I worked alone these days, still keeping a small list of faithful clients and even dabbling into day-trading. Turns out I hadn't lost my touch. Those boys at the firm had nothing on me. Best of all, I had balance in my life. Wholeness. Letting go of the old Erin had been the best career choice I'd ever made.

"You should've seen what your two rascals did today," I went on. "The plumber had quite a laugh saying they take the prize for most bars of soap jammed down the toilet with a plunger."

"Oh, no." He lifted his head. "Where are they?"

"Asleep."

He took me by the hand and we walked quietly into their shared room.

"Such angels," I whispered, amazed at how the right light on a child's soft cheek could erase all the troubles of the day.

He kissed the side of my forehead. "Let's wake them."

"Oh, no you don't. It's my first moment of silence all day."

"Please."

"Nothing doing. Go change and I'll warm your dinner. Rosa made one of your favorites."

I stopped on my way to the kitchen. "Holy cow! Someone's sawing logs."

The ruckus was coming from *Señora* Botello's (or Nana's, as we called her now) room. She had fallen asleep in her favorite chair, a book open across her lap, snoring without a care in the world. Placing the book on her nightstand, I pulled the lap-blanket up and tucked it around her tiny body.

She looked good. Not so frail anymore. With the new medication she was taking, she seemed normal. There were a few rare moments of strangeness, but mostly she was a regular, sweet granny to the kids, in a constant battle with my mom for Grandmother of the Year Award. They both spoiled the twins mercilessly. I'm sure I would pay for it in the teenage years.

Nana and I got along swimmingly. She always had liked me even when I thought she was trying to kill me. Really she had been giving me clues about the poisoned tea, doing her best to sneak out of Maria's tight clutches. Sadly, I didn't figure it out until too late.

"Night, Nana." I kissed the top of her head and turned out the light.

Warming Santiago's food in the microwave, I poured two glasses of wine. *Where is that man?*

On a hunch, I went to the kids' room. My heart melted. The world's most handsome man was wrapped in tiny arms and legs, in a little girl's bed. He had moved little Andrés so he could lie between them. It was a crowded spot of heaven.

"Want to snuggle?" he whispered in the glow of the nightlight.

"No place I'd rather be." I wiggled in between the pink princess sheets.

I thought briefly about my pale blue notebook. I had written just one more entry in it before I put it away four years ago. Every line had been accomplished, including number five: No more nightmares, only sweet dreams from now on. The last line was my favorite.

Snuggling closer, I kissed my husband. I didn't need a journal to get a life anymore.

I already had one.

Get a Life Journal

1) I am not crazy. I will trust everything will work out for the best and go to Spain.

2) Relax. Flirt. Enjoy a man, just because. Become a goddess.

3) Be the goddess. Be the goddess. Be the goddess. And don't go crazy.

4) Get through to Santiago, if it kills me. And stop flipping out.

5) No more nightmares. Only sweet dreams from now on.

6) Find Santiago before it's too late.

7) Forget about being a goddess. Let him love you for the woman you are.

About the Author

Kimberley Troutte has been a substitute teacher, caterer, financial analyst for a major defense contractor, aerobics instructor, real-estate broker, freelance writer, homework corrector and caregiver to all the creatures the kids/hubby/dog drag in. She lives with her husband, two sons, one dog and three snakes in Southern California.

Please visit her at www.kimberleytroutte.com or come blogging at http://kimberleytroutte.blogspot.com.

GREAT CHEAP FUN

Discover eBooks!

THE FASTEST WAY TO GET THE HOTTEST NAMES

Get your favorite authors on your favorite reader, long before they're out in print! Ebooks from Samhain go wherever you go, and work with whatever you carry—Palm, PDF, Mobi, and more.

Samhain Publishing Ltd

WWW.SAMHAINPUBLISHING.COM

LaVergne, TN USA
24 June 2010
187296LV00003B/34/P

9 781605 047317